ACTS OF REVISION

MARTYN BEDFORD

DOUBLEDAY

NEW YORK   LONDON   TORONTO
SYDNEY   AUCKLAND

ACTS OF

REVISION

PUBLISHED BY DOUBLEDAY
a division of Bantam Doubleday Dell Publishing Group, Inc.
1540 Broadway, New York, New York 10036

DOUBLEDAY and the portrayal of an anchor with a dolphin
are trademarks of Doubleday, a division
of Bantam Doubleday Dell Publishing Group, Inc.

Book design by Dana Treglia

Library of Congress Cataloging-in-Publication Data
Bedford, Martyn.
Acts of revision / by Martyn Bedford. — 1st ed.
p.   cm.
1. Men—England—London—Psychology—Fiction.   2. London (England)—Fiction.
3. Revenge—Fiction.   I. Title.
PR6052.E31112A28   1996
823'.914—dc20   95-44372
CIP

ISBN 0-385-48273-6

First Edition

FOR DAMARIS

ACKNOWLEDGEMENTS

I am grateful to the following friends and critics for their comments on this and other pieces of writing: Ian Buffery, Tom Guest, Jim McClure, Alistair McNaught, Dave Peak and Sally Worboyes. Thanks also to my fellow creative writing students at UEA (1993–94) and to my tutors: Terence Blacker, Malcolm Bradbury, and Rose Tremain. I am indebted, too, to my agent Jonny Geller, at Curtis Brown, and to Broo Doherty and Patrick Janson-Smith, at Transworld Publishers. Finally, special thanks to Phil Whitaker for his unfailing friendship, encouragement and criticism over the years.

The word "education" comes from the root *e* from *ex,* out, and *duco,* I lead. It means a leading out. To me education is a leading out of what is already there in the pupil's soul. To Miss Mackay it is a putting in of something that is not there, and that is not what I call education, I call it intrusion, from the Latin root prefix *in* meaning in and the stem *trudo,* I thrust. Miss Mackay's method is to thrust a lot of information into the pupil's head; mine is a leading out of knowledge, and that is true education as proved by its root meaning.

—*The Prime of Miss Jean Brodie,*
Muriel Spark

Clever, but schoolteacher beat him anyway to show him that definitions belong to the definers—not the defined.

—*Beloved,* Toni Morrison

PROLOGUE

They burned her.

It was a cold morning, January; twelve months ago. It was cold but the burning of her was not for warmth.

They gave me a small urn and we went outside where the sky was grey-white and our breaths hung in the air like visible whispers. We followed a gravel path to the flower beds. A rosebush, brown and spiky bare, was indicated and I knelt before it in the frost. Her name had been printed in black on a plastic label stuck in the hard soil: MARION LYN.

They'd misspelled the surname: one *n* instead of two. I removed the lid from the urn and took a handful of ashes. I uncurled my fingers. The ashes, distressed by the wind, made silver confetti in people's hair and left smudges on their dark coats as they brushed themselves down.

Lower, someone said. Hold them lower before you let go.

I took another handful, raised it to my mouth. The flakes were smooth and silky, they dissolved on my tongue and made my throat dry when I tried to swallow. Wafery fragments of her, and of coffin. They tasted of nothing.

Gregory, don't. Here.

Hands on my shoulders, and I was being made to stand up; to come away. Someone released my grip on the urn and it fell onto the whitened grass at the path's edge. An arm at my back, stiff scratchy hair against the side of my face, catching on the stubble where I hadn't shaved. A woman's bony hand wiping my lips with a handkerchief. Smell of perfume and of lipstick.

Cry, love. That's it. You cry as much as you want.

I wasn't crying. The noise was not the noise my throat makes whenever I cry.

Sandwiches. Cheddar cheese and tomato, fish paste and cucumber, ham; sliced white bread. Packets of crisps tipped into glass bowls. Cups of tea. People mumbling between silences. I sat watching them eat, waiting for them to go. Auntie, who'd seen to the food, was the last. She washed up and returned all the chairs to their proper places, she put on her coat and scarf and gloves and hat. She said things on the front doorstep, she said Marion would be with the Lord now. She pressed me to her, then she left and I closed the door.

Upstairs, in my room, I took the notepad and pencils from the locked drawer in my desk and turned to the first blank page. I wrote the day and date. I drew the boxes—six, in two sequences of three—then the scenes, then I did the colouring. No speech bubbles, no thought bubbles; that way you have to make the pictures tell the story. People wearing black, sitting in rows in a chapel; coffin disappearing behind a curtain (hard, sketching the curtain to suggest motion); flames: oranges, yellows, reds, thick black spirals for smoke; people clustered round a rosebush; one man—apart from the others—kneeling, dispersing ashes at the base of the bush; the man crying, tears light blue against the pink of his face. On the facing page I sketched a beautiful dark-haired woman—upright, arms by her side, dressed in a summer frock; her head tilting upwards and feet pointing down sharply like a ballerina's. Her eyes were closed. She was ascending into heaven; only I didn't know how to draw heaven, so it became a picture of a woman floating in the air. Adrift.

. . .

My name is Gregory Lynn. I am thirty-five years old. I am an orphan, a bachelor, an only child from the age of four and a half. My feet are size 12, I am six feet two inches tall and weigh thirteen stone eight pounds. I am not clumsy, it's just that my body sometimes misinterprets the signals emitted by my brain. I have one brown eye and one green.

I no longer have the notepad in which I recorded my mother's funeral. I don't have any of the books anymore. They've been confiscated for use in evidence, though it is unclear whether this will be of most benefit to the prosecution or the defence. My barrister is more preoccupied with their illustration of my "personality" than in any question of artistic merit. Their significance is also lost on him; at least, he perceives a different significance. I am quite sane, but these cartoon strips, apparently, might enable him to suggest otherwise. Mitigation, he calls it. If this man is on *my* side, then I am curious to hear the case for the Crown. I ask if any of the drawings will appear in the newspapers during or after the trial and he assures me they won't. But I remain hopeful. There were fifty-seven of the books in my room, each containing 150 pages, spanning the last twenty-three years and six months of my life. The court, however, will confine its interest to the most recent volumes. Dozens of notepads and loose sheets besides these: sketches, paintings, collages, my collection of scrapbooks; in drawers or cupboards or boxes or under the bed or on top of the wardrobe or on the floor or pinned to the walls. And, of course, they discovered the maps, photographs, and files, the accounts of each of the incidents, although a conviction would be inevitable with or without such incriminating exhibits. Motive and state of mind may be hard to establish, but the forensic and circumstantial evidence is incontestable. Fact: I did it. Me, Gregory Lynn (orphan, bachelor, only child from the age of four and a half). I was there, the eye witnesses confirm this, the tests prove it. I did it. The who, what, where, when, and how are matters of fact; the only unanswered question is why? But "why?" is not relevant to the verdict, merely to the sentence. A mitigating factor. The irony will be of no consolation to him now, but Mr. Boyle was right: it all comes down to facts, to logic, to science; everything, always. Facts eliminate doubt. Nevertheless I intend, against the advice of my barrister, to plead not guilty. This is not to deny the commission of the acts from which the charges arise, it is rather that I have no idea what they mean when they talk of guilt and innocence as if they were opposites, as if they were mutually exclusive. I have one brown eye and one green.

While counsel and I differ in the assessment of my "predicament," he acknowledges—albeit begrudgingly and with a hint of surprise in his voice—that I have demonstrated a quick grasp of the rudiments of the legal process and its nomenclature. The point is, if something interests me, I immerse myself in it. I absorb. I learn. If it doesn't, I don't. This doesn't make me unintelligent. Teachers (some of them—Mr. Boyle, for instance) would tell me to work at my weaker subjects, to knuckle down, to fulfill my potential. What they meant was: you can't switch intelligence on and off like a light. And I think: the fuck you can't. The way I planned and carried out the acts. Originality and creativity which Miss McMahon and, it goes without saying, Mr. Andrews would recognise and appreciate; harnessed with a precision, calculation, and methodical thoroughness that Mr. Boyle and all the other bastards wouldn't credit me with being capable of.

Mr. Andrews.

He has seen the drawings, the cartoons. He sees their artistic merit, and he sees beyond it to their significance. He is closer to understanding the "why?" than anyone, apart from me. He ought not to talk in terms of victim and perpetrator, guilt and innocence. He should know, as I do, that they seep into one another as the past seeps into the present. He should know, as I do, that the swathes of books and papers in my room contain the real evidence in this case, even though they are unadorned with

4

hard facts. Mr. Andrews, however, is to be a witness for the prosecution.

Alone. Drawings done and no need to lock the pad away in the drawer now. No need to keep to my room. Even so, I stayed there all afternoon and evening with the door closed, as if Mum was still in the house.

In the night I descended to the kitchen for toast and jam and a glass of milk. That was the last of the jam, and the loaf was nearly finished. Plenty of milk. She'd forgotten to cancel it before she died. I would have to go out, to the shops. I would have to go outside. I drew a picture of outside. An empty box, a box filled with white. I drew the inside of a supermarket, Auntie carrying a wire basket laden with tins and packets and jars. Sometimes by drawing something I make it happen, I make it come true. And Auntie had told me she'd pop round in a day or two, make sure I was all right. See if there was anything I needed. It was one of the things she'd said on the doorstep when she left. In my head, I told her I'd sooner fucking starve than have her lipstick here. Her perfume.

I drank my milk and went to Mum's bedroom. The bed was made, the thin yellow counterpane pulled up over the pillows and tucked in tight. The room was cold and smelled of stale smoke. On the dressing table I found her perfume in a glass bottle the shape and size of a cigarette lighter. She used to dab it behind her ears and on the inside of one wrist and then rub her wrists together. When it was in the bottle the perfume was the colour of whisky, but on her skin it became colourless. I removed the cap and fragranced my hands, my face, my neck.

In the morning, the day after the burning, the phone rang. I didn't answer it.

I made sure both doors were locked and bolted and checked

5

the catches on all the windows. Then I went to Mum's room again. I went to every room in the house. Barefoot, trouser cuffs rolled to midshin; the texture of carpet against the soles of my feet. For hours I drifted from room to room; not touching anything, just sitting on a chair, a sofa, a bed, or on the floor. On the floor was best because the room looked bigger, the ceiling would be higher and the windows would stretch and the furniture would become tall, like when you are a child. Sitting on the floor you can make yourself smaller. In this way the rooms became like I remembered them. I stood up and started to touch things: a china dog, a magazine of knitting patterns, a yellow vase (empty), a pair of pink slippers, a black-and-white photograph in a metal frame. I studied the photograph. We were in swimming costumes, standing in an open-air paddling pool. Janice was holding Mum's right hand and I was holding her left. My head came up to her thigh. I was squinting because of the sun. Dad must've taken the picture, you could see his shadow on the water if you looked closely. "Butlins, Bognor Regis, 1962," written in ballpoint pen in the top left-hand corner, where the sky was. There were other photographs, on a shelf in Mum's bedroom. Me on my own, in school uniform; Mum and Dad on their wedding day; Janice, skipping—one sock pulled up and the other round her ankle.

Janice called me Jeggy, because when I was born she was too little to say my name properly. Janice went away when she was seven—when I was four and a half—and came back as a baby. Then she went away again forever.

The phone rang a second time.

Gregory?

Nn.

Hello, Gregory?

I hung up. When the phone rang again I didn't answer it. I went up to my room and drew a picture of Auntie talking into the mouthpiece, saying my name over and over.

Auntie came. Uncle was with her, dressed as a bus driver. When they gave up thumping the door and calling my name and started peering through the windows, I let them in. He was angry but when he went to speak Auntie stopped him. She whispered, but I heard her.

Leave him. It's Marion.

Miss McMahon taught me the art of words. Mr. Andrews taught me the art of meaning. He taught me about proportion and perspective. He used to say: never confuse proportion with quantity, or perspective with relativity. Art is not an exact science, Gregory. I've given this a great deal of thought recently and I'm not certain I agree with him. Art isn't a science at all. They are opposites, as Mr. Andrews and Mr. Boyle are opposites. Were.

When I try to discuss this with my barrister he says our time would be more usefully spent in focusing on the matter in hand.

What if this is the matter in hand?

He ignores this. He wants me to start at the beginning, and to speak slowly and clearly for the benefit of the solicitor, whose pen is poised over the notebook resting on her lap. I smile. She looks away. I wonder why the barrister and I get to sit across the desk from one another when the only person taking notes has nothing to lean on.

Can we begin, please?

I start to speak. The problem is that my idea of the beginning is not the same as his. He tells me to stop, to confine my contribution to what is relevant; to the specifics. He proposes a method: he will ask questions and I will answer them. This is called legal aid. He leans forward, elbows on the desk; he becomes avuncular.

Gregory, my only concern is with the issues which have a direct bearing on your case.

I think: I was involved in my case before you were and shall continue to be involved with it long after you've gone. What I say is:

Tell me, why do you fasten your bundles of case notes with pink ribbon?

At the conclusion of the interview we shake hands and I am escorted to another room. In some respects it is similar to my room at home: private, secure. I'm assured that in due course (post-trial, pre-sentence) I shall have the opportunity to cooperate in the preparation of a social inquiry report. It is then, assisted by a suitably qualified professional, that I can raise any "peripheral matters"; to substantiate the mitigation. To begin at the real beginning, I take this to mean. I have spent time in the company of suitably qualified professionals. Shrinks. None would recognise a real beginning if it jumped up and bit them.

After the visit with Uncle, she came round every day for a while. She cleaned, she hoovered; she brought food. I gave her money out of Mum's purse. Which was my money now. The money in the bank, the building society, the post office; that had become mine too. Not much, Auntie reckoned, but enough to cover the rent and bills and keep me for a good few months. The house belonged to the Council. She wasn't sure what would happen now there was just one of us; but what they didn't know couldn't hurt them.

You stay here 'til someone tells you different.

That was me, the solitary tenant. If any of Mum's customers phoned I told them she couldn't do their hair because she was dead.

A week after the burning I started an inventory of the house. Every ornament, every vase, every book, every towel, every chair, every cushion, every dishcloth, every spoon, every clock, every plate, every photograph. I listed them in a scrapbook. I drew a picture of each item alongside its number and title. I drew grid maps of each room and gave every item a map reference. It took days. When I'd finished I could go where I liked—any room, any cupboard; even the unfriendly ones had become familiar.

On the last day I went into the loft (room H). The light didn't work. I fetched a torch (item D 17) from the cupboard under the stairs (grid ref. D–H5). I pointed the torch. Cardboard boxes, old carpets, a suitcase, toys, a table lamp, empty picture frames. Dust everywhere, and spiderwebs; a chink of light where one of the roof tiles was missing. A water tank so big I couldn't light it all up at once. Some of the toys looked familiar: an Action Man with no arms, a blue car and stacked sections of Scalextric track, a painting-by-numbers kit. I remembered to walk on the beams so my feet wouldn't go through the floor. Between the beams there were rolls of orangey-coloured glass-fibre matting that came away in candyfloss clumps when I picked at it. It felt scratchy and went on feeling scratchy even when I'd let go of it. I could see bits glinting when I shone the torch on the palm of my hand. I wasn't allowed in the loft on my own, but Dad used to take me up with him sometimes. And Janice and I played there, when Mum and Dad didn't know. Janice could lower the metal steps by standing on a chair to reach up and release the catch. You had to let the steps down slowly so they didn't make a noise. The loft was our secret place. The light used to work then, but we liked to leave it off and play in the dark.

Now the loft was too small. My head banged against the wooden rafters unless I stooped or kept to the middle. The dust made me sneeze and cough and made my eyes sting. I sat on a beam and went through the cases and boxes one at a time, took each item out in turn and held it in the torchlight before entering it on the inventory. The locks on the suitcase were rusted and I had to press hard to make them click open. Old bedding: a quilt made of knitted squares of wool, striped nylon sheets that smelled of damp. The first box split as I dragged it closer. It was full of board games and jigsaw puzzles. Jigsaw pieces were loose in the bottom, along with two dice, a plastic racehorse with a number 6 on its side, and a card saying "Manchester United," followed by the handwritten words "are shit."

I pushed the box to one side and pulled the other one in front of me. A pile of *Woman's Own* and *Woman's Realm* magazines, a mail-order catalog and glossy brochures full of photographs of women's hairstyles. Underneath all these was a plain plastic bag. I lifted it out of the box and shone the torch inside. Exercise books. Some with pink covers, some with green. I thought they were my old schoolbooks, but when I pulled them out I found they were end-of-term reports. There were nine of them, winter and summer; the pink ones were from my primary school and the green ones from my senior school. I sorted them into date order: December 1966 to December 1974. Several were missing. The cover of each report bore the name of the school, the school badge, the name of the Borough Education Committee, my name (in ink) and the words: "This Book is the property of the School." The pages were thin, oniony; scrawled with ballpoint in blue, black, red. I read them. I read them by torchlight. I read for so long the batteries started to lose power and the small circle of light dimmed from white to yellow to dull orange and I had to strain my eyes to make out the words. I read about me, and what the teachers said. And I remembered.

A beginning. Beginnings within a beginning, at least. Still not the start of it all, if such a moment can ever be isolated and identified; but a clue. Something which may be deciphered by those who do not care to be constrained by the terms "relevant," "specific"; by the science of facts.

Those reports were about me, Gregory Lynn (orphan, bachelor, only child from the age of four and a half). They told of what I was and what I became, they contained the story of this transition. With my one eye of brown and my one eye of green, I read those reports; I read the names of those who had written them and I remembered their faces. I saw them, the teachers. I saw what they had done. My barrister has also read the reports. He fails, naturally, to perceive the connection between them and the incidents. That is, he perceives *my* making of a connection, but not the connection as such. I quibble with him, but he is insistent. He says twenty years is a long time. I inquire:

Relative to what?

The court will not be persuaded to accept that these were "legitimate acts of revenge," if I may borrow your description. Nor shall I attempt to, ah . . . persuade it of this on your behalf.

Acts of re*vision* is what I said. Ask her, she wrote it down.

The solicitor looks at the barrister, then at me. Her face is flushed. She clears her throat before speaking.

Why don't you explain that subtle distinction to Mrs. Boyle?

Mr. Patrick, Mrs. Davies-White, Miss McMahon, Mr. Teja, Mr. Hutchinson, Mr. Andrews, Mr. Boyle. Tracking them down was the most difficult aspect. Some were easy to find, others required a greater degree of ingenuity.

W hen I had finished in the loft, I took the reports to my bedroom. I made a large wall chart and wrote each name and subject on it in capitals, leaving space for any additional information and photographs. There would have to be photographs. I opened files. I went to the newsagent and stationery shop on the corner; it wasn't far, I was only outside for twelve minutes. I bought maps—one of Greater London and one of the United

Kingdom—and taped them to the wall, either side of the chart. I bought felt-tip pens, pencils, folders, a 12″/30cm ruler, a pad of ruled A4 paper and a pad of unruled. I bought a packet of coloured pins and selected seven different colours, one for each of them. Then I began.

history **1.** (chronological record of) significant past events **2a.** treatise presenting systematically related natural phenomena **2b.** account of somebody's medical, sociological, etc. background **3.** branch of knowledge that records the past **4.** past events **4a.** unusual or interesting past **4b.** previous treatment, handling or experience

My name is Gregory Lynn. I was born on October 22, 1958, at exactly five o'clock in the evening. Weight: nine pounds two ounces. Like giving birth to a sack of potatoes, Mum used to say; in the days when she still said things like that. In the same month: French Guinea was proclaimed the Republic of Guinea. Pope Pius XII died, women peers were introduced into the House of Lords, the State opening of Parliament was televised for the first time, and the USSR, Britain and the U.S. opened a conference in Geneva on the suspension of nuclear tests.

I am a Libran. If I'd been born seven hours and one minute later I would have been a Scorpio. Famous Librans include John Lennon and Margaret Thatcher, which just goes to show.

I am famous too. I have achieved a certain notoriety. My name is in the newspapers and on radio and I have been the lead item on *News at Ten*. They have to be careful because my case is sub judice. The *Daily Telegraph* devoted half of page three to a report of my arrest, with what I believe is called a "snatch" photograph of me being escorted into the side entrance of a police station. The officers flanking me were made to appear short and spindly by comparison with my bulk. One of them was holding a blanket over my head, contrary to my express instructions.

Facts:

1. At primary school I was always in the top class in my year. *Tick. v.g.*
2. I consistently finished below halfway in class exams. *Cross. See me.*

They tested us on arithmetic, reading, composition and comprehension, history, geography and science. My marks were never poor enough for them to relegate me to a lower class, never high enough for me to be ranked up there with the real brainboxes.

December 1966
Lynn, Gregory. Form 1a
No. in form: 42
Pos. in form: 35

July 1968, form 2a, position 38th; December 1968, 3a, 38th; July 1970, 4a, 31st. Nevertheless, all the time there was an "a" after my form number I remained—relative to those in forms b, c, d or e—among the brainies. To my classmates, however, I was a thicko (not to be confused with the divvies, mongs and spasoids in the lower groups). Between the ages of seven and eleven, I had yet to receive the benefit of Mr. Andrews's wisdom in matters of proportion and perspective.

. . .

The primary school was red brick with blue doors and window frames. All single-storey. On the wall inside the main entrance, a stone tablet with gold lettering said the school was officially opened on September 3, 1960, by B. J. W. Biggs, J.P., chairman of the Borough Education Committee. Janice went to infants, but she never went to juniors because the summer before she was supposed to move up was the summer she went away. You could tell which part of the building was infants because there were paintings in the windows: trees and dogs and chickens, people with sticky-up hair and arms coming out of their necks; smiling yellow suns, lopsided houses. When I was small Mum walked me to school, she held my hand. From our house you went along the street, past the parade of shops and across the green to the highway. An underpass came out by the school gates. Older boys climbed the railings, crossed the road. If a teacher saw you, you got caned. One boy was run over by a lorry and his head popped like a melon.

We wore uniforms: white shirt, royal-blue V-neck jumper, blue-and-white-striped tie, black or grey short trousers, grey socks, black or brown shoes, a black blazer with a badge on the breast pocket and a blue cap. You didn't have to wear the cap, and on hot days you could take off your blazer and jumper in class. I had a brown leather satchel. In the infants, you sat cross-legged on the floor for assembly. The floor was wooden and shiny and made your bottom ache. In the juniors, we sat on wooden chairs. We sang hymns. The words were printed in white on big sheets of coarse black paper hung from pulleys above the stage. The hymn sheets were kept in a cupboard, some torn and patched up with thick strips of Sellotape. "Onward Christian Soldiers," "All Things Bright and Beautiful," "He Who Would Valiant Be," "Love Divine All Loves Excelling," "Jerusalem . . ." When it was your turn for assembly duty you had to find the right hymns, clip them to the pulley and wind them up into the air while the headmaster was making the morning announcements. Once I hung one of the hymns upside down

15

by mistake and the headmaster turned to see what everyone was laughing at.

Lynn!

He grabbed me by the wrist and smacked the back of my legs. Hard. I was made to stand on the stage for the whole of assembly. When the hymns ended everyone said the Lord's Prayer. The headmaster had a deep, loud voice; louder than anyone else in the hall.

In the classroom, my seat was by the window. I could see across the playing field to the woods at one end of the estate. In winter, the trees were bare. Spring and summer were best, when the windows were open and you could feel the breeze and hear the noise of the mower and smell the new-cut grass. Sometimes a bee or a wasp would float in and the teacher would try to scoop it out the window before one of the boys killed it. Morning break we each got a small bottle of milk and two Rich Tea biscuits. The desks were wooden, with tops that lifted up so you could put your books inside. In the corner of each desk was a hole for a small white inkwell. We were given pens made of plain wood with scratchy metal nibs. The desks were pushed together so we sat in fours. I sat next to a girl called Janice. She had the same name as my sister, but she didn't look like her because she had long blond hair in plaits and my sister's hair had been short and black. Not black like black people's, but browny black. After bathtime her hair used to shine and smell of apricots. The other two on my table were boys, I don't remember their names. If you needed to go to the toilet you had to raise your hand. Janice—the one who wasn't my sister—wet herself once because the teacher made her wait until break. There was a puddle on the floor under her chair and she was crying and swinging her legs back and forth.

We didn't do much history at primary school. It was mostly English and arithmetic. History was cavemen, dinosaurs, Henry VIII. He was fat and had six wives and chopped off their heads when he didn't love them anymore. Pterodactyl is spelt *p-t-e-r-o-d-a-c-t-y-l*. Dinosaurs died because they had brains the size of a walnut, or because the climate changed or because a giant meteor crashed into the planet and they all burned up. I forget which. In the end–of–term tests, history, geography and science were on the same question paper.

July 1967
Lynn, Gregory
Form la
History/geography/science: (C)
Gregory must try to seek out relevent material for himself.
E. Robertson (form mistress)

I reread that report twenty five and a half years later, by torch light in the loft of a house whose occupants had recently been reduced in number from two to one. My reactions to the report were onefold:

1. E. Robertson (form mistress) can't fucking spell.

Dad taught me this song:

> *Hitler has only got one ball,*
> *the other is in the Albert Hall;*
> *Himmler is very similar,*
> *and Goebbels has no balls at all.*

Dad was eleven years old when the Second World War started. There were bombs that made a droning noise, he said, and when the noise stopped you knew they were going to fall out of the sky and blow up. You couldn't see them, just hear them. If the droning stopped right overhead you might be killed, or the bomb might drift and land somewhere else.

Brown-pants time.

Patrick.

Mum called him Patrick when she was angry with him, otherwise she called him Pat.

What's brown pants?

Never you mind, Mum said.

Dad put his mouth to the side of my face and whispered:

S' when you shit yourself.

Dad said we'd beaten the Krauts in two world wars and one World Cup. We got our first telly for the '66 World Cup. Black-and-white, with wooden doors that you closed over the screen when you weren't watching it. 1966. You say "1966" to someone English—even people who weren't born then—and they think: World Cup Final. Wembley. England 4, West Germany 2. Geoff Hurst. *Some people are on the pitch, they think it's all over . . . it is now!* I used to have a picture on my bedroom wall, torn from a magazine: Bobby Moore sitting on someone's shoulders, holding the Jules Rimet trophy. His shirt was red, the trophy was gold. That's football. That's history.

Bobby Moore is dead now. So is Hitler. There is no "West Germany," and the Berlin Wall, erected in the same year as my primary school, has ceased to exist except in photographs, memories and museums, or as souvenir lumps of masonry on mantelpieces all over Europe. The Cold War and the Second World War were quite unalike: the Cold War wasn't really a war at all, and the Germans were on our side (some of them). We won that one as well, you ask anyone. Capitalists 1, Communists 0 (after overtime).

History is written by the winners, Mr. Andrews once told me.

Mr. Patrick did not endorse this assessment. When I mentioned Mr. Andrews's observation to him, he smiled and said:

Mr. Andrews, you must remember, is an *art* teacher.

Mr. Patrick taught history at my senior school. The syllabus covered British and European history, 1760 to 1945. Mostly wars and revolutions: Agrarian, French, Napoleonic, Industrial, Crimean, Indian Mutiny, Franco-Prussian, Boer, WWI, Bolshevik, Spanish Civil, WWII. A Bolshevik was a member of the radical wing of the Russian Social Democratic Party that seized power in 1917. According to the dictionary, Bolshevik is also a derogatory term for a communist. From this word we have the adjective "bolshie." A bolshie person is obstinate and argumentative, or stubbornly uncooperative.

Words. Names.

St. Petersburg became Petrograd became Leningrad became St. Petersburg, because Lenin is now one of the bad guys, and a proud city can again honour its founder: Peter I (Peter the Great), warmonger, butcher of the serfs, creator of a capital on soil littered with the bones of the thousands who slaved, literally, over its construction. But that was three hundred years ago.

The language of history, written by the winners.

We didn't study the Cold War at school. It was still going on, and history is—by definition—concerned with the past rather than the present. As Mr. Patrick expressed it:

Interpreting events while they are in progress is like trying to shoot a moving target. No matter how good your aim, you may be wide of the mark.

The implication of this typically Patrickian aphorism being that it *is* possible to interpret events which have a clearly defined beginning and end (1914–18, 1939–45). Historical events themselves are factual; any apparent contradictions or misunderstandings in interpretation can only be the fault of an erroneous historical perspective.

Another aphorism:

History is like life, it makes sense in retrospect.

Bollocks, is what I say.

. . .

19

I know a joke about the Cold War:

A journalist asked Mikhail Gorbachev whether things might have turned out differently if Nikita Khrushchev had been assassinated instead of John F. Kennedy. Mr. Gorbachev thought for a moment, then replied: "Yes. I do not believe Aristotle Onassis would have married Mrs. Khrushchev."

I tell this joke to my barrister. He says he's heard it before.

Mr. Patrick was tall. He wore dark suits: navy, charcoal, brown. He had dandruff. When he leaned over your desk he smelled of aftershave and pipe tobacco. Teachers weren't allowed to smoke in the classrooms, so he used to suck on the empty pipe. It clicked against his teeth. His hair was grey and thinning, and stuck up at the crown, the way Billy Whizz's did. Billy Whizz was a boy who could run very fast, which was good for escaping from angry adults or catching baddies. He was in a cartoon strip in a comic. All my pocket money went on comics: *Whizzer and Chips, Dandy, Hotspur, Scorcher & Score, Shoot!, The Beano.*

Mr. Patrick couldn't run fast. One of his shoes had a thicker sole than the other, like a moon boot. We called him Hopalong or Hoppy or the Hop. The skin on the back of his hands was as thin and pale as tracing paper, with thick purple knots where the veins stood out. Long, pointy, knuckly fingers like a skeleton's. If he caught you talking or mucking around or not paying attention, he'd jab the top of your head so hard it made your eyes water and you could feel his sharp fingernail in your scalp for hours afterwards. We had double history on Monday afternoons and Thursday mornings. On the first day of the first term, when he took the register, instead of him calling our names and us saying "yes" or "sir" or "here," he told us to shout out our names so he would get to know who was who.

Surnames then first names, if you would be so kind.

They never said "Christian" names, because of the Asian kids. When it was my turn I said:

Lynn. Gregory.

Lynn Gregory? Lynn, that's a girl's name, isn't it?

Everyone laughed. Mr. Patrick was standing at his desk, looking at me over the rows of heads, most of which were turned in my direction. He was grinning.

Lynn. Is that short for Linda or Lynette? Or Lindsay?

More laughter.

It's my last name.

My last name . . .

Sir.

Sir. Sir or Mr. Patrick, either will do; neither will not. All right, settle down. Joke over. Thank you, Miss Gregory.

At home, I drew the boxes then the pictures, then coloured them in. I drew Mr. Patrick, at the front of the class. A speech bubble is saying: "Lynn. Isn't that a girl's name?" No one is laughing except him. I draw me. I am saying: "Mr. Patrick, were you born a cunt or did you take lessons?" Now everyone is laughing. I draw HA! HA! and HO! HO! above their heads. They are holding their sides, tears streaming down their faces. I draw me, talking. "All right, settle down. Joke over."

Lynn, Gregory
Form 4-3
History
Gregory really must learn to accept constructive criticism more graciously. More careful revision and a stricter adherence to the question at hand are also required.
Mr. A. Patrick

Two weeks and one day after the burning I rang my old school and asked for Mr. Patrick. I didn't want to speak to him, I just wanted to know if he still worked there and it was the only way I could think of to find out.

Mr. who?

Patrick. He teaches history.

Hang on a moment.

I heard her asking if there was a Mr. Patrick teaching there. History. Another woman's voice in the background, I couldn't make out what she said. Then the first woman again, talking to me.

I'm sorry, but apparently your Mr. Patrick retired years ago. Can I . . .

I hung up. I tried to remember how old he was when I was at school and figured he must've been in his early fifties. That was twenty years ago. On the wall chart, in the column beneath his name, I wrote "retired" alongside the words "presently employed at." I sat at my desk. I tore a page from a pad and wrote his name, I drew him and I drew a house. I opened the phone directory again and turned to the letter *P*.

Fifty-eight people listed under the name Patrick, four with "A" as their first initial: Patrick A, Patrick A D, Patrick A J, Patrick A S. One of them, Patrick A D, had the word "chiropodist" alongside his name. I rang the other three in turn. There was no answer on the first two numbers and, on the third, a recorded message said, "Hi! Sorry, Angela and Brian are out at the moment, if you . . ." I waited until evening and dialled the other two numbers again. A woman answered the first call, a man the second. Neither of them had heard of Mr. Patrick, retired history teacher.

Just after the joke about the Cold War, I ask my barrister:

What was it like, d'you suppose, being Mrs. Jackie Onassis?

I'm not with you.

You know, John F. dies and she marries someone else. She

22

copulates with him, wakes alongside him each morning between silk sheets, they dine at exclusive restaurants, attend cocktail parties, they're photographed by the paparazzi, they cruise the Mediterranean, drink champagne, sunbathe, and . . .

Gregory.

. . . all the time she's thinking—d'you think she ever stops thinking this?—on November 22, 1963, I was riding in the back of a convertible in Dallas, Texas, with part of the president's brain in my hand.

How many books have been written about the Kennedy assassination? How many films made, how many TV documentaries? And still no one knows for sure who killed him or why. I was five years and one month old when he died. I used to think I remembered seeing the news of his death on television, but I couldn't have because we didn't get a TV set until 1966. Perhaps it was the shooting of Robert, in 1968, that I saw. I would have been nine or ten, more likely to take it in. Or perhaps I've seen the footage of those last seconds of the Dallas motorcade so many times I am no longer able to divorce the actual event from my image of it. What I see is not the assassination of a president, but a man having his brains blown out. What I perceive is not History, but two histories; one factual, one fictional.

Fact: a dead president
Fiction: a president's death

My dad said the Kennedys were a bunch of fucking micks.

Mr. Patrick wrote history books. Some were on our O-level reading list. I remembered this as I sat at my desk, wondering how to find him. He wrote about the French Revolution; about

Danton and Robespierre, and Napoleon Bonaparte. When he said their names he said them with a French accent.

I waited until morning. I drew pictures of outside and filled in the blank boxes; I drew me, outside. It was cold, the last week of January. I put on my thick coat and my scarf and gloves—the ones I was wearing in the cartoon strip—and went out. It had been snowing overnight and the fallen snow on the pavements was already packed hard and rutted with dozens of footprints. There was a line of greyish-brown slush down the middle of the street. I saw an old man, a neighbour, clearing the path to his front door with a shovel. Red face, and clouds of white when he breathed. He stopped shovelling to look at me. He didn't nod or smile or say anything at first, just looked. He used to work at the same place as Dad. Denis, his name was. Den. Saturday mornings, when the boss was off, Dad sometimes let me go to work with him, just to watch or to fetch things from the stores or to run back from the pub at one o'clock and clock off for Dad and his mates. I would've been ten or eleven. Dad worked in the paint shop and Denis was in the plating shed. He did car bumpers and overriders. The parts went in a metal tank full of stuff that bubbled and smelled like hot vinegar. Denis said if I stuck my head in while the current was on it'd make my green eye go brown to match the other one. At morning break we'd sit on wooden benches in the goods yard and eat our rolls, Dad, Denis and me. Black thumbprints on soft white bread. This morning he was wearing woollen gloves.

Hello, Gregory.

I slowed, half turning my head towards him as I walked alongside the low brick wall at the front of his garden. His face was sweaty, unsmiling.

Nn. Nnng.

I looked away. I kept on walking, speeding up, past his front gate; aware of him at the periphery of my vision, watching me. Then, when I could no longer see him, there was only the sensation of still being watched. I passed another two or three houses beyond Denis's before I heard the scrape of the shovel as he went back to shifting snow.

I waited eleven minutes and twenty-seven seconds for a bus. There were two women waiting, one had a child in a push-chair. A girl with short, dark hair. I stood away from the bus stop. I put my hood up and pulled the cord tight so most of my face was hidden. Cold toes, wet socks where the snow had soaked through. When the bus came, I sat downstairs in a window seat and kept my hood up the whole way. With Mum, we always had to go upstairs so she could smoke; even on short trips. The seats were orange, yellow and brown checks, not red and black like they used to be. I had a notebook, but the bus was jolting too much for me to draw or write anything. I looked out the window and counted the cars coming the other way. I counted one hundred and seventeen.

They had three of his books in the library, in the history section. I took them to a table in one corner, partly hidden from the reception desk by a set of shelves and a display stand of leaflets on evening classes. Two of the books were paperbacks and the other a hardback. I opened my notebook and wrote down the titles: *Robespierre, Biography of a Revolutionary; The King and the Guillotine: The Last Years of Louis XVI (1791–93);* and *Russian Roulette: Napoleon's Advance on Moscow.* I took the first one, a hardback, and read the dust jacket. "Maximilien-Marie-Isidore de Robespierre (1758–94), country advocate turned revolutionary under whose ruthless leadership France was to endure the most terrible days of her bloody transition from . . ." I opened the book. At the foot of the rear flap was a solitary paragraph:

Anthony Patrick is an historian, teacher and author whose series of books on the French Revolution have become an invaluable resource for students at secondary schools and sixth-form colleges all over England and Wales. Educated at Durham University, he taught history for forty years at schools in his native Newcastle-upon-Tyne and in London before retiring to concentrate on his work as a writer, reviewer and education consultant. He lives in Orpington, Kent.

No photograph. There was a list of other titles by the same author in the *French Connections* series, eight in all. I looked around. The library was quiet, two or three people browsing in the fiction section, someone using the photocopier; no staff in sight except for a woman at the main desk. She had her back to me. I took a pair of scissors from my coat pocket. Scissors beat Paper, Paper beats Rock, Rock beats Scissors. We played it at primary school, in the playground. One, two, three . . . go! The other boy is holding his palm out flat, you have two fingers in a V. You trap his hand in the V and pretend to snip. You laugh. If you are careful, scissors make hardly any noise at all when they are cutting paper.

At home, there was a note from Auntie; an envelope folded in half and pushed through the letter-box. The note said she'd popped round but couldn't get any answer. She asked me to phone. There were kisses after her name. I crumpled the envelope and threw it in the pedal-bin in the kitchen. I made a cup of tea and a ketchup sandwich and went up to my room. On a large sheet of unruled paper I drew a set of boxes. I had to remember how Mr. Patrick used to look. I made him tall and dandruffy, I gave him one big shoe. He had a pipe in his mouth, unlit. In the first box, I drew a market square; I made it French by writing Charcuterie and Boulangerie and Salon de Thé over the shop-fronts and drawing a Tricolour on a pole above one of the buildings. The square was crowded with children, all dressed in school uniform, and in the middle was a wooden platform with a guillotine. Two of the children were marching Mr. Patrick up the steps, his bony hands tied behind his back. At the foot of the guillotine, he was made to kneel and place his neck on the block.

A wicker basket awaited his severed head. Just as the blade was about to fall, a lone horseman in a red cape and mask galloped through the crowd, dragged the condemned man from the platform and rode off with him.

Scene: a clearing in a forest. The horseman unties Mr. Patrick's hands. The teacher, weeping, begins to thank him; but the horseman jumps down from the saddle, pulls a sword from inside his cape and presses the tip against the man's throat.

Asseyez-vous!

A chair, a desk, paper, a quill. Mr. Patrick sits down. With the sword against his neck all the while, he is made to take up the quill and write the words "Liberté, Egalité, Fraternité" at the top of the first sheet of paper. He is made to write these words a hundred thousand times. He is made to write until his long thin fingers bleed and his hand, papery and veiny, seizes with cramp. When he is no longer able to write, the horseman slices off Mr. Patrick's hand with his sword and makes him use the other one. Another hundred thousand lines, another bloody stump. The lone horseman remounts and rides off, leaving the teacher in the clearing: tall, dandruffy, an unlit pipe in his mouth; a stack of paper being scattered by the wind.

I picked up the telephone and dialled.

Directory inquiries, which town, please?

Orpington, Kent.

And the name?

Patrick. Initial "A."

Do you have an address?

No.

One moment, please.

A recorded voice gave me the number and told me to stay on the line if I required any further information. I stayed on the line. When the operator came back on I asked if she could let me have the address listed in the directory for Mr. A. Patrick. There was a pause, then her voice again. I noted down what she told me. Upstairs, I added the details to the column beneath his name on the wall chart. I studied the map of Greater London and stuck a pin in the bottom right-hand corner, next to the word "Orpington." Using a ruler and a red felt-tip I drew a line from the pin to his name.

The journey would have been relatively straightforward: two bus rides, a short walk. These days I wouldn't hesitate (not that I'll be boarding any buses in the foreseeable future). But I was not then the Gregory Lynn that I have become. "Outside" contained too many blank boxes, too much whiteness to be filled. Even after a morning at the crematorium, a trip to the shop, the library —even after these tentative outings, Orpington remained out of bounds. But my physical presence was not necessary to effect a successful outcome to this first act of revision. By drawing things, sometimes I make them happen.

I picture a scene: a wintry morning, a suburban postman cycling in a snow flurry, his collar turned up against the biting wind, cap pulled firmly onto his head. He dismounts, walks along a tree-lined road of large semidetached houses with bay windows and front gardens enclosed by hedges. At No. 27 the scrollwork gate squeaks open and he hurries up the white-dusted path. With gloved hand, he removes an envelope from his bag and pushes it through the polished brass letter-box. I picture the occupant, a tall, elderly man, limping along the hall and stooping with difficulty to collect the delivered item. He straightens. He is expecting, perhaps, a royalty check for one of his books, or a request to speak at a history society luncheon, or a gas bill, or a letter from a daughter who, say, is living in New Zealand. But the writing on the envelope is unfamiliar, block capitals in red felt-tip. He takes the letter through to the kitchen, where his toast and coffee are going cold. Is there a wife? No, I imagine him alone; widowed.

He sits down stiffly at the breakfast table. Using a butter knife, he slices open the envelope and removes the contents—a single sheet of A4 paper, which he unfolds. A frown. He fumbles for his spectacles. It takes a moment for him to register the series of coloured drawings, to piece together the story they tell; to recognise the character with an unlit pipe in his mouth, a clubfoot, no hands. I picture the old man's expression as the sheet of paper falls to the floor.

Within a week, this man begins to dread the delivery of the post. Each morning, without fail, an envelope will arrive with the name and address written in red and bearing a South London postmark. No more cartoons, no note, just fragments of text and sketches which appear to have been cut from the pages of books, his books. Descriptions of beheadings, a drawing of a guillotine and coloured illustrations in which there are holes where people's hands should be. One morning, the hands are delivered. Dozens of them, paper-thin, no bigger than a thumbnail; loose in the envelope so that when the occupant of No. 27 opens it they flutter about him like confetti.

Facts:
1934. Hitler, chancellor of Germany, assumes role of dictator; Austria's chancellor murdered by Nazis; Chairman Mao's Long March.

Mum was born on March 8, 1934. Her name was Randall. In 1955 she got married and she wasn't Marion Randall anymore, she was Marion Lynn. Two *n*'s. She was a hairdresser. Then she stopped being a hairdresser because of Janice and me. By the time I started senior school it was just the two of us and she had to go out to work again. She got a job in a grocer's. Supashop. She wore a blue-and-white-check apron and flat shoes and had to wear her hair up if she was on the cheese and meat counter. Smoking wasn't allowed at the shop, except in the rest area. They let her work odd hours so she could see me off to school and be there when I came home. When she was making my breakfast or cooking tea she always had a cigarette in her hand, or her mouth, or balanced on the edge of an ashtray. Tea was egg, chips and beans, or sausage and mash, or boil-in-the-bag cod with potatoes and peas; unless she fetched something from work like frozen pizza or ham and mushroom flan—damaged, or past its sell-by date. One teatime Mum burnt her arm on the oven door, dropping a pizza face-first on the floor.

Jesus Christ all fucking mighty!

She tried to scrape the food onto plates, but the cheese and tomato topping came away from the base and was stuck with bits of hair and dirt. The whole lot went in the flip-top bin, plates and all. Mum swore again. She grabbed a dish cloth, bent over the mess on the floor and started to scrub the tiles in a vigorous circling motion that became slower and slower until her arm was still. When she raised her head, her eyes were red-rimmed and puffy and there was snot down her mouth.

Facts:
1928. Earthquake in Greece destroys Corinth; German airship crosses the Atlantic; Captain Kingsford-Smith flies the Pacific; women in Britain enfranchised on same basis as men.

Dad was born on August 18, 1928. His hair was the blackest of all of us. He was big, like me. He said I got my brains from Mum and my brawn from him and I should thank fuck it wasn't the other way round. Dad read the *Mirror* and the *Sporting Life*. He did crosswords. He supported Chelsea. His favourite player was Charlie Cooke, even though he was a Jocko. Peter Osgood was a fucking pouf.

Dad voted Labour, said the only good Tory was a lavatory. The greatest man who ever lived was Winston Churchill.

He was a Tory, Mum said.

Politics don't come into it when there's a war on.

What about Spain? You know, Franco.

Spain's got fuck all to do with anything.

Mum, who was washing up or ironing or sewing, told him not to use that language in front of Gregory.

She was always telling me I had to be a good boy or when Dad came home he would smack me or I'd be sent to bed early or I'd get no pocket money or he wouldn't take me with him to work on Saturday.

Dad's job was to paint bits of car—bonnets, doors, wings, boots—after they'd been mended in the panel shop. He used a spray gun and wore a wad of cloth over his nose and mouth, held in place by two loops of elastic round his ears. He'd try the gun out on the wall to make sure the colour was right before pointing it at the metal. The wall was puke-splatted with paint: green, red, yellow, blue, black, brown, silver, gold.

Like one of them fucking arty-farty paintings, Dad said.

Facts:
1956. Khrushchev denounces Stalin; Suez crisis; Soviet forces crush Hungarian uprising; Britain has coldest day (February 1) since 1895.

Janice was born on April 2, 1956. Janice was my sister. She always had scabby knees from falling over, always had one sock pulled up and the other round her ankle. Janice remembered Grandpa Randall. He had white, scratchy whiskers that hurt your face when he kissed you, she said; he'd been a soldier in the war. He'd met Queen Victoria, Elizabeth I and King Edward—the one who invented the potato. Grandpa Randall was old, then he died. There are babies, children, grown-ups and old people. Babies get older and become children, children get older and become grown-ups, grown-ups get older and become old people. Old people die.

Janice said an old person had died in our house before we moved in. He died and went to heaven, but his ghost stayed

31

behind. The ghost lived in the loft. You couldn't see him or hear him or touch him but, when the light was off and the loft was dark, sometimes you got goose bumps on the back of your neck. That was him, Janice said, breathing on you. She went:

Huuuuh. Huuuuh.

Like a wheeze. It wasn't scary in the loft. Unless it went quiet and I thought Janice wasn't there anymore, and then I'd say her name out loud to make her tell me to shush. When we asked Mum, she said she didn't remember what the old man was called. And anyway he hadn't died, he'd gone into a home. That was a fib, because we'd both felt him breathe on us. Me and Janice. We called him Mr. Mistry Man, because Janice said Miss Coote had read them a *mistry story* about a ghost who made friends with two children. You had to talk in whispers in the loft because you weren't supposed to be in there. You had to keep very still, and not giggle or sneeze or cough. If Mr. Mistry Man didn't come, we took turns to breathe on each other's neck and make believe it was him. If my lips touched her skin, she'd say:

No touching, Jeggy. Ghosts can't touch.

Janice wasn't old when she went away. She went away when I was four and a half, came back as a tiny baby; went away again. When I see her in my head I see her the way she is in my drawings. The way she was then.

Mum never smacked us, but Dad did. No belts or canes or anything, just the flat of his hand on your legs or the side of your head. The barrister seems indifferent to this information.

I am too big to hit now. When it is necessary for me to be escorted from place to place, I am always accompanied by the burliest of guards. I am always in handcuffs. Now that my hair is shaved to a charcoal stubble, now the ponytail is gone, my appearance makes all the more impact. I alarm people. They see the discrepancy in the colour of my eyes, see my face, my size, my scalp, and they are like a rabbit caught in the dazzle of car head-lights. Of course, this is also symptomatic of their cognizance of my reputation, my notoriety. I am held in awe. I am awesome. When people meet me they experience an encounter with an historic person. Me, Gregory Lynn (orphan, bachelor, only child from the age of four and a half).

The first time I cut my own hair, I was ten. It was my birthday, there was to be a party on the Saturday. My friends were coming, and their mums and dads. Mum spent all morning getting ready for their arrival. She laid the table in the back room, made sandwiches and cakes and puddings and put little sausages on sticks, and chunks of cheese and pineapple; and made tea and jugs of orange juice. She dusted, hoovered. She wiped around the door handles with a yellow duster until Dad's grey fingerprints smudged and then disappeared. The party was in the afternoon; Dad had time to come home at lunchtime and change out of his work clothes. That morning at breakfast, Mum said:

I'll put the water on for later.

Why?

Why. Why d'you think?

I had a bath *last* month.

Dad was reading the paper and drinking tea. He hadn't shaved yet, or combed his hair. He winked at me, smiling. Mum said:

I'm not having you get your nice clothes all smelly and messed up.

That shirt? That shirt's older than him.

There'll be people here.

And the trousers for that matter. My overalls are in better shape than those trousers.

I'll put the water on.

Two o'clock.

33

Patrick.

Two.

They're coming at half past.

Do I smell?

Dad put the paper down, lifted the front of his pyjama top to his nose and sniffed. He looked at me, raising one arm above his head and pulling me by the neck so my face was pressed into his armpit. The cloth was damp and yellowy brown. He let me go.

Do I?

If I catch a whiff of beer on you, Patrick Lynn.

Mum came to find me. She stood outside the bedroom door and called my name. I didn't answer. I was sitting on the edge of the bed with a pair of scissors from her hairdressing kit. The curtains were drawn.

Gregory, they'll be here soon.

I didn't say anything. The door opened. Mum asked what was I doing sitting in the dark like that? She went over to the window and opened the curtains.

Jesus Christ.

She sat beside me on the bed. She was saying things, touching me. I felt her hand on my head. I felt her stroking the thick clumps of hair on the crown and at the back; the spiky, stubbly bits above my ears and where the fringe used to be; and—gentler, gingerly—the bald places, where the skin stuck to her fingers. And her fingers came away red and wet.

December 1970
Lynn, Gregory
Form 1-3
Attendance: poor
Punctuality: fair
Gregory's attendance record has shown a slight improvement in

Form 1–3 meant I was in the first year, form three. Senior school was different to juniors: the forms weren't streamed, only the subjects. Form 1–3 was the same as 1–1 or 1–6—just a number, a room where we had to meet for morning register. Then, after assembly, you'd go off to lessons and some children from your form would be in the same class as you and some wouldn't. I was in the top group for English, the bottom group for maths and science. Art wasn't grouped according to ability because, Mr. Andrews said, you can't give marks for pictures.

At lunchtime on the first day, one boy walked up to another boy in the playground and punched him in the face. He didn't say anything, just hit him and walked away. The other boy's lip was bleeding. I didn't know them, they were in the second year. The second years were the oldest because the school had only been open twelve months when I went there. They hadn't finished building the sports hall, and one end of the playground was still being laid with Tarmac. If a football landed there a workman would knock it back with a long piece of wood and you had to pick off the bits of black which stuck to the ball, like gobs of chewed liquorice. Where the school was built there used to be a hill with grass on it and a few trees. It was the Common. People walked their dogs there, or flew kites, or dumped rubbish. In winter, if there was enough snow, kids from the estate went tobogganing. Dad made me a sledge from old chipboard and strips of metal from the scrap bins at work. A Christmas present. My hair had grown back by then, except where the stitches had been, so I didn't have to wear a woolly hat anymore. Mum made me wear one anyway, because of the cold. It was January. I'd been back at school for weeks, but it was the first time I'd been allowed out to play since my birthday; since the party that never happened. The tests had stopped, but we still got visits

from a woman from the Council—Antisocial Services, Dad said
—and a man he called a shrink, though Mum said he was nothing of the sort. The man showed me a book of pictures made up
of ink dots and asked what I saw, and I said dots. And when he
kept on, I made things up and he wrote my answers in a notebook. He asked who I liked best—John, Paul, George or Ringo
—and wrote that down as well. At school, I told the other kids
I'd had an operation on my brain and nearly died and my dad had
saved me with the kiss of life. That was in the juniors. By the
time I went to senior school my hair was long enough to conceal
the scars.

The hill disappeared. When they built the school the Common was dug up and levelled by bulldozers. The dumper trucks
came past our house, rattling the windows and leaving stones and
lumps of mud in the road. The mud became flattened like plas-
ticine, tyre-tracked. I tried to work out where the hill would've
been that time Dad and I went tobogganing; but I couldn't. It
was as though the Common hadn't existed; as though all there'd
ever been was the school, square blocks of glass, chrome and
concrete, the playground with its white lines and the netball posts
with tatters of net hanging from the metal hoops. The uniform
was green and grey. My nickname was Odd Eyes.

When Mr. Patrick asked a question you had to raise your hand
before answering. If you didn't, if you shouted it out, he'd say:
Hands. Hands.

If you put your hand up and he picked you, you had to say
"sir" or "Mr. Patrick" at the end of the answer or he'd say
WRONG! and ask someone else, even if you were right. And if
you said names wrong he'd say them back at you and everyone
would laugh.

Dan Tunn? Who is this Dan Tunn chappie, if you please?

Danton, sir.

I take it you are referring to Monsieur *Danton*. Beheaded he
may have been, but that is no reason for you to behead his name,
Mlle Gregory.

He said it *Dongtong*. He always called me Miss Gregory, or Mlle Gregory if we were doing the French Revolution. Or Linda. Or Lynette.

The way he taught history was to dictate notes or write things on the blackboard for us to copy into our exercise books, or hand out worksheets on paper covered with purple handwriting and which were slightly damp from the copier and smelled of methylated spirits. Or we'd make notes from our textbooks while he sat at his desk, marking essays. At the end of the class there'd be ten minutes for *questions, queries, quandaries and quibbles*. If no one asked anything, he'd *recapitulate*.

Patrickian aphorism: History is the study of cause and effect. If we are to understand a period or moment in history, we must examine the events preceding it—i.e., the cause—and those succeeding it—i.e., the effect. Thus we establish the chronology, the order. History is "this happened, then that happened"; the study of history—its beauty—is "that happened *because* this happened."

Is it, fuck.

Historical Fact (1):

The Japanese attack on Pearl Harbour occurred on the morning of Sunday December 7, 1941.

Historical Fact (2):

The Japanese attack on Pearl Harbour occurred on the morning of Monday December 8, 1941.

Two facts. Only one of them can be correct, yet they both are. How is this possible? How can the same single event take place on two different days? It is possible because when it is Sunday morning on one side of the international date line it is Monday morning on the other. Pearl Harbour is bombed: in Hawaii it's Sunday, in Tokyo it's Monday. Your plane takes off from Los Angeles at 11 P.M. on Friday, flies across the Pacific, and lands in Sydney, Australia, at 3 P.M. on Sunday. What about Saturday?

Saturday didn't happen, it didn't exist. You were born on February 29. You are twenty-four years old and you've had six birthdays, which makes you six. According to your watch it is two minutes to midnight, the clock on the wall says it is two minutes past. Which is the correct time, or are they both wrong? The sun sets; somewhere, simultaneously, the sun rises. Mr. Patrick, our watches are not synchronised. What I say, then, is: if there is a discrepancy over something as straightforward (as certain, as factual) as "when?," how can we be clear about "why?" Who are we to determine cause and effect when we don't even know what fucking day of the week it is?

I try to discuss this with my barrister. He is uninterested.

Lynn, Gregory
Form 3-3
History
I realise that Gregory is not especially interested in this subject, but he will find it a useful asset in the future provided he is prepared to make the necessary effort to learn the material thoroughly.
Mr. A. Patrick

In W. H. Smith, in Waterstones, and in Dillons, I removed certain books from the shelves in the history sections. In the quieter corners, out of sight of customers and cashiers and with my back to the security cameras, I knelt. I opened the books at the appropriate pages, I cut them. Pictures, text. Hands. Scores of papery pairs of hands. I put the fragments in my coat pocket and replaced the books. I returned home. Daily, I sent another delivery, carefully placing the pieces in the envelope and drawing the cartoons. Each cartoon was the same: a single frame (scene: a classroom); a tall, dandruffy old man sitting at a desk; a horseman in a red mask and cape writing on the blackboard. Only the words on the board changed with each drawing:

Mr. Patrick must learn to accept constructive criticism more graciously.

More careful revision and a stricter adherence to the question at hand is desirable.

I realize that Mr. Patrick is not especially happy with this subject, but he will find it a useful asset in the future.

Mr. Patrick must make the necessary effort to learn the material thoroughly.

History is the study of cause and effect.

Employment History

Dates	Employer	Position	Reason for Leaving
May 75–Sep 75	Supashop (grocers)	shelf-filler	emotional
Oct 75–Oct 76	H.M. Govt (Youth Opps Prog.)	skivvy	inevitable
Nov 76–Mar 77	H.M. Govt (DHSS)	claimant	financial
Apr 77–May 78	Borough Council	cleaner	hygienic
Jun 78–Nov 79	H.M. Govt (DHSS)	claimant	political
Nov 79–Feb 80	Borough Council (Leisure Services)	art gallery attendant	aesthetic
Feb 80–Aug 84	H.M. Govt (DHSS)	claimant	implausible
Sep 84–Sep 85	Borough Council (Leisure Services)	assistant to community artist	unpalatable
Oct 85–Jan 94	H.M. Govt (DSS)	claimant	criminal

Fact:

The community artist to whom I had been assistant from September 1984 to September 1985, inclusive, was a Mr. A. W. Andrews. Andy Andrews. Former art teacher at ———, a large South London secondary school, future witness for the prosecution in the case against me, Gregory Lynn.

Although trivial compared to the other alleged offences, I am to be charged with criminal damage in relation to a quantity of hardback and paperback books. A compensation order is being sought on behalf of various shops and the Library Services Department of the Borough Council. I am also informed that Mr. Patrick contacted his local police station twelve months ago, when all this started, to report the receipt of an offensive letter. Initially, the police showed little interest, taking a statement and —after a cursory examination—filing the envelope and its contents. When the retired teacher began to receive similar deliveries on a daily basis, a more concerted effort was made to identify and trace the sender. However, the inquiries drew a blank and when, after a few weeks, the letters ceased, the investigation was suspended pending further evidence or information. My arrest and forthcoming trial have reactivated the matter and it is to form part of the prosecution's case.

All this I learn from my barrister. For an hour he has questioned me closely about the *Patrick letters* while the solicitor, in her customarily methodical manner, has taken notes. At one point, early in the interview, my description of the first cartoon prompted an exchange of glances—a palpable unease—between the two lawyers. Initially, I put it down to my graphic account of the punishment meted out by the caped horseman—bloody stumps, etc. But the significance of the look that passed between them, I have come to realise, was more than mere shared distaste. Nothing the Crown can pin on me, of course, beyond the damage to the books, the sending of offensive and threatening material through Her Majesty's postal service and the causing of a nuisance to one Mr. Anthony Patrick, historian. Even my representatives, despite their epiphanic inkling of the true manifestation of this act of revision, retreat from its implications. They deny, they resist, they explain it away. But they know. I detected it in their eyes during that exchanged glance, I sense it now in their manner. They fucking well *know*.

Is Mr. Patrick to give evidence?

Not as such.

Meaning?

My information is that the gentleman is excused attendance due to, ah, ill health.

Ill health?

A sworn statement is to be presented instead. To the court.

In pressing my barrister to elaborate on the nature of Mr. Patrick's illness, I am met with silence. He averts his gaze from mine. Finally, it is the solicitor, after a moment's deliberation, who answers. Her tone is flat, efficient; she is dispensing information in response to a formal request. She informs me that during the early part of last year the witness—that's to say, Mr. Patrick—developed Parkinson's disease. She says he has, for several months, resided in a private nursing home. The onset and progression of the disease have been swift and, apparently, the tremor is so pronounced that he has to sit on his hands to prevent them from shaking. He is unable to hold a pen, or a knife and fork, or a cup of tea, nor can he manage to perform the most basic of bathroom necessities unassisted. Mr. Patrick can't use his hands at all.

2

geography **1a.** science that deals with the earth and
its life; esp: **1b.** description of land, sea and air
1c. distribution of plant and animal life, including
human beings and industries **2.** geographical features of an area

The estate was an island, a triangle; four hundred homes bordered on one side by a highway and on the others by a small
copse and an industrial estate. The houses had pebble-dashed
walls, the flats—in six eight-storey blocks—squatted over a parade
of shops; there was a row of maisonettes, an old folks' home, two
pubs, a health centre, a boy scout hut, a church and a playground.
The scout hut was burnt down, rebuilt, burnt down. A sign outside the church carried messages like: "Give Jesus Your Presence
This Christmas" or "Nazareth Carpenter Seeks Joiners." There
once were fields and woods where the estate stood, and a common where they built the school. The copse was all that remained—tall trees huddled on a rise of land overlooking the
rooftops. The copse floor was shingle and pebbles. Dad said it was
seabed, millions of years ago, before people. We moved to our
house when I was three months old; a transfer from another part
of the borough because the flat where we were living before was
too small now there were four of us. The estate was new then,
some of it still a building site; the noise of the lorries used to
wake me and make me cry, Mum said. We had a bright red front

door, like every house in our street. A path at the front, and flower beds, and a concrete yard and strip of lawn at the back which Dad dug over to grow vegetables. He wanted to keep chickens but the bastard Council wouldn't let him. Denis next door kept pigeons in a shed with wire mesh for windows. You could smell them from our garden. He talked to them, they had names. He held them to his face and kissed their beaky heads. Every afternoon he'd let them out—twenty or thirty—and they'd swoop and soar over the back gardens, settle for a while on the surrounding rooftops, then return to their shed. They always came back. He used to say:

You don't train a homing pigeon by keeping it in the loft.

On race days he'd stand outside for hours, watching the sky. Waiting for black dots to appear against the white, the grey, the blue. Dad said pigeons were flying vermin—rats with wings. If we played outside, Janice and me, we had to stay off the flowers and vegetables. I had a trike and she had roller skates. We played in the yard, or up and down the front path. Mum left the door open so she could keep an eye on us. When I was older and had a proper bicycle I rode all over the estate and where the factories were, and over the copse, using the tracks where shingle had been compressed into the mud by people walking. I climbed trees. I wanted an air rifle so I could shoot things: squirrels, birds. Mum said no. I wanted to line up empty drinks cans on a fence and shoot them off one by one.

I stopped playing outside when I was nearly twelve. The only time I'd go out was to go to school. Go to school, come home, eat my tea, go to my room. Then I stopped having tea in the kitchen and got Mum to bring it up to the bedroom instead. She wasn't allowed in, so she had to knock and leave the tray by the door. If the food wasn't nice I'd throw it down the stairs. If Mum came into my room I'd scream at her to fuck off. I skipped school some days, or I'd go in the morning and come home at break or lunchtime. I'd tell Mum I wasn't well; or not say anything at all, just ignore her. On the mornings I decided not to bother with

43

school I'd make her phone and say *Gregory is under the weather.*
When I went in the next day or a couple of days later, she'd
write a note for the form teacher.

December 1971
Lynn, Gregory
Form 2-3
Geography
Gregory produces good neat maps and diagrams but must be sure
to listen to instructions more carefully.
E. R. Davies-White (Mrs.)

I didn't resume my exploration of the estate until after the business with Mr. Patrick. I went out every other day to start with,
then every day—each time for a little longer. I'd draw a picture
of a place—the shops, or wherever—and draw me; then I'd walk
there, always in the clothes I was wearing in the picture. Once I'd
made the estate familiar again I began to venture further afield. I
travelled by bus to where the shops are. I sat in a park: lunchtime,
the eighteenth of March, there were people eating sandwiches—
office workers, shop staff. Didn't talk to anyone, just sat on a
wooden bench. It was sunny. I lowered my hood. Another time I
went right into London, into the centre. On the train, I sat opposite a woman, a stranger. She wore a green coat with black
lapels, a magazine open on her lap. I spoke to her. We had a
conversation:

Excuse me, is this train going to Victoria?

Yes it is.

Auntie was pleased I was getting out and about. She said
Marion would've been pleased too, it was what she would've
wanted. Marion was my mum, she was *on the other side* now.

. . .

I read about this in the local newspaper:

A businessman leaves his office in Birmingham at 9:05 and sets off in his company car for an appointment in South London. At 10:47 the same morning, a young woman leaves home in Purley to collect her parents at Heathrow on their return from holiday. At 11:12 both cars are on the M25, London orbital. The businessman is heading anticlockwise at 81 mph, the woman is travelling clockwise, 70 mph. On the anticlockwise road a car veers into the fast lane without indicating; the businessman brakes sharply, his car goes into a skid, clips the rear of the other vehicle and flips. It clears the barrier and collides head-on with a car coming the other way. That car contains the young woman from Purley. Both drivers are killed instantly.

I've invented some of the details. In the paper there was a quote from a paramedic saying "neither of them stood a chance." Didn't they? What if the businessman had left his office at 9:10 instead of 9:05, what if he'd stopped at a service station for coffee, what if he'd had a cold and phoned in sick that day, what if he hadn't jumped those red lights on his way out of Birmingham, what if his car had broken down, what if he'd been doing 79 mph instead of 81? Or what if the young woman's car had started first time, what if she'd forgotten her purse and had to go back to the house to fetch it, what if her parents had chosen a holiday which meant flying into Gatwick instead of Heathrow, what if she'd been driving in the middle lane instead of the fast lane? Or what if . . .

What if what if what if.

I put this question to my barrister. Don't mention the story in the newspaper, I just say "what if?" He is puzzled.

What if what?

What if anything.

I went to places where I'd been before, where things had happened but where nothing was happening now except me being there thinking about what had happened those other times. Making ghosts.

1. The copse: at the rim of a hollow, looking up at an overhanging branch. Janice and me used to climb into the tree and shin out along the branch and jump onto an old mattress which had been dumped in the hollow. The mattress was split, showing its innards. You weren't allowed to hang from the branch by your hands and let yourself drop, you had to stand up and jump. You'd shout Geronimo! I was four. Too young to be climbing trees, Mum said. So she wasn't to know. I wasn't to tell. Janice was two and a half years older than me, bigger. Scabby knees. Whoever went first had to get out the way quick before the other one jumped. Sometimes I pretended to have my foot stuck in the hole in the mattress so Janice would land on me.

The mattress was gone. Nothing in the hollow except dead leaves. The branch wasn't so high anymore, if I stretched I could reach up and touch it. My fingers came away green.

CONTINENTAL DRIFT

The continents are carried along on the top of slowly moving crustal plates which float on heavier liquid material (the lower mantle) much as icebergs do on water. The plates converge and diverge along margins marked by seismic and volcanic activity. This is called plate tectonics. About 200 million years ago earth's original landmass (Pangea) began to split into two continental groups—Laurasia to the north, Gondwanaland to the south. These further separated over time to produce the present configuration. Two hundred million years ago there were no people, no countries, no borders. The planet is 4.6 billion years old, we've been here 40,000 years. The earth's crust accounts for 1.5 percent of the planet's volume, it is where we live. We are one race: *Homo sapiens*.

We opened our exercise books and drew pictures of volcanoes: brown for soil; grey for rock; red, yellow and orange for lava. Magma. Magma is like the word smegma. We drew continents, we drew arrows to show which way they moved; we drew fault lines. Mrs. Davies-White got us to lower the blinds and switch off the lights for a film about earthquakes. An earthquake is a series of rapid vibrations originating from the slipping or faulting of parts of the earth's crust when stresses within build to breaking point. In 1906 more than five hundred people in San Francisco were killed in an earthquake measuring 8.3 on the Richter scale. There could be another one at any time. People living in San Francisco are aware that, one day, they might die. I put my hand up:

So how're they different to anyone else?

Gregory, we are studying *physical* geography, not *meta*physical.

Mrs. Davies-White had dark brown curly hair and brown eyes. When she smiled, her mouth went up at one corner more than the other. She wore tight white trousers, or skirts and frocks you could see through in the right light. She wore perfume. You could make out her bra through her blouse. Pointy tits. When I wanked, I dreamed of Mrs. Davies-White.

She was Welsh, from a place none of us could say without bringing up a gobful of grolly. She showed us her hometown on the map. Sixteen letters, no vowels. She had a Welsh accent, especially when she was angry. Her name was Davies and her husband's was White and when they got married they put their names together. He was English.

Dad knew a joke about Wales:

An English tourist is driving through a Welsh village. He stops at the roadside, winds down the window and calls out to a passerby: "Oi, Taffy, which way is Caerphilly?" The man looks up and says: "How d'you know my name was Taffy?" The driver says: "I guessed." And the man says: "Well, guess the fucking way to Caerphilly."

I told this joke to Mrs. Davies-White. She said if I ever used that word in front of her again she'd send me to the head of year. Being sent to the head of year meant a bollocking, a letter to your parent(s) or guardian. Being sent to the headmaster meant the cane or suspension or expulsion. When I was in the fourth year two boys got expelled for smoking dope in the toilets. In the fifth year a boy in my form hit a teacher. Punched him in the face. I didn't see it happen, only heard about it. He was the best fighter in the school, even the sixth formers wouldn't fight him. After he hit the teacher he got caned and expelled. I didn't see him again until years later, after the Mr. Patrick letters. He had dreadlocks instead of Afro, but I recognised him. He was on a bus, with a woman and three children. The youngest, a girl, was on his lap. She was sucking her thumb, her index finger curled over the bridge of her nose. He was reading to her from a story-book.

2. The school: outside the perimeter fence, looking across the playground to the Humanities Block. Sunday, no children. I tried to work out which of the second-floor windows was the geography classroom. I remembered maps on the wall, diagrams, photographs, posters. Countries were different then: Yugoslavia, Czechoslovakia, the Soviet Union. In Russian, USSR is CCCP. The hydrological cycle is: it rains, water evaporates, clouds form, it rains. A boy in my group was from Hobart. He had a badge with a huge Tasmania on it and a tiny Australia-shaped blob above it marked "North Island." If we had to draw maps and diagrams I always finished mine first—they were always the best, Mrs. Davies-White said so. But she wanted facts: tonnes of coal per annum, average rainfall in inches *and* millimetres, an arrow pointing north, a scale showing miles and kilometres. She'd say:

Labels, labels, labels.

Eight kilometres equal five miles. They are the same distance. They are different ways of saying the same thing.

I held the fence. It was twice my height, metal posts with spiked tops and a sign with the name of a security firm. There

48

was a picture of a dog's head in silhouette, and big red letters saying WARNING. When I was a pupil, there was only a low chain-link fence hidden by a hedge. There were gaps, trampled-down places where we took shortcuts. "Security" was a care-taker. He wore blue overalls and brown boots and a woolly hat. He fixed things when they broke, he shouted OI! when we went where we weren't supposed to, when we ran along the corridors, when a window broke. He grew vegetables in the garden of his bungalow in the school grounds.

Mrs. Davies-White put coloured stickers on the map of the world and a code showing which crops grew in which coun-tries; where coal was produced; where the people spoke Spanish; where the Muslims lived. She wrote the name of every capital city of every country, the currency, the population. She asked questions. We'd be in the middle of something—coastal ero-sion, or whatever—and she'd suddenly call your name and say: "What's the capital of Syria?" or "In which country is the zloty the currency?" And you had to know. If you didn't, she'd send you to the back of the room and make you look at the map on the wall until you found the answer.

Learn your labels. Labels are no use if you don't learn them.

From the fence, I couldn't make out any of the rooms. I could see a long row of windows. I could see reflections of clouds and sky. My hands were cold against the metal posts, knuckles showing white through bluey-purple skin. I'd forgotten my gloves, even though I was wearing them in the picture I'd drawn before going outside.

My barrister is curious to know why I waited so long before tracking her down. Nearly two months elapsed between the Mr. Patrick episode and my pursuit of Mrs. Davies-White. Why the delay? Once I'd committed myself to the acts of revision, was it not—in the terms of my own logic—simply a matter of picking them off? We quibble over "committed" and "logic." No common ground here, an agreement to differ. He persists with his why? why? why? and I explain the necessity of my training regime, the time-consuming nature of these preparations and the logistical difficulty I encountered in tracing my next subject. He is neither satisfied nor convinced.

There must be more to it than this, Gregory.

Write that down!

The solicitor, of course, does nothing of the sort; doesn't even look up from her pad. Her instruction is to record only *my* comments, to note only those utterances which help establish *my* thought processes; which give clues to *my* personality. Which mitigate. Which diminish my responsibility. Counsel tries another tack:

Very well, why the, ah . . . urge actually to *visit* your victim (a raised hand to still my objection) . . . your subject, this time? Were you bored with the strategy of revision by correspondence?

Letters. Their wank factor wears off after a while. (Now I have the solicitor's attention. I smile at her.) That's *w-a-n-k*.

According to my calculations, Mrs. Davies-White—thirty-something when I was her pupil—would've been in her midfifties around the time I was attempting to locate her. If she was still teaching, she was no longer at my old school. I checked. She'd left five years earlier. On requesting details of her current place of employment, I was informed that the school was not at liberty to divulge such information.

The loft was a spaceship, a submarine, a cave. It was a tree house. If we made believe it was any of these, the Mistry Man wasn't there because he was only there when it was the loft; when it was real. If it was a cave, we had to take our clothes off and pull the

old blankets from one of the boxes and wrap them round ourselves like animal skins. We had to turn the light out, because
caves are dark. We had to talk in grunts, quiet grunts so the
mammoths and sabre-toothed tigers and dinosaurs wouldn't hear.
It was cold in the cave, we had to huddle together. Janice was
warm under the blanket and she smelled of skin and old blanket
and soap. Her skin was warm and soft where it touched mine.

Ug. Ug.

Ugga–ugga.

Cavemen and cavewomen rub noses, like Eskimos, instead
of kissing. We rubbed noses. When Janice touched my willy it
got bigger and she asked if it hurt and I said it didn't, it felt
funny. Tickly. She said did I want to touch her and I said yes
and she let me, but my fingers were cold and she had to rub them
between her hands and breathe on them before I could touch her
again.

What is it?

S'where girls widdle out of.

But . . . what's it called?

Isn't called anything.

She let me touch her a bit longer, then pushed my hand
away and said I was too rough. My willy was still big and when I
widdled, it went on my tummy and made the blanket wet and
went on Janice's hand. She giggled and said she wanted to widdle
too and did I want to feel while she did it? I said I did, and she let
me.

Time of departure: 9 A.M. On foot to the bus stop, bus to the
station, train to Victoria, tube to Paddington, train to Cardiff.
Time of arrival: 1:05 P.M. Rain.

Cardiff (Caerdydd): Loc. Govt. dist. South Glamor-
gan, cap. of Wales; at mouth of R. Taff on Bristol
Channel, one of world's great coal-shipping ports;
univ. colls, cath., cas.; iron and steel wks, flour mills;

freeport (1984) to help redevelopment of docks; pop.
279,500.

Orange buses, not red. One had an advert down the side
saying "It's Brains You Want." Brains is a beer, the landlady of
the guesthouse told me. You go into a Cardiff pub and ask for a
pint of Brains. Ordinary or SA. SA stands for Strong Ale, or Skull
Attack. Brains goes straight to your head. I don't drink. If I go in
a pub I have Coca-Cola or Fanta. I don't smoke. Drinking and
smoking kill you. Outside the railway station I raised my hood,
crossed the taxi rank and went into a café. People were talking
funny. Not Welsh, funny English; like Welsh people on the telly.
I ordered pasty and chips and tea and sat at a window seat,
watching the orange buses. I asked the waitress which bus went
to Cathedral Road. She had to ask the woman on the till. The
woman told me the bus number, then a man at another table said
how far up Cathedral Road was I going cos it wasn't far to walk
like, and the woman said look at the rain and did I have a brolly
and I shook my head and she said never mind she expected my
hood would do just fine and wasn't I hot with it up, here, in the
warm? And where was I from? Oh, London, she said. Her sister
lived in London. Pinner. Handy for the M4 it was. Too big,
London. Too many people. Nobody talks to anybody.

The man gave me directions, he drew a map on a serviette
with a Ladbrokes pen. He drew a big oval to show where the
rugby stadium was, and a wiggly blue line for the river. No scale,
no contour lines, no arrow pointing north. It was a good map. I
found Cathedral Road, where the man who'd sat opposite me on
the train said there'd be plenty of B&Bs. I ought to ask for a
room at the back, away from the road, he'd said. Was I up for the
international rugby match? No. He asked other things, we had a
conversation. Later, I wrote it down in my notepad, made a cartoon of it. I drew the people in the café as well, and wrote speech
bubbles. I drew the man drawing the map. My head ached with
all the listening, all the thinking of what to say. I could hear the
rain on my hood as I walked: across the bus station, past a swim-

ming pool, over a bridge, turn right along the river with the rugby stadium on the other bank, left at the main road, right at the lights. Cathedral Road. The first four places were full, the landlady at the fifth place said I was lucky—late cancellation. She let me have a double room at the single rate. *En suite facilités.* She asked how many nights I'd be staying and I said I didn't know. It all depended.

I got her to fetch me a telephone directory. She talked a lot, then went away. I locked the door. Half past two. They wouldn't be out of school for another hour. I sat on the bed and unfolded the map I'd bought at the railway station. I looked up Davies-White in the phone book—pages of Davies, only one Davies-White—and copied the address. I looked up the address of the school and wrote that down too. I undressed and went to the bathroom; cleaned my teeth, had a shower. I thought about Mrs. Davies-White and soaped my prick until I spunked.

She was the first of the seven to have her photograph on the wall chart in my room. A cutout from a photocopy of a five-year-old newspaper cutting—she was much older than I remembered, but you could see it was her. Black hair as dark as Janice's. Curly, though; longer. I stuck a green pin in the map, where Cardiff was. When I was cutting the picture I had to be careful with the scissors so I didn't make her head a funny shape. The rest of the photograph showed a schoolgirl handing Mrs. Davies-White a bouquet. In the background, two dozen children stood in a semicircle; grinning, pulling faces. Above the picture was a headline: "Geography Teacher Maps Out Career Move." The caption read:

> Pupils at ——— school said a fond farewell this week
> to the deputy head of geography, Mrs. Elizabeth Da-
> vies-White, who is leaving after 21 years to return to
> her native South Wales. Mrs. Davies-White, aged 51,
> takes up a new post at ——— school, Cardiff, in Sep-

tember. She is pictured (above) receiving a bouquet from 12-year-old . . .

The cutting was date-stamped in red. It was in a small brown envelope with "Davies-White, Elizabeth (teacher)" typed on the front. There was one other cutting. No picture this time, just an article dated October 3, 1987, about a twenty-four-hour sponsored Geographon quiz Mrs. Davies-White had organised at the school to raise funds for famine relief in Africa. The envelope was in a drawer marked "Dace–Duggan" in one of a row of tall metal filing cabinets in the library at the local newspaper offices. Easy. All you have to do is go into reception and ask. The receptionist gives you a security tag and gets you to sign in (you make up a name). She makes an internal call, and a librarian escorts you to the library, explains the filing system. There's a desk and writing paper, or you can make photocopies. I made three copies, one for my own files, one for the wall chart and one to take to Cardiff.

The day after the visit to the newspaper offices, Auntie came round. I locked the bedroom before going downstairs to let her in. She'd brought chocolate biscuits, she made tea. She made me sit in the front room and talk to her. It was okay; practice conversation, part of my training. I was very polite, cordial. After a while, I told her:
I'm going away.
Away? Where?
Just for a few days.
On your own?
Yes. A holiday.
Where?
. . . Brighton. A guesthouse in Brighton. Near the sea.
She asked me questions and I made up some more stuff. She smiled, patted me on the knee. She was glad I was getting back to normal. I asked what she meant by that. She got flustered and said something about how Marion's passing to the other side had

54

been hard for all of us. I said yes, it had. She drank her tea. If I left her a set of keys she could mind the house for me while I was away; dust, hoover, air the rooms . . . I thanked her. I said no. I said:

Thank you, Auntie, that will not be necessary.

The school was a thirteen–minute walk from the guesthouse. The rain had stopped, but I kept my hood up. I stood under a tree opposite the front gates and watched the children coming out. They wore red jumpers, they screamed and yelled. They climbed into cars, pushed and shoved onto buses, they cycled, they walked in ones, twos, threes. Some of them noticed me and muttered behind their hands. A girl called out:

Hey, give us a flash, will you? Show us your dick!

Her friends laughed like they were having a fit, they had their arms round each other. I took my hands out of my coat pockets. I watched them go, staring at them. They kept looking over their shoulders, not laughing anymore; walking faster. Teachers were leaving too. I peered through the windscreens but the glass was too shiny to make out faces, too full of trees and clouds and fragments of lamppost. I crossed the road to observe the teachers as they walked from the main doors to the car park. Close enough to hear them say good-bye, have a good weekend, see you Monday, then. Enjoy the game.

Seventeen minutes to five. Cold, damp. No more children, only three cars remained. The colour of the sky had deepened from pale grey to slate and the streetlights had flickered into life. A ground-floor window bled yellow onto the wet grey concrete of the car park. Five o'clock. Half past. Eight minutes to six. A door opened and clanked shut; not the main door, one I couldn't see—round the side of the building. Footsteps coming closer, the sharp click of a woman's heels, a figure moved into the lamplight. Shreds of yellowy white on the roof of a car, the figure beside it; jangle of keys. The white of breath. A head went back to shake long curls from a face. And it was her face. It was her. She got in and slammed the door. She tossed a bag and some books onto the passenger seat, took off the steering lock and fastened her seat belt. The engine started, coughing grey out of the exhaust. Revs. Lights on. The car backed away from the building in a loop, halted and moved forward; through the gates, stopping again at the kerb. She leaned forward over the steering wheel, looking left then right, left then right. I stood in the shadow of the gatepost, near enough to touch the side of the car, the shiny door handle, if I'd wanted to. She didn't see me. The shoosh of wet tyres on Tarmac, red taillights growing smaller, dimmer. Gone.

> *Lynn, Gregory*
> *Form 4-3*
> *Geography*
> *Gregory's test results show he does not always revise thoroughly.*
> *He has to really start working hard if he is to successfully*
> *complete the course.*
> *E. Davies-White (Mrs.)*

I reread these words by torchlight as I sat alone in the loft that time, after the burning, with the reports—oniony pages of my school days—spread about me, open on my lap. Mrs. Davies-White, through the words she'd written in green ink, was there. So were Mr. Patrick, Miss McMahon, Mr. Teja, Mr. Hutchinson, Mr. Andrews, Mr. Boyle. All of them, present in the loft of a house which once had four occupants and now had one—me, Gregory Lynn. A boy grown into a big man with odd eyes. As I itemised the report books, giving each a reference code on the inventory of household contents, I read them. I reread them, have gone on rereading them over the past twelve months, prior to their confiscation. I know each entry by heart.

> *Gregory's test results show he does not always revise*
> *thoroughly . . .*
> *. . . to really start working hard . . . to successfully*
> *complete . . .*

Not *one* split infinitive, but *two*. What would Miss McMahon say? And what would Mrs. Davies-White say now, about my capacity to revise?

The Davies-Whites had a cat, still have for all I know. Ginger tom. It prowled the flower beds and bushes outside the house; it lay in the spring sunshine on a downstairs window ledge, it sat on the low brick wall arching its back for a stroke from passersby. When she stood on the front doorstep calling its name, beating the inside of an empty tin with a spoon, the cat would stop whatever it was doing and run indoors, darting between her legs. I monitored all this. Each day, dawn until dusk, I stood at a bus stop or in a phone booth, or sat on a bench or in a park, or in a launderette, or I walked slowly down one side of the road and back along the other; places from where I could observe, unobserved. Places which afforded a view of the red-brick semidetached with its leaded windows, its curtains. Sometimes I glimpsed her at a window, or her husband. Bald, older than her. He wore indoor slippers to walk to the newsagent's. The Davies-Whites read the *Guardian* and the *South Wales Echo*, on a Sunday they took the *Observer*. They had two pints of semiskimmed and a carton of orange juice delivered daily.

The postman usually arrived before 8:20. They had a son, about my age. He visited on the Saturday, the morning after I'd seen her leaving school. He parked his car on the grass verge. He wore a red and white woollen scarf and had a toddler with him, a dark-haired boy on reins. Hugs and kisses on the doorstep. I sat in the launderette, on a bench by the window, pretending to read a newspaper. I ate the sandwiches I'd bought from the supermarket. At 1:12 P.M. the son and the husband came out, both wearing red and white scarves, waved good-bye, got in the car and drove off. Mrs. Davies-White remained indoors, with her grandson. I took out my sketch pad and pencils: a door opening; a woman and small boy stepping outside; a woman and small boy, holding hands, walking along a street; a man in a hooded coat, following. Sometimes, by drawing things, I make them happen.

Fiction (1):

I am on detention, just me. Mrs. Davies-White is supervising. I ask for help with the work I've been set and when she comes over to the desk she sees that I have my prick out and I'm playing with myself. She smiles, she puts her hand over mine . . .

Fiction (2):

I take a message to Mrs. Davies-White from one of the other teachers. She is alone in the staff room, I am wearing gym clothes. She can't help staring at me, at my hairy arms and legs and where the front of my shorts sticks out. She smiles, she kneels on the floor in front of me and, slowly, lowers my shorts . . .

Fiction (3):

Mrs. Davies-White is off sick. I am told to take some books to her home. I knock on the door. She opens it. Her hair is wet from the shower, she is wearing a white bathrobe. She smiles, undoes the belt . . .

Fact:

A summer afternoon, the windows were wide open, the geography classroom was flooded with brightness. Mrs. Davies-White was wearing a thin white, short-sleeved blouse and a beige cheesecloth skirt that clung to the contours of her legs, her buttocks. She was drawing a diagram on the board for us to copy into our exercise books under the heading "Classification of Clouds." On the left-hand side she drew a vertical line, marked in metres by thousands, and the label "altitude at which clouds are formed." On the right, she used the side of the chalk to draw the clouds: a wispy swirl for cirrus, cotton-wool clumps for cumulonimbus, horizontal streaks for stratus. She dictated.

Clouds form when damp, usually rising air is cooled . . .

I was sitting in the corner at the back, a desk to myself. I wasn't looking at the diagram, I wasn't drawing the clouds, I wasn't writing down the words. What I was looking at was Mrs. Davies-White. What I was drawing were pictures of her, naked; of me fucking her, being sucked and wanked by her. The words I wrote down were in speech bubbles, her saying: fuck me, go on fuck me. What I was doing with my other hand was spunking myself beneath the desk. Slowly, quietly; rubbing. I shut my eyes.

When I opened them again, Mrs. Davies-White was standing beside me. All the others were looking, heads twisted. Silence. I leaned forward against the desk, fumbling sticky-fingered with my zipper; I shut the exercise book. Too late. She stood there without speaking and each second lasted an hour and each hour lasted a day and she was still standing beside me, looking down. I turned my face to the open window. The sky was blue, cloudless.

Get out.

Nn . . . nn . . .

Now!

Her hand slapped the desk, scattering pens and pencils. I stood. She stepped back to let me pass. I walked along the aisle between the rows of desks, opened the door and went out into the corridor. I closed the door behind me. The corridor was empty, every door shut. The striplights made ghosts on the polished floor. I could hear voices muffled by walls, teachers talking; somewhere—a long way away—children were singing.

59

At 2:44 P.M. Mrs. Davies-White and her grandson left the house, turned left out of the front gate and walked along the pavement. At 2:44 P.M. I left the launderette, turned right. It was cold, they were wearing woollen hats and gloves. I kept to the opposite side of the road, slightly behind them. At the crossing, she lifted the boy up so he could press the button. I slowed. When the lights changed, they crossed. The boy was imitating the *bleep-bleep-bleep* and swinging from her arm. She made him walk properly. They were coming towards me, fifty yards away. Thirty, twenty. I could see their faces. Wrinkles around her eyes and mouth and plump cheeks caked in blusher. Grey hairs among the black. Too late to turn round or cross the road. I pulled the cord to tighten my hood and kept going, head down. We passed. I walked on a short way and then looked back, in time to see them going into the park.

I watched her again on the Sunday, as she weeded the flower beds in the front garden. Her husband was there but the son and grandson had gone the previous evening, after the international. Wales beat England, the landlady at the B&B told me. She said rugby hadn't been the same since J. P. R. Williams, Gareth Edwards and Barry John. Had I been to the match? No. Well, I was certainly getting out and about. Yes. Did I know anyone in Cardiff? Sort of.

There is a bronze statue of Gareth Edwards in a shopping mall in the city centre, I saw it when I followed Mrs. Davies-White on the bus on the Monday morning. Tried not to catch her eye as I walked past her seat, but I couldn't help it. She stared at me, as though startled. I thought she'd recognised me from the other day, outside the park, or remembered me from school all those years ago; but it wasn't that sort of look. It was my eyes: the brown and the green. They unsettle people. People are unsettled by abnormality. People are afraid of the abstract, Mr. Andrews said; afraid of what can't be made to fit their understanding. Thing is, Mr. A., who's to say what is normal and what isn't? My eyes, for instance. My eyes aren't abnormal, to me. They are familiar.

Mrs. Davies-White went to school in the afternoon. I returned to my room at the guesthouse and drew the bus ride, the shopping trip. In each picture, she was naked. I had to imagine what her tits and cunt looked like. I made her younger, slimmer. When I'd done the cartoons, I waited until it was time to return to the house, ready for her. Ready for a moment when she'd be outside, alone: no grandson, no husband, no bus passengers, no crowds of shoppers. Just her and me, the man in the hood. Odd Eyes.

They teach you about weather patterns: cold fronts, warm fronts, isobars and isotherms, areas of low and high pressure, precipitation, mean temperatures, chill factor. What they don't teach you, what you have to learn for yourself because no one's worked out a way of measuring it, is:

> The scent of rain in the woods
> The cold sting of the wind on a shaven scalp

My barrister is hanging a waterproof cagoule above the radiator to dry. He is stamping his feet, rubbing his hands; commenting on the foulness of the day. I say to him:

You know, the best part of the TV weather forecast is when they show a child's picture of a woman with a yellow face and a big purple umbrella.

We settle down, we turn our attention to the matter in hand. I am to confine my description of the pursuit of Mrs. Davies-White to the relevant details. Enough time has been spent on incidentals, it is the ending which is of most concern to my legal representatives, the denouement. Motive and method have been more than sufficiently established (albeit insufficiently appreciated, in my view). They want me to say what happened.

• • •

It's raining, it's pouring,
The old man is snoring.

Dad snored when he'd been drinking. Saturday afternoons,
after the lunchtime session, he'd fall asleep in the chair in front of
Grandstand. If Mum changed channels to watch a film, he'd wake
up—gummy-lipped—and ask what the fuck she thought she was
doing. He'd switch back, and fall asleep again, mouth hanging
open. Snoring.

Listen to that, Mum said. Like water going down a drain.

When it rained heavily, Dad said it was *pissing down.* He said
rain was God, pissing on people.

Tuesday evening. I'd been in Cardiff four days, waiting. Watching. I was within sight of the school gates at 5:30 when Mrs.
Davies-White drove out, and I walked to the road where she
lived in time to see her draw the thick brown curtains of the
downstairs front room. The cat, the ginger tom, was curled asleep
on the bonnet of her parked car, tail twitching. I was still there an
hour and a half later when she left, on foot. I followed, at a
distance. It wasn't fully dark yet and I could see her walking
quickly in the quiet side streets, hear her shoes on the flagstones.
At the main road she turned left, out of sight behind a hedge. I
hurried to the corner and looked along the road. A man at a bus
stop, youths eating from paper bags outside a burger bar, a
woman walking a dog. No Mrs. Davies-White. I started to run,
then stopped. I looked for side turnings, a building she might
have gone into. Nothing. A horn blared as I stepped off the
pavement. I scanned the dull yellow glow of a street flanked by
parked cars and neon-lit shopfronts. Then I saw her: on the opposite pavement, a hundred yards ahead. I jogged along the kerb,
waiting for a break in the traffic, then crossed the road, slowing to
a brisk walk, closing the gap. I was ten yards behind her when
she turned up a set of steps and through a doorway. I halted
outside, the heavy wooden door still creaking shut. I was sweating and out of breath. I hesitated before going inside. The walls

of the brightly lit lobby were pinned with posters and leaflets. I toured the corridors, peering through glass-panelled doors. Some rooms were empty and unlit, others busy with people in leotards, in sweatshirts and shorts, or sitting at rows of desks. I found her in a small gym with a dozen other women. She was taking off her coat and scarf, draping them over the back of a plastic chair among a stack at the back of the hall. She stripped down to a baggy red T-shirt and black leggings, with leg warmers. Her feet were bare. Through the chequered glass in the door, I saw the instructor, a man, move to the front and beckon the women. They spread around the room, each in her own space, facing him, imitating his pose: upright, straight-backed, feet apart, breathing deeply. I watched Mrs. Davies-White do yoga.

She was a brunette, like Mum. Like Janice. If Mum had cut Mrs. Davies-White's hair it would've made dark ringlets on the kitchen floor. But Mum never met Mrs. Davies-White, she never did her hair. Her custom came by word of mouth: neighbours, friends, family, clients from the days when she worked at the salon. At a Snip. I went there on one of my outings, but the place was closed down. White swirls in the window; a notice saying "To Let" and giving the name and telephone number of an estate agent. Mum had gone back part-time, after Dad died; then the Supashop job came up so she packed in at the salon and worked from home. They came in the evenings, after her shift at the shop, and at weekends; or she would go to theirs. Women, mostly. Sometimes I stayed in the kitchen to watch. I liked perms best, because of the smell. And I liked the hair, the way Mum cut and curled it and washed and dried it. The way she cocked her little finger when she was cutting, the *snip-snip-snip* of the scissors, the wisps of black or blond or auburn that stuck to the soles of your feet when you walked barefoot across the tiled floor. It was the women I hated, with their cigarettes and their sticky pink lips and their conversation. The way they looked at me, their smiles. Or if I was out of the room and they thought I couldn't hear them: How's-Gregory-these-days? and It's-his-dad-he'll-get-over-it and Have-you-thought-about-you-know-speaking-to-the-doctor? Then they'd talk about their own children; or their husbands, except Mum had to talk about hers in the past tense. Some of the women brought their children with them and we had to go into the garden or up to my room to play. Play *nicely,* Mum would tell me. If I didn't feel like playing I'd make them cry, even the older ones.

Perm is short for permanent wave; only the wave isn't permanent, it grows out after a few months. Mrs. Davies-White had a perm, she used hair spray. I got close enough to smell the chemicals and to feel the stiff tight curls between my fingers.

Nine o'clock when she came out of the community centre with two women. I was across the road, in a shop awning. I followed them into a pub and sat in a corner of the lounge, sipping Fanta; watching them through the smoke and the cluster of drinkers. Mrs. Davies-White drank (half a pint of lager and lime) but didn't smoke, though her companions did. I was too far away to hear their conversation, but they were laughing a lot. Laughter made her look younger, prettier, the way she did when she taught us geography. After a while one of the women stood up, holding her purse and pointing to the empty glasses. Mrs. Davies-White shook her head. She felt around on the seat for her handbag and stood up as well, putting her coat on. They were talking and nodding. She kissed both friends on the cheek and made her way towards the door, turning to wave good-bye as she stepped out alone into the night. I counted to 20. I left the pub.

The main road was too busy, too bright. I waited until she'd turned into the side streets. I stayed close this time, near enough for her to hear my footsteps. She half turned once or twice to look over her shoulder. I had my hood up. She began to walk more quickly. So did I. Ahead of us lay an alley which ran between the backs of two banks of houses; I'd noticed it earlier as I trailed her from the house. As we approached the mouth of the alleyway I moved closer still, until we were only a few paces apart, the sharp slap of my footsteps in rhythm with hers. She was fumbling with the clasp of her handbag, searching for something. Something metallic, red and silver; glinting. Two strides. I gripped her by the shoulder, one hand over her mouth, and yanked her towards me. The object fell to the floor—a small canister like a deodorant stick. A rape alarm. In the struggle, her foot kicked the canister and it rolled away out of reach. Muffled words, the sharpness of teeth biting into my hand; but I held tighter, pulled her off balance so that her feet were dragging, scuffing, stumbling along the brick cobbles of the alleyway. She was heavy, but I was heavier, bigger. Stronger. It was dark there, the ground strewn with damp litter from a split refuse sack, and hidden from the rear windows on either side by wooden fences. There was a stench of cats. I thrust a hand under her jumper, working my fingers inside the elasticized top of her leggings. She was sobbing into my other hand, still biting, gagging on my sweat and blood and flesh. Trying to scream. Her fingers were scratching at air. Her thumbnail caught the soft skin at the corner of my left eye and I had to grab her wrist. I forced her onto the ground face-first, and started again on her clothes. The coat was rucked up around her shoulders now, the leggings round her knees. She was groaning, her face pressed into the hard dirty brick. I tugged at her knickers until they ripped, exposing her buttocks, pale in the dim light; skin as white as paper, like a blank page. I shoved a hand between her legs. Wet. Wet flesh, hairs. The wet was streaming over my fingers and down the insides of her thighs and splashing onto the ground, making rivulets in the cracks between the cobbles.

I stopped, stood up. I let her go. She was sobbing, breathing in panicky gulps; her hair messed up and face streaked with tears and the sticky blood she'd drawn from my hand. She didn't say anything, didn't look at me, just straightened her clothes and set off in a loping, knock-kneed run to the end of the alley and out into the street. I heard her footsteps grow fainter and fade until the only noise was the heavy, irregular sound of my own breathing. I picked her scarf from the ground, rolled it up and put it in my pocket.

The scarf was a mistake, I recognise that now. When they found it in my bedroom months later it was one of the conclusive pieces of evidence which connected me to the assault. Along with the cartoons, of course, and the written accounts. And my confession. The investigating officers in Cardiff didn't have the benefit of any of this at the time. To them, it was another unsolved sex attack on a lone woman. The victim's description of her assailant gave them little to go on: a tall, well-built man with a hooded anorak. Colour of skin, white; colour of hair, unknown; colour of eyes, unknown; approximate age, twenty? thirty? forty? It was dark, he kept his hood up, he attacked her from behind. He never spoke. The police were searching for a man with a cut hand and, possibly, an injured eye. The perpetrator, meanwhile, had checked out of his guesthouse in Cathedral Road the morning after the incident and boarded a train to London, Paddington. By the time the landlady at the B&B read the report of the attack in the *South Wales Echo*—and recalled, no doubt with a certain chill, the nasty scratch on the face of her recently departed guest —the assailant was 160 miles away, in his room in a Council house in South London. The name and address he'd entered in the register proved to be false. All the guesthouse proprietor could tell detectives was that he was English—she couldn't place the accent—had black hair tied up in a ponytail and, oh the strangest thing: he had one green eye and one brown. Based on her description, a composite picture was issued to the press. The English papers didn't carry the story. It was a busy news day. The attack happened in Cardiff. It wasn't part of a series of incidents. And the woman hadn't actually been raped. Or killed.

. . .

I tell my barrister it will not be necessary for Mrs. Davies-White to testify at my trial. This charge is one to which I intend to plead guilty. He says I am being sensible. There is one aspect of this particular act of revision, however, which continues to arouse his curiosity. Why stop? Why let her go? I can tell, as I begin to enumerate the reasons, that he is puzzled to the point of exasperation; but I continue, counting them off on my fingers as the solicitor writes down what I say:

> The fact that she didn't smoke
> The whiteness of her buttocks
> The alleyway
> Fear (mine)
> Fear (hers)
> Power (mine)
> The smell of perming solution
> Wetness . . . the sensation, the smell, of her wetness on my fingers

Counsel, typically, fails to appreciate the wholeness of these factors—their interconnectedness—seeking to isolate them in order to assess the relative significance, to extract one overriding truth from an entanglement of several truths. Or to unearth an altogether different one.

You weren't disturbed.

Emotionally?

During the, ah, attack, I mean. No one interrupted you.

I shake my head.

Footsteps? Voices?

No.

(A pause while he refers to the solicitor's notebook.) Her fear. What do you mean when you say *her fear*?

That's sort of tied in with the sixth point.

(Another glance at the notes.) Power?

Exactly.

What, exactly?

She was afraid of me, that was good. I was in control. I could carry on or I could stop and there was nothing she could do about it. She was powerless, I took away her power.

Ah. I see. Yes, I think I'm with you. But what about *your* fear? What do you mean by that?

(I shrug.) Inadequate training. Being "outside," being among people—I tried to do too much too soon. The physical contact with her made me quite ill, actually.

The solicitor exhales loudly, causing a second exhalation as her back comes into abrupt contact with the back of the chair. She lets her pen fall onto the table. For a moment I think she's about to say something, but the barrister raises his hand and she remains silent. I continue, intending to explain the significance of Mrs. Davies-White's being a nonsmoker, the whiteness of her skin, the alleyway, the odour of perming solution, the wetness . . . I'm keen to expand on the wetness factor, but counsel stops me in midsentence. And I realise there is a pecking order of impatience, of anger. He's pulled rank on the solicitor. And on me. Except he can't pull rank on me because *I'm* the reason we're here. Me, Gregory Lynn (orphan, bachelor, only child from the age of four and a half). So fuck him.

Each time I reflect on the incident in the alley—each time I draw it—I remember it differently and it becomes harder to separate what happened from what didn't happen. Sometimes I am fastidious in my efforts to capture the events accurately; sometimes I invent, I falsify. But, whichever way I remember it, each version seems equally real because it occurs in my head and is therefore true to itself.

Fact:
Mrs. Davies-White pissed herself.

68

Fiction:

Mrs. Davies-White had an orgasm.

She could've reported me, but she didn't. She could've told the head about the cartoon and about me spunking myself under the desk in the middle of a geography lesson. She could've got me caned, expelled, referred back to the educational psychologist. But she didn't. What she did was leave me standing in the corridor until the end of class, until the other children had filed past with their stares and their giggles and their snide jokes; then she summoned me into the room. She tore the drawings from my exercise book and ripped them to shreds. She made me sit at a desk and copy the information about clouds: diagram, words, labels. She stood over me while I worked, my head down—not catching her eye. And, without a word, she let me go.

The copse, the school, the salon. Places I'd been before. Places where things had happened. Places where nothing was happening now except me being there thinking about what had happened those other times. Making ghosts.

3. The alleyway: where it joined the road, the road Dad followed from work to pub. A Saturday, the week before I went to Cardiff. Saturday, just like the other time, when I was eleven and three-quarters. Early spring now; summer then. I stood at the end of the alleyway and looked along it, as Dad's workmates had done on an August afternoon in 1970. No people now, no blood; just a rusty stove, a supermarket trolley, a crate of empty beer bottles, walls kaleidoscoped with graffiti. It was raining, pouring down. I tried to remember if it was raining that other time, when I came along the road after clocking off for Dad and his mates. I'd been gone an hour, sitting in the empty paint-spraying shop and reading comics. When I realised the time, I let myself out and hurried back towards the pub. I saw the crowd before I reached the mouth of the alleyway. Children, youths, men in work overalls, a

policewoman. An ambulance stood at the kerb, blue light swirling but no siren. Denis, from the plating shed, was there. When he saw me, he held my wrist and wouldn't let me any nearer no matter how much I struggled. Through the arms and legs of the onlookers I made out fragments: an ambulanceman kneeling; a body, clothing soaked with red; a motorcycle on its side; another body; a face. The face was Dad's. Eyes closed and mouth open, as though he was asleep.

Later, I sat on the stairs at home—eavesdropping—while Denis told Mum what happened. They left the pub at the usual time—okay, they'd had a few but no more than usual. Pat wasn't drunk, none of them were. Not at all. They were walking along the road, the four of them, and Pat decided he was dying for a leak. You know how it is. The men waited while he ducked into the alley and went against the gate to someone's back garden. He was still zipping himself up as he stepped out of the doorway into the path of the motorcycle.

Right into its path. *Bouf!*

I heard the smack of one palm against another. The motorcycle was nicked, Denis said. Kawasaki 950. The rider was *sixteen* years old. Doing sixty, the police reckoned. Eighty, more like. Stupid little bastard. They'd tried to shout, to warn Pat. But it was all so quick. I heard Mum crying. Denis was sorry, he really was so sorry. Daphne and him were just next door if there was anything . . . Mum said something I couldn't make out. Then I heard footsteps along the hall and retreated to the top of the stairs, out of sight. The front door clicked open. Mum thanked him for coming round.

Marion, love, he didn't stand a chance. Not a chance in hell.

3

English **1a.** Germanic language of the people of Britain, the U.S., and most Commonwealth countries **1b.** English language, literature or composition as an academic subject **2.** people of England **3.** (characteristic) of England

Beginnings. A beginning. In the beginning was the word.

The cartoons started then, after the accident. I was eleven and three-quarters. I drew the boxes, then the pictures: an alley; a man pissing in a doorway; a youth on a motorcycle—difficult, drawing the cycle to suggest speed; men shouting, warning the man as he zips his trousers.

Endings: (1) collision—youth dies, man dies; (2) collision—youth dies, man lives; (3) collision—youth lives, man lives; (4) collision—youth lives, man dies; (5) no collision.

Lynn, Gregory
Form 4-3
English
Gregory's essays are generally good—the only major fault being that he sometimes gets so carried away that he wanders close to the limits of the subject, thus losing the perspective and control that are essential in such an exercise.
Miss J. McMahon

Miss McMahon was Scottish, she taught English. Both lang. and lit. English words derived from Scottish Gaelic include clan, slogan, cairn and trousers. This is called etymology. Words, too, have origins. Beginnings. There was a time when the words we use now didn't exist. We invented them, gave them meaning. We borrowed them from other languages, we changed them. We gave things names—tree, moon, river, house—and that is what they are. You say "moon" to someone and they picture the moon, unless they're Spanish or French or Russian and they don't know what the fuck you're talking about. You say "house" to someone and they picture a house. But it might not be the same as the one you have in mind. It will be different.

When we read aloud, Miss McMahon said:

Let the words flow from your mouth like honey from a spoon.

Or she would tell us to roll our *r*'s, only we'd laugh because she said it "arse." She made us pronounce the *h* in "why" and "where" and "when." Whenever we read aloud she'd close her eyes and listen, her lips smooth and smile-shaped. A dictionary sat on her desk, big as a doorstep. She called it her bible. Her hair was carrot-blond and fine, her pale face pricked with freckles. She always wore a perfectly white blouse with a ruffed collar, a navy cardigan and a pleated tweed skirt. Brooch, necklace, no rings. When one of the boys asked why she wasn't married, she said she'd never met a man as beautiful as Shelley.

After Cardiff, I cropped my hair close to my scalp; I cut off my ponytail. I didn't wash or shave or brush my teeth for two weeks. I didn't change my clothes. I bit my nails until my fingers bled. I went days without eating, or made food for myself and left it half eaten to go stale and mouldy. I slept fully dressed, or not at all. I didn't go out, I didn't answer the phone or the door. Each day, I stood for a while before the mirror in Mum's bedroom, looking at myself. Or I drew cartoons. Always the same subject, the same setting: me, in the alleyway with Mrs. Davies-White. I drew dozens of them. Sometimes, while I was drawing, tears dripped onto the page and caused the colours to run.

My barrister suggests:

You were, ah . . . lying low for a while, were you? You were afraid of the consequences of your action.

I look at him.

It's possible you were ashamed of what you'd done. Guilty. Would you say you were feeling guilty?

I don't answer.

What, then?

I shrug.

Gregory, you're not being very helpful.

You have to be helpful, lend a helping hand. You have to help others to help you. You have to help yourself. Can I have some more, please? Help yourself. Help yourself to a second helping. Auntie said:

God helps those who help themselves.

To be helpful is to be of service or assistance, to be useful. It is an adjective, a word that describes a noun. Verb. to help. I help (first-person singular), you help, he helps, she helps, we help, they help. Past tense: I helped. I couldn't help it. *Help me if you can I'm feeling down.*

When my barrister asks me to be helpful, what he is seeking is my cooperation. It is the cooperation between a driver and a passenger. I am the one reading the map; he is the one with the steering wheel, the brake, the accelerator, the gears. He is the one at the controls. If I fail to navigate correctly, or hide the map in the glove compartment, or make a grab for the steering wheel, I am being unhelpful; I am not enabling us to reach our destination. This assumes that the driver's destination is the same as the passenger's. I begin to sing:

A spoonful of sugar helps the medicine go down . . .

My barrister terminates the interview.

Back in my room, the one with the metal door and the barred window, I continue the discussion in his absence. I imagine a cartoon client and a cartoon lawyer. In the final frame there is a speech bubble above my head. I am expressing the opinion that hatred is like a bowl brimful with water—carry it around with you and there's always the risk that you will be the one to get wet. This is the sort of thing Mr. Andrews would say.

L̲ay, lie.

You lay your cards on the table. A hen lays eggs. Yesterday, the hen laid an egg.

If you are tired or unwell, you should lie down. I am lying down. Last night I lay down. I have lain in bed all day.

If you got them mixed up, if you said "lay" when you should have said "lie," Miss McMahon would say: Are we a hen?

To lie is to be or to stay at rest in a horizontal position. It is to have as a direction (the route lies to the north); or to occupy a specific place (the river lies behind us). It is also to remain at anchor, becalmed.

To lie is to make an untrue statement with intent to deceive, to speak falsely; to create a false or misleading impression.

To lie heavily is to have an adverse or disheartening effect (responsibility lies heavily on his shoulders). To lie low is to stay in hiding, to bide one's time.

After two weeks, I showered and shaved. I put on clean clothes, except socks; I had adopted the habit of going barefoot about the house, my trousers—my trews—turned up at the shins. I liked the feel of the floor beneath my feet, the different textures: carpet, linoleum, floor tiles. The splintery beams of the loft. I rang Auntie and told her I was back from holiday and yes I'd stayed away longer than I'd said and I was sorry she'd worried and yes

I'd had a good time and hadn't I been lucky with the weather? In Brighton. I opened windows to let the air in and the smell out. I went outside, to the launderette. I went to a barber. He saw the state of my hair and laughed. He asked who was my last barber, and did I want him beaten up? I said I'd had a brain operation. He apologised; said he could've bitten his tongue off, he really could.

April. The trees were in blossom, there were daffodils and tulips and forget-me-nots in the front garden and the sun made different shapes in the house. Brighter. In the mornings the window lit up the yellow counterpane on Mum's bed so that the thin cloth was warm when you pressed your face against it. Smell of cotton and dust and warmth. The stale tobacco odour wasn't so strong now, but if you sprinkled her perfume on the pillow it was as though she'd slept there the night before. If you lay on the bed for a while and then got up, it left a depression like the one her body might've made, only bigger. Outside, I no longer needed my heavy anorak with its hood. But I wore it, sometimes. I resumed my training regime: walks, bus journeys, conversations with strangers. I learnt to make people comfortable with my behaviour and appearance, putting them at ease. If they had no fear —if they were lulled into a false sense of security the impact would be all the greater when I gave them reason to be fearful. Slowly, gradually, I prepared myself. I updated the wall chart and began planning the next act of revision.

On Good Friday Auntie phoned.

Our Lord is dead, she said.

On Easter Monday she visited, with Uncle. She gave me a chocolate egg.

Our Lord is risen.

Miss McMahon made it easy for me to find her. In class, she was always going on about Aberdeen and how the granite buildings sparkled like frost in the sunlight and the wind off the North Sea filled your nostrils with the scent of salt as you walked along the strand. She would go back there one day, she said, when her teaching days were over. She would go home.

I took the bus to the library. A different one, not the one where I'd cut the books. In the library, there were telephone directories for every part of the country. I found the one for Aberdeen and North-East Scotland and wrote down all the McMahons with the initial "J" or J-something. I copied addresses as well as phone numbers. When I got home I rang each in turn. It took several days to tick them off, I had to ring some of them again and again to get an answer. None of the McMahons was her. I looked up the local newspaper in Aberdeen, the *Press and Journal,* and copied down its address. A few days later I sent a letter, for publication. Said I was organising a reunion for former pupils and staff of ———— school, South London, to mark its twenty-fifth anniversary. I believed that a Miss J. McMahon— who'd taught there for many years—had moved back to the Aberdeen area on retirement. I wrote that I would be grateful if she, or anyone who was *acquainted with her whereabouts,* could contact me. I gave my name and address. The name was my real one, Gregory Lynn, the address was a box number issued to me, for a fee, by the post office.

Me and Janice played trampoline on the bed in Mum and Dad's room. It was bouncy, big enough for both of us. I could touch the paper light-shade with my fingertips if I jumped high enough. Janice could bang it with her head. We bounced up and down at the same time, giggling, colliding, trying to push each other over. If I fell, she'd lift me up again. Or, as I lay on my back, she'd jump high—feet together—and pretend she was going to land on me, then open her legs at the last second so her feet landed either side. And I knew that if I kept perfectly still I was safe, but if I moved or tried to roll to one side she really would land on me.

Eyes open, Jeggy! Eyes open!

I kept my eyes open, like she said, even when I thought she

was going to land on my face. I didn't blink or flinch at all. Even when she opened her legs so late I felt the breeze of her feet on my cheeks.

Janice went away when I was still at nursery school, and again when I was in the infants. Mum took her away the first time—in an ambulance. Janice couldn't say ambulance, she said it "ambliance." I wanted a ride in the ambliance as well, but Mum said I couldn't. There was a bed on wheels and Janice lay down on it and Mum sat on a seat that folded out from the wall, and Dad got in and sat on another seat. I waved, but one of the men shut the doors before Janice could wave back. Auntie held my hand tight and told me to stop it, to stop showing myself up. The second time Janice went away, she was lying with Mum on the big bed in their room; red against the white of the sheet. Dad hid her. He wrapped her in a pillowcase. When they saw me in the doorway, I was made to go away. Janice was smaller than the time before, smaller than me. Tinier than a baby.

Dad's funeral was on a Wednesday. It was still the summer holidays so I didn't have to miss school. Mum held my hand the whole time. I could feel her shaking. When the music started and the curtain came across, she had to let go of my hand so she could blow her nose. She used a tissue, a pink one. She always kept a tissue tucked inside the sleeve of her blouse or cardigan. It made a lump there, like she had something wrong with her wrist. A growth. She was shaking harder. We were sitting at the front, with Auntie and Uncle. Auntie had her arm round Mum. The chapel smelled of wood polish and fresh flowers and Uncle's aftershave, which was the same as the stuff Dad used. I wanted to ask if men's whiskers kept growing after they'd died, but I didn't. There was an empty seat at the end of the row. I said:

That for Janice?

Auntie leaned forward, whispering at me across Mum. She told me to shush. To show some respect. Denis was there, in a suit, and some other men from the factory and their wives. Outside, in the sunshine, Mum put a cigarette in her mouth and Denis lit it for her, then lit one for himself. He rested his hand on my head. His hand was hard and heavy.

When I started senior school, I didn't have a dad. If any teachers or kids asked about him I said he was a motorcycle racer who'd died in a crash or that he'd drowned trying to rescue my sister in the sea at Bognor Regis. Or I made my face serious, like the chaplain's at the funeral service, and said my dad had made *a tragic and untimely departure from this world*.

Dad swore when he was angry or when he'd been to the pub or when him and Mum were fighting. From him, I learnt the words fuck, shit, bollocks, bastard. I wasn't to say them, not even "bloody." Dad would hit me, hard, on the legs. If I said them in front of Mum she'd threaten to tell Dad. Once—when I was too big to hit, when Dad was dead—I called her a cunt, just to hear how it sounded. Just to see her expression.

I wished I'd found my exercise books, my essays. I wished I could read what I'd written for Miss McMahon. But these books had not been kept in the box in the loft with the school reports; they must've been thrown out long since. I could picture them, with their blue covers, dog-eared and worn at the spine from being shoved in and out of bags, lockers, desks. Scrawled over. Drawn on. I could feel the pages, see them—the pink margins and the faint grey lines, the neat rows of handwriting with its loops and swirls and dots. Blots and smudges patterned with blue fingerprints, the comments in red ink. "V. Good." "Excellent." "Imaginative!" I liked essays better than comprehension or dictation. In essays there wasn't so much right and wrong. There would be ticks in the margin, not because you'd got something "right" or "correct" but because she liked the way you'd used a word or the way a sentence had been phrased or the way you'd described something. She liked ideas, images. She liked smells and colours. Tastes. Sounds. The feel of things. In essays, you could tell stories, you could make believe. Making believe wasn't the same as lying. If "truth" was what you imagined to be true, then truths were to be found in your imaginings.

An essay, she used to say, is an act of composition. When you write an essay you are a composer, you have the freedom to express yourself.

There were rules, of course. Spelling, punctuation, grammar. They were necessary, we were not permitted to break them. But Miss McMahon never gave anyone a *tick v.g.* for putting an apostrophe in the right place.

When we were first-years, the first piece she asked us to write was a five-hundred-word essay on "The Inside of a Table Tennis Ball." Everyone groaned when she put the title on the blackboard. I started the essay as soon as I got home. I wrote in the first person, as if I was living on the inside of a table tennis ball. I called it the Land of Ping. I wrote about how I was one of thousands of molecules making up the smooth inner surface and how dark and boring it was in Ping and how we went to war with the molecules on the outside so we could take over—so we'd be on the outer surface instead of them. I called the outside the Land of Pong. No sooner had we conquered Pong, however, than we were being whacked by table tennis bats, smashed onto wooden tables, blinded by harsh overhead lights, drowned in sweat from the players' palms. So we started another war, another invasion, to reclaim our place on the inside.

Miss McMahon gave me an A.

I looked at the photograph again, the one of us in the paddling pool at Butlins, Bognor Regis, 1962. I studied the writing where someone had printed the place and date in neat block capitals. Mum's handwriting. The ink had cracked and faded with age. She had held the photograph, as I was holding it; she had written on it. The words would remain as long as the photograph existed. Mum and me and Janice would remain, holding hands as we stood in the shallow water; posing. Me, squinting in the sunshine.

And Dad's faint shadow would remain fixed on the water, his outline fractured and distorted by the broken surface of the pool.

Ten days after I wrote to the paper I received a letter, postmarked Aberdeen. I waited until I was home from the post office before opening it. A brief handwritten note on beige paper enclosed in a matching Oxfam envelope. Recycled. I read the letter. In the top right-hand corner was the address and date, no telephone number. The note was headed "Dear Mr. Lynn" and signed "Janet McMahon." I added certain details to the wall chart, inserted a blue pin alongside Aberdeen on the U.K. map and drew a line in matching felt-tip connecting it to her name on the chart. I made space on my desk, took a pad from one of the drawers and, using my best pen and resting my hand on a sheet of paper to avoid smudges, I composed a letter.

> Dear Miss McMahon,
>
> Thank you for responding to my letter in the newspaper—I can't tell you how pleased I am that I've managed to track you down. I'm delighted you are willing to attend the proposed reunion, although I am unable to confirm a date or venue as the arrangements are still to be finalised. It all comes down to numbers, as Mr. Teja would've said. The main thing is that we have established contact, you and I.
>
> As well as organising the reunion, I have taken it upon myself to produce a twenty-fifth-anniversary magazine to which staff and pupils—past and present— are invited to submit articles, photographs, anecdotes, etc. As one of the school's longest-serving teachers, any contribution you care to make would be gratefully received. Perhaps you would also be so kind as to send a photograph of yourself, for inclusion in the magazine?
>
> As for me, I was a pupil at ——— from 1970 to

1975 and was in your group for English (lang. and lit) during that time. You may not remember me, but I remember you. I remember you as if it were yesterday. You met my mother at an open evening and told her she had a budding poet in the family. I am not a poet, as it happens; I am between jobs at the moment. Mum died in January. Lung cancer. At night, her coughing still keeps me awake. To be honest, the reunion and the magazine are helping to take my mind off her. It's good to keep oneself occupied at times of upset, don't you agree?

I digress.

Please write soon with your article, photograph, etc.—forgive the P.O. box number, but I'm in the process of moving and anxious that no correspondence should go astray. Your phone number would also be helpful, for my files.

Yours sincerely,
Gregory Lynn

P.S. What is your view on the splitting of infinitives? I received an item of correspondence from Mrs. Davies White—geography, as you may recall—in which she split two infinitives in one sentence. When I undertook this project, I little imagined the *teachers* would require so much revision!

The prosecution has this letter now. All of them, hers and mine. My barrister keeps the photocopies among the sheaf of papers which he fastens with strips of pink ribbon. We are going through them together. He is impressed by the neatness of my handwriting.

I tell him about the time Miss McMahon asked us each

to write a poem. She'd read Shelley to us, and Keats and Wordsworth and Byron. Gerard Manley Hopkins. We'd done Dylan Thomas, Walt Whitman and John Clare. Stevie Smith. Emily Dickinson. Sylvia Plath. She'd taught us haiku. Haiku is an unrhymed Japanese verse form made up of three lines containing five, seven and five syllables respectively. She told us:

Haiku is distillation and discipline. It is the beauty of perfection.

We'd learnt about rhyme and rhythm and meter. Alliteration. Free form. Rhyming couplets. Blank verse. We were familiar with iambic pentameters. Now it was our turn to be poets. To compose. To express ourselves. For the benefit of my legal representatives, I recite the limerick Dad had taught me and which I wrote in my English exercise book:

> *There was a young man from Nantucket,*
> *Whose prick was so long he could suck it.*
> *He said with a grin,*
> *Wiping cum from his chin:*
> *"If my ear was a cunt, I could fuck it."*

My barrister does not smile, nor does the solicitor. He asks if I got into trouble over that poem. I tell him Miss McMahon was disappointed in my lack of originality.

I made a hideout in the copse, where I used to go when I should have been in school. In the thick undergrowth between the base of a tree and a holly bush, I cleared out the scrub to make a hollow, a cave enclosed by a canopy of foliage. You had to crawl in on your hands and knees. Inside, you could look out through the chinks in the branches and leaves and nobody would know you were there, even if they walked right by. The floor was soft earth spread with dead leaves and ferns and an old blanket from the loft. It was dry in there, even when it rained. I liked rainy days best, I liked to sit in my shelter and listen to the rain-drops on the leaves. I liked the smell when the rain stopped, and how the birds would start to sing again. I liked to watch columns of ants carrying tiny bits of leaf or bark or fragments of dead beetle. If you crushed an ant with your thumb the others would stop, panic, nuzzle the broken body, then make a detour; a new route where ant-death hadn't occurred. If you didn't crush an ant properly, bits of it would go on twitching. Or it would stumble in circles. Helpless. Crippled. There were spiders in there, and worms. I drew them. I'd dug a hole to hide a small tin where I kept a rolled-up pad and pencils so I could make my cartoons. If something bad happened at school I would make it happen again, differently. Or I'd draw me and Janice. We would play games, climb trees, ride our bikes; she'd tell me about heaven. There were no schools in heaven, she said, no teachers. I had to draw Janice the way she was the first time because I couldn't picture how she'd be now. And I had to draw me the way I was then, otherwise I'd have been older than her; bigger and that wouldn't have been right. Sometimes I drew Dad, in bloodied overalls, staring glassy-eyed at me through a jumble of people's arms and legs. I'd draw him, then poke holes in the page with the point of the pencil. I liked to sleep in my hideout, to curl up on the blanket and sleep and breathe in blanket-smell and fresh air and trees.

When I got home, Mum would want to know why my uniform was crumpled or how I'd muddied my trousers. I'd tell her to mind her own fucking business.

Lynn, Gregory
Form 3-3
English
Gregory continues to express his ideas fluently in written work and sets himself a consistently high standard. It is a pity that his

contribution to discussions in class is not greater, as he has more
to offer than he gives himself credit for.
Miss J. McMahon

Dear Gregory,

I must apologise for failing to respond more promptly to your letter, but my elder sister—with whom I reside—has been unwell of late and I am much occupied with attending to her needs. As you will see, I have enclosed a photograph for your magazine (why do those dreadful booths give one the demeanour of a startled rabbit?) but have been rather too pressed for time to make a start on the requested article. Late with my homework!

It amused me to read of dear Lizzie's (Mrs. Davies-White) split infinitives—I only hope my own effort will give you no cause to wield the editor's scalpel. If we English teachers (ret'd) cannot set an example, who can? Your letter has rekindled some fond memories of the early years at ————, and—yes—I do indeed remember you, Gregory. How could I ever forget the great Battle of Ping-Pong? It may have been twenty-odd years ago, but certain matters do stick in one's mind!

I was sorry to learn of your recent bereavement. I shouldn't worry unduly about being kept awake at night by her coughing—my own mother died seven years ago and we still have daily conversations (although she is somewhat hard of hearing these days).

I was sorry, too, to learn that you are without work at present (an increasingly common phenomenon among those of my former pupils with whom I am still in contact). Aberdeen, as you may be aware, has enjoyed something of a boom in recent years (thanks to North Sea oil), but Scotland in general has suffered severely in these times of economic recession. I have never been a devolutionist, but since my return to these parts I have come to realise just how remote the government is (and not merely in a geographical sense). As a teacher, I always believed that authority without respect was untenable. Unfortunately, it seems that certain of our politicians share the view of some of my former colleagues: that government and education are primarily matters of discipline and the imposition of order. Here I am, on my soapbox! Perhaps this could provide the theme for my contribution to your magazine, or had you envisaged something rather less contentious!?

I should sign off. I shall, I promise, endeavour to compose something suitable for publication when time permits. In the meantime, do please keep in touch with regard to the anniversary reunion. In answer to your request for my telephone number, I'm afraid we had ourselves disconnected last year in protest at the outrageous standing charges imposed on we pensioners. (Shelley had the right idea: die young.) By the by, I hope the move goes well—do let me have your new address when you are able.

Yours with fond regards,
Janet

I pasted the photograph of Miss McMahon onto the wall chart. It was in colour. Her hair was mostly grey now and her face wasn't as freckly as I remembered it. Very pale. If the dark curtain wasn't pulled across behind her, her face would've been lost against the white wall of the booth. Her mouth was turned up at the corners.

Mum went grey. She went grey a lot towards the time of the burning. And her hair started to fall out because of the chemotherapy. It made her sick, too. I heard her. I saw her once, bent over the toilet, when she'd forgotten to lock the door. Talking to God on the big white telephone, Dad used to call it. He did that sometimes, after the pub. He didn't go grey at all, or bald. He had *a fine head of hair.* He used to make me tug on it as hard as I could. He'd laugh:

That's not a syrup, is it? That's not an Irish.

Dad died when he was forty-two. When I was eleven and three-quarters.

Syrup of fig, wig. Irish jig.

Dear Janet,

I've been reading about Shelley, a library book. Did you know, he died when he was twenty-nine? Drowned in a boating accident. His wife wrote *Frankenstein.* After Shelley died, his heart was removed from his body and she slept with it under her pillow. Medical evidence now suggests it wasn't his heart, but his liver. The book I'm reading devotes a great deal of space to this anatomical discrepancy. What it seems less interested in is:

1. Mary Shelley *believed* the organ to be her husband's heart;
2. She *slept with it under her pillow.*

This is a book about a *poet,* and the author is preoccupied with medical facts. Science. A widow sleeps with one of her dead husband's vital organs under her pillow and we are meant to wonder: Hmmnn, heart or liver?

Excuse my French, Miss McMahon, but for fuck's sake!

So I've skipped all this biography crap and started reading the poems. I read them aloud, like you taught us. And as I read I think: yes, I'd sleep with a part of this man under my pillow and imagine it to be his heart. When Mum died they burned her and gave me the ashes. Mum liked you. She said I ought to listen to you, to pay attention; you could be my salvation. This isn't what I meant to write about, what I meant to

86

write about was the article you are contributing to the magazine. There's no word limit, no title, no deadline. There doesn't have to be a beginning, middle or end. It doesn't have to be neat. You can write what you like. Did you ever set your pupils an assignment like this? Did you ever say to them: there are no rules. If there are no rules, do you see, it is impossible to transgress. It is impossible to be a transgressor. If there are no beginnings, middles or ends there is nowhere for transgression to be located.

I look forward to hearing your views on this. I have explored similar issues with Mr. Patrick, my former history teacher, and Mrs. Davies-White. Neither of them, I have to say, provided a satisfactory response.

Lizzie, you called her in your letter. Does this mean you were friends, you and Mrs. Davies-White? Did you ever talk to her about granite, I wonder? And if you did, did she say it sparkled like frost in the sunshine; or did she describe it as a hard granular igneous rock formed of quartz, feldspar and mica and used especially for building?

I will keep in touch.

Yours sincerely,
Gregory

Primary school reports (extracts):

Gregory writes well but is hesitant and lacking in confidence when reading aloud.
Gregory has a wide vocabulary.
. . . compositions show originality and are well expressed.
The original and interesting ideas in his written work are spoiled by very careless errors.
. . . written work is interesting and original, but little effort is made in presentation.

Gregory finds oral expression difficult.

His work will become less disjointed and more interesting when he learns to organise his thoughts more carefully.

Organisation. Presentation. Confidence. The necessity for absence of error.

English Literature

Mock O level, Jan. 1975

Question 5: Who is proud and who is prejudiced in *Pride and Prejudice?*

Three questions out of five. Austen, Hardy, Dickens, Lawrence, Eliot. All English, all dead. Eliot was a woman, even though she called herself George. Her real name was Mary something but she had to use a man's name because women weren't supposed to write novels in those days. She wrote *Silas Marner.* It's about a miserly hermit who has all his money stolen and then finds a little girl with hair the same golden colour as his coins and he adopts her and raises her like she was his own daughter. In the end he gets his money back, but doesn't hoard it or spend it on himself because he's discovered the true meaning of treasure. Jane Austen wrote *Pride and Prejudice.* Elizabeth Bennet is the heroine. She meets a bloke called Darcy and doesn't like him at first, but then finds out that the reason she doesn't like him is due to a misunderstanding. So they fall in love.

These are the Victorian realists, said Miss McMahon. This is realism.

Lawrence wrote about sex. Dickens wrote about poor people. Hardy's books were set in Wessex, which doesn't exist anymore. We had to do papers on Chaucer and Shakespeare. Chaucer wrote in Middle English, the language of the fourteenth century—except for the ruling classes, who'd used French since the Norman Conquest. Henry IV was the first English-speaking king (1399–1413) to rule England since 1066. William Shakespeare wrote plays: tragedies and comedies. Plays about history. Miss McMahon took us to see *Henry IV (Part I)* at Stratford. We went on a coach, we ate our sandwiches in a park next to the river Avon, then watched the play; we sat high in the upper circle. The Gods, she called it. Every time Hotspur's name was mentioned, one of the boys in my class shouted "Come on, you Spurs!" The play went on for hours. I couldn't understand a fucking word.

Essays. Essays about books. Words about words. It wasn't enough just to read a book or a play or a poem; you had to study it, analyse it, understand it. You had to learn the right passages to quote in your essay. A lot of the time I didn't know what to write, or my head was full of words but I couldn't put them down the way you were supposed to.

What is it, Gregory?

Nn.

I don't understand what it is.

I looked away.

You write wonderful essays in the other class, but when it comes to English lit . . .

The classroom, at breaktime; Miss McMahon had asked me to stay behind. She'd pulled up a chair and was sitting beside me. Smudge of chalk dust on the elbow of her cardigan. Mock-exam papers lay fanned out on the desk, the Austen on top. I reread what I'd written.

> Jane Austen is proud of her cleverness, I am prejudiced against that.
> (word count: 12 approx.)

It's not as though the material is beyond you.

I didn't respond.

Is it?

No, miss.

89

Have you read the books?

Yes.

All of them?

Yes. Twice.

Well, then.

Well.

(Exhalation.) You'll fail if you do this in June. You know that.

I nodded.

Does that not bother you?

Not really.

Miss McMahon sat back in her chair and folded her hands in her lap. She turned her head slightly, towards the window. Children were playing outside. There was shouting and squealing, the scuff of a plastic football on concrete.

Nor me, she said.

I looked at her. She was smiling.

Gregory, no one's going to throw you in jail because you haven't an O level in English literature.

Her smile faded.

But this (she gestured at the exam papers) worries me. This isn't just a case of being flippant or rebellious or lazy. Is it?

I shrugged. I was prodding the desk with the tip of my pen, scoring a thick blue line along the grain of the wood. I made the line into a square and the square into a box and the box into a dice. I was aware of Miss McMahon watching me.

You like stories, don't you? You like telling them. Your essays in the other class are full of . . . of invention.

Nn.

But you don't like other people's stories. Jane Austen. George Eliot. Dickens. You're not interested in what they have to say. Am I correct?

I don't know.

Do you *like* the books? Do you actually like them?

I like *reading* them.

But *yours* are the only stories that really interest you.

I can make people do things in my stories.

What d'you mean?

I can make people.

You can make people?

Yes.

I'm not sure I understand, Gregory.

I joined up the dots on the face of the dice, began filling it in with a series of crosshatches. But fragments of wood from the desk accumulated around the inky brass point of the pen and it stopped working. I scribbled back and forth on the exam paper but the nib left no ink, just a zigzag of deep white grooves picked out against the white page by the light from the window. If you moved your head slightly, the grooves disappeared.

Can I go, miss?

You want to go?

I shook my head.

What, then?

I don't know. I don't . . .

Here.

She handed me a handkerchief. It was soft and white and scented, edged in lace. Her initials were stitched into one corner. J.M. She kept the handkerchief inside the cuff of her cardigan.

Janice used to try on Mum's dresses, shoes, jewellery, makeup. She'd totter around the bedroom in a pair of high heels, a smear of pink across her mouth and her eyelids thick with blue; treading on the ends of a long skirt. She made me wear Dad's clothes. His jackets were rough against my skin, his shoes were smelly and sweaty and my feet slipped around inside them when I tried to walk. I had to put on a deep voice, I had to shout at her. Or I had to call her "love." If I tried to kiss her, she'd push me away and say "Mind my lipstick!" Janice liked clothes. She liked to cut pictures out of Mum's mail-order catalogues and hairdressing magazines and paste them into a scrapbook. Men in suits, women in sparkly frocks, children in bright reds and greens and yellows. She gave the people names, made up stories about them and wrote them next to the photographs. I was allowed to watch, but I wasn't to touch anything because boys are clumsy and have grubby fingers. Boys spoil things. She told me the stories, she read aloud to me as she wrote them down.

I went to the post office every day. It was two weeks before the next letter arrived. The envelope was light, no more than a couple of pages. I could tell before I opened it that there was no article inside. I read the letter on the bus. I read it again and again.

> Dear Gregory,
>
> Well, what a curious letter! It would be fair to say that it is some time since I received such diverting correspondence! Of course, it is good to have one's thoughts provoked, even at my age (especially at my age!). Actually, your letter reminded me of your essays: somewhat disorganised and with a tendency to stray from the point, but remarkably alive and original. Unmistakably you. I suspect your involvement with the anniversary reunion and magazine is a convenient excuse for you to chew over old times, as it were, with some of your former teachers. Am I correct? In any event, please do not think ill of me for failing to respond more promptly; but my time is not entirely my own. If it is a "pen pal" you are seeking—as the tone of your letter seems to suggest—I'm afraid my reliability as a correspondent may not be all you would wish.
>
> However, I should like to offer my observations on one or two of the points you raise. With regard to Shelley, I too am inclined to focus on the poetry rather than the man himself or the more sensational elements of his pitifully brief life. Though, naturally, I am aware

that the relationship between an artist and his work is something of a grey area these days! For example, what diverts me about your letter is not so much the content as the insight it gives into the person who wrote it (i.e., you). As far as the question of "rules" is concerned, I must say I do not share your view that, without rules, there can be no transgression. Surely rules, in their various forms, arise out of a prevailing consensus of "right" and "wrong" and simply to do away with rules does not undermine the conceptual possibility of "rightness" and "wrongness"?

Similarly, I do not subscribe to your implied belief that a scientific appreciation of something (e.g., granite) is inferior to an aesthetic one. The two, to me, are not mutually exclusive and I certainly do not choose my friends on the basis of their enjoyment—or otherwise—of igneous rock formations! Talking of which, I really must write to Lizzie—I've been characteristically neglectful in this respect since she left ————.

I have not forgotten the article you requested, indeed I hope to be able to send you something shortly. In the meantime, feel free to divert me again!

With best wishes,
Janet

P.S. I am flattered to learn that your dear mother thought so highly of me, though I confess to being at a loss to know how I might have been your "salvation." Salvation from what, or from whom?

prescribe   *(vb):* to set down as a rule or guide
proscribe   *(vb):* to denounce or prohibit

One letter makes all the difference. I say this to my barrister, who shuffles the pile of papers and asks which of the letters I'm referring to: one of mine or one of Miss McMahon's?

The letter O.

He doesn't know what the fuck I'm talking about. I relish this lack of communication, this failure of language between us. It's one way in which he will learn to appreciate my point of view. My case. However, when I try to explain, he interrupts; he urges me *yet again* to please keep to the point. We continue to discuss the letters—mine and Miss McMahon's—and I'm not allowed to talk about the small, subtle way in which prescribe can become proscribe. How a word can be a fraction away from meaning something quite different. Insert the letter *e* into dad and you have dead.

Words are signs, Miss McMahon told us. They represent things, they are not the things themselves.

When I am describing to my barrister the events of the past year—the incidents—I am assembling a series of signs. I am telling stories. No actions, only words. The court will sit in judgement not on the events, but on the evidence. Written and spoken testimonies; photographs, documents. Tape recordings. Diagrams. I will be judged by a series of representations. And when the verdict is announced, I will be neither guilty nor innocent; I will be "guilty" or "not guilty." My photograph will appear in the papers and on TV, and that will be me. Gregory Lynn (orphan, bachelor, only child from the age of four and a half). In the black-and-white pictures it will not even be apparent that I have one brown eye and one green.

Another thing I am not permitted to share with my barrister: education is like the law, both prescriptive and proscriptive. Its primary concerns are with setting down rules of learning (what you can and can't know) and restrictions on behaviour (what you can and can't do); with punishing you when you err in either respect. With the making of model citizens.

Exceptions: Mr. Andrews. Mr. Andrews was neither pre nor

pro, he was ascriptive. Miss McMahon. Not sure about her. The jury is still out on Miss McMahon.

Dear Miss McMahon,

You see, you tell me nobody will throw me in jail if I fail English lit and then you write a report saying you're sure I'll "acquit myself creditably" in the English Language O level; and I think what is it with these fucking exams anyway that one minute they're a load of bollocks and the next they are worthwhile. Important. Necessary. And when I think along those lines, it makes me wonder whether you are any different from the rest of them.

Are you? Were you?

This stuff about transgression, in your letter. You

Anyway, what do teachers know about transgression? It's your duty *not to transgress,* to set an example. If I don't want to write an essay about Jane Austen, that is a transgression because you can't just

You can't

I may screw this letter up and throw it in the bin. There: I have screwed up the page and smoothed it out again and I will send it to you all creased so you know you're reading something that could just as easily have been thrown away and never read. Did you know that Kafka wanted his manuscripts destroyed when he died, but his friend—Max someone-or-other—reneged on the deal and had them published? What I want to know is: would Kafka have been a brilliant writer even if all his works had been burned without being read, or did he become one only because he was *recognised as such?* What do you think, Miss McMahon?

Max Brod is who it was, Kafka's friend.

I didn't take English O level, lit or lang. Or any other fucking exam for that matter. You don't even remember that, do you? You remember my essays, you remember meeting Mum. You remember *me* but you don't remember what happened when I left ————. Why I left.

I have a map on the wall in my bedroom. I know where Aberdeen is.

Dad liked Charlie Cooke—he was a Jocko, like you. He played for Chelsea.

My dad is dead and so is my mum and so is my sister. Mum liked you.

She said you

I know where Aberdeen is, I know how to get there. If I draw a picture of Aberdeen and draw myself in the picture, I'll be in Aberdeen. By drawing things, sometimes I make them happen.

> Yours sincerely,
> Gregory

Dad read the *Sporting Life,* the *Daily Mirror.* You weren't to talk to him when he was reading, or when he was doing the crossword. He sucked the end of the pen, said it helped him think. All the pens in our house were short and splintered and leaked ink, or they didn't work at all, so Dad had to swear and throw them across the room at the wastepaper bin. If he got stuck on a clue he'd shout it out to Mum.

Incomplete. Seven letters, blank blank *R* blank *I* blank blank.

He only did regular crosswords, cryptic ones were a load of fucking gibberish. When he'd finished with the paper he'd take out the TV section and wedge the rest under the seat cushion of his chair. Every few weeks Mum would have a clear-out, chuck the back copies in the bin. She'd find pens jammed down the side of the cushion; coins, betting slips, pools coupons. Bits of food. A plastic comb, greasy and knotted with clumps of black hair.

You're a pig.

Oink!

You are. Filthy. It's like living with an animal.

Oink, oink!

He would wink at me, and call her a nag. She wasn't happy unless she'd something to moan about. She was a moaning old mare.

In winter, Dad lit the coal fire as well as the gas fire. He'd pull a couple of old newspapers from under the cushion and scrunch up the pages in the bottom of the grate and stack bits of kindling on top, then the lumps of coal. He lit the paper with Mum's cigarette lighter and watched while the flames took hold. If they didn't catch, he'd blow on them or spread one of the double pages of newspaper over the mouth of the fireplace so the air from the chimney would suck the fire into life.

I liked newspapers. I liked the big black headlines, the photographs of famous people. I liked the way the print stained my hands, leaving bits of sentences on the damp skin of my palms, my fingers. You had to hold your hands up to a mirror to read what the words said.

No "Dear Gregory" on the final letter, no Oxfam notepaper; just a note in blue ballpoint on two ruled sheets peeled from a spiral-bound pad. After I'd read the letter I tore narrow strips from around the margins of the pages—careful not to remove any of the words—placed the pieces in my mouth, one at a time, and chewed them. When the paper had formed into a small wet wad I took it from between my teeth and pressed it against the underside of my desk, one piece after another, leaving a line of pellets to dry and harden.

You clearly went to some trouble to contact me, Gregory, and I would have been grateful if you had been courteous enough to tell me the *true* reason. Since receiving your last letter, I have been in touch with the school, and the secretary informs me that she has no knowledge of the reunion you say you are organizing. She is also unaware of any magazine being published to coincide with the anniversary. Indeed, when I mentioned your name it meant nothing to her. All of which, I confess, leaves me somewhat perplexed as to your purpose in writing to me.

It is apparent that you still harbour some ill feeling with regard to your days at ———, though you are correct when you say that I do not recall the exact circumstances of your leaving. Whatever happened—and I have a vague recollection—it was a very long time ago and surely best forgotten, don't you agree? For what it's worth, whenever I find that I am brooding on the past or wallowing in nostalgia, I remind myself of a piece of advice a dear friend gave me: "It's all right to look back—but don't stare."

Reading between the lines, Gregory, I can't help but suspect that all this is connected in some way to the recent upset of your poor mother's death. As someone who has been similarly bereaved, I cannot tell you how to grieve; but I do urge you to hold on to what is *real* and to trust in God to grant you the wisdom to know what that is.

I'm afraid I shall not write again. Nor do I think it would be a good idea for you to come to Aberdeen, as you seemed to suggest in your last letter. My dear sister and I, in our advanced years, have grown rather unac-

customed to receiving guests. I do hope you understand.

Janet McMahon

God. I was to trust in God. Auntie could've written that, it was the sort of thing she would say. He is our Redeemer, He delivers us from Evil. He frees us from the consequences of Sin. When Auntie tells me this, I ask: (a) why? (b) when? She answers: (a) because He loves us, (b) on Judgement Day.

God is the Word and the Word is with God, she said.

Auntie was under the impression that I had a job, as a security guard at a warehouse on the business park next to the estate. I told her I had to work nights. I told her I slept during the day and that was why I left the phone off the hook and why the curtains were drawn and why I hadn't come to the door right away. She was happy for me, that I had some money coming in; that I was making a fresh start. It was what Marion would've wished. She apologised for disturbing me and said she'd phone in the evenings from now on, or at weekends. As long as she knew everything was hunky-dory, that was the main thing. Auntie told me that I was always in her prayers.

After she left, I made a round of fried-egg sandwiches and a mug of coffee and returned to my room. I removed Miss McMahon's note—frayed and misshapen at the edges—from my files and reread it as I ate. A drip of egg yolk made a sticky yellow stain on the page, next to her signature.

I took my pad and my pencils, I drew the boxes. I coloured them in.

Walk to the bus stop, bus to the station, train to Victoria, tube to King's Cross on the Victoria line; the royal-blue one. Five stops. It was a bright spring day, I wore a T-shirt. I carried a plastic holdall containing a change of clothes, soap, toothbrush and paste (Colgate), a packed lunch (sandwiches, crisps, Fanta), a paperback novel (police procedural), a pad and pencils, the "McMahon, J." file and a street plan of Aberdeen. After purchasing a return ticket I had enough money left for an evening meal, one night's accommodation in a cheap B&B and bus fares to and from the street where she lived.

The departures board flickered: Leeds, Edinburgh, Newcastle. Aberdeen. My train was not due to leave for another twenty-five minutes, the platform number had yet to be displayed. I sat in the main concourse and watched people hurrying. I watched their confusion. I watched them being confused within themselves and within their surroundings, with each other. I watched the people at the margins. Three seats along from me a woman was slumped asleep, head lolling; her thick coat held together at the waist by a length of twine. An old man was stooped over a waste bin, rummaging. A youth on roller skates slalomed among the seated, standing, walking; their baggage, their trolleys. His head was shaved high at the sides and back, his black face was beautiful. It gleamed. Across the concourse, by the news kiosk, a small girl was crying. A paper bag lay on the floor at her feet, prettily coloured sweets scattered. Her mother slapped the bare backs of the girl's legs. They were too far away, there was too much noise, for me to hear the smack of flesh on flesh; but I saw the fat white hand, moving, moving. Mum never smacked Janice, or me. It was Dad who did the smacking. Whenever he hit Janice, I would cry as if it was me who was being hit. I would scream. I would wet myself.

Didn't talk to anyone at the station. By the time I'd finished my packed lunch, the departures board displayed the platform number for the Aberdeen train, it listed all the stops and the connections to other towns and cities. I zipped the holdall, stood up and walked towards the platform. The train was already half full. I found a window seat in one corner of a nonsmoking car. I removed my paperback and stowed the bag overhead. I didn't get out my notepad and pencils because if you make pictures on buses and trains, people will peek. They'll try to see what you are drawing, they'll ask you about it. Or they won't say anything, just look at the person they're with and make faces. They'll smirk. You will have to hide the pictures with your hand, like when you're at school and someone is trying to copy. Miss McMahon told us:

If you copy, you will not cheat me, you will cheat yourselves. If you can't think of anything original to write, I'd sooner you handed in a blank piece of paper.

Miss McMahon, English teacher.

As the train waited at the platform, I drew her in my head. I pictured her asleep; me standing at her bedside, waking her. The pale, freckled face—confused and fearful, like a startled rabbit—as she recognised me. I saw the pillow drenched in blood.

A RECITATION

Sweet Spirit! Sister of that orphan one,
Whose empire is the name thou weepest on,
In my heart's temple I suspend to thee
These votive wreaths of withered memory.

Poor captive bird! who, from thy narrow cage,
Pourest such music, that it might assuage
The rugged hearts of those who prisoned thee,
Were they not deaf to all sweet melody . . .

Shelley. The opening lines from "Epipsychidion," she told us, written in 1821. She read the whole poem aloud, in her soft voice; her Scottish voice. And the room was quiet, so that there was only her voice, his words. It was a long poem. When she'd finished, she didn't say what it was about, she didn't ask questions. She stood smiling silently at her desk for minute upon minute, until it was time for us to leave.

・・・

You, ah, say that this cartoon was drawn "in your head"?

Yes.

And yet (he searches among the documents) I have here a copy of one of the drawings recovered by the police . . . here it is . . . When was that drawn?

Afterwards. When I was back at home.

Not on the train?

No.

But is this not the cartoon you have just described for us, the one you said you didn't actually draw?

(I don't look at the paper which he offers, hand outstretched across the table.) No it isn't.

Miss McMahon—I assume it to be her—lying in bed . . . the blood-soaked pillow?

And me, Gregory Lynn? Where am I?

(The barrister reexamines the picture.) Very well. But in all other respects it is essentially similar, is it not, to the *imagined* cartoon?

No.

Look . . .

The blood is dissimilar.

The blood? In what way?

Essentially.

Gregory, the prosecution will dwell on the fact . . .

While I sat on the train, drawing pictures in my head, I saw that the pillow was stained red not by her or by anything I'd done to her, but by the dead heart concealed beneath it.

Doors slammed, there were shouts, a whistle, and the train jolted into motion. One minute late. People waved to one an-

102

other, passengers settled themselves for the long journey north. The train gathered momentum, piercing the arch of sunlight where the grey of the platform petered out into shiny ribbons of track. Faces blurred, smiles and waves distorted into streaks of pink and white. I watched the train go. I stood on the platform and watched it disappear from view.

4

mathematics   **1a.** science of numbers, their operations, interrelations and combinations   **1b.** science of space configurations and their structure, measurement, etc.   **2.** mathematics or mathematical operations involved in a particular problem, field of study, etc.

Mr. Teja was a Paki. Mr. Teja was not a Paki, he was from Kenya; his parents were from India.

Mr. Teja brushed his teeth with curry powder. Mr. Teja did not brush his teeth with curry powder, his breath—when he stood close to you—had the faint fragrance of turmeric, of cumin, of coriander, of garam masala.

Mr. Teja rode to school on an elephant. Mr. Teja did not ride to school on an elephant, he drove a mustard and chocolate Austin Princess.

In conversation with my barrister, I ponder the discrepancies between what can be demonstrated to be true and what is perceived to be true; the authority of rumour, gossip and slander. The power of falsehood. How it can be possible for Mr. Teja and Curry Breath to be one and the same person. I endeavour to make it plain that my own antipathy towards Mr. Teja was not motivated by such schoolboy bigotry; it was not born of cultural or racial prejudice, nor of peer-group pressure, but of a resistance to his religion. My legal representative raises his eyebrows, he prompts:

His religion being?

Mathematics.

Gregory . . .

The God of Numbers. The verifiable fact. Fixity.

You prefer to side with the, ah, gossipmongers, the slanderers?

(Shake of the head.) I tread the middle way, between facts and fiction. "Truth" and "untruth," as absolutes, are equal partners in the conspiracy.

Which conspiracy is that?

The conspiracy to delude.

Naturally, I am wasting my time; my barrister regards this dialogue as another digression from what is relevant to my case, he suggests we *shift the focus*. I am helpful. I discuss what he wishes to discuss. I do not show him the newspaper clipping in which I read these words: "So far as the laws of mathematics refer to reality, they are not certain. And so far as they are certain, they do not refer to reality"—Albert Einstein. According to the article, this has long taxed the designers of "complicated control systems" (no clue as to what the fuck these are)—the difficulty being to apply mathematically logical regimes to complex, ill-defined or nonlinear problems. Solution: fuzzy logic. Precision is out, imprecision is in.

Mr. Teja would not have been one for fuzzy logic.

Something of which I was unaware at the time, but I now learn from my barrister, is that the continuation of my acts of revision was made possible by a failure of communication between Miss

McMahon and Mrs. Davies-White. The former wrote to the latter, as she'd said she would, and my name was mentioned, along with a brief résumé of my letters to Aberdeen. In reply, Mrs. Davies-White said the name did not ring any bells, and she'd certainly not been contacted regarding a school reunion or anniversary magazine. The matter warranted one sentence in a long letter, a substantial part of which was taken up with an account (abridged) of her shocking ordeal in a Cardiff alleyway, and subsequent recuperation (psychological and physical). Mrs. Davies-White did not make a connection between Gregory Lynn and her attack, nor did Miss McMahon. If either had done so, and had reported their suspicions to the police, it is probable, counsel observes, that I'd have been apprehended at that stage. Before the Teja incident, and those involving Mr. Hutchinson and Mr. Andrews. Before Mr. Boyle. I'd have been *stopped in my tracks*. However, neither woman made the connection. They did not put two and two together.

Denary: 2 plus 2 equals 4.
Binary: 2 plus 2 equals 100.

I've seen a photocopy of the last letter I received from Miss McMahon. There is a small grey circle, slightly misshapen, alongside her signature: the mark made nine months ago by a dried blob of yolk from an egg sandwich. Counsel for the prosecution has the original document, with its torn edges, the original ink which spells out her name, the original egg stain. Yellow, crusty. It could, I imagine, be removed with the flick of a fingernail.

> *Lynn, Gregory*
> *Form 5-3*
> *Mathematics*
> *Gregory does not have his heart in this sort of work. He has ability when he cares to use it—unfortunately, he seems to enjoy spending time distracting others.*
> *S. Teja*

On Saturdays, Dad would stop off at the betting office on the way home from work. Usually he told me to run along, but sometimes I was allowed to go in with him. The bookie's, he called it. A bookie is a bookmaker, a turf accountant. When Mum wanted to know where he'd been, he'd say:

I've been consulting my accountant.

Dad hated Grand National day, when once-a-year gamblers crawled out of the woodwork to put a couple of bob each way on a 150–1 shot because they liked the sound of its name. Ben Nevis, because they'd been to Scotland on their holidays that year; or Highland Wedding, because their daughter had got married the previous Saturday. National day, you couldn't move in the bookie's for women with shopping bags, blokes putting bets on for the missus and the kids and the old biddy next door. They'd be queuing halfway down the street, and some giggly doris would be asking you what-does-that-mean? and how-am-I-supposed-to-fill-this-in? Or they'd want to know which horse Lester Piggott was riding and you'd have to tell them he wasn't a National Hunt jockey; and then you'd have to explain what that meant. Or there'd be a delay at the counter because some dozy wanker had written the bet out wrong. And at 4:30 they'd be back, lining up to collect their winnings. A quid. Ten bob. Seven-and-six. They'd be grinning fit to piss themselves.

Dad, what's a hundred and fifty to one?

You put on a quid and win a hundred and fifty.

What's four-to-six?

Six-to-four on. You bet six to win four.

So you lose two quid?

Pounds. No, you get your stake back as well.

What's each way?

Bloody questions! You're giving me earache.

People said hello to Dad in the bookie's. Old men, men in overalls. Big black men. They nodded, smiled. All right, Paddy. Right, Pat. Paddy boy. He would talk to them about horses, dogs, football; they'd mutter and scratch their noses and tilt their heads to one side and look around, like when you say things behind Teacher's back; like when you pass notes or bubble gum from desk to desk. There were TV screens on high shelves; racing pages from the newspapers pinned to boards around the walls; rows of high stools; a narrow Formica-topped ledge scarred with cigarette welts and littered with metal ashtrays, ripped betting slips and dozens of tiny plastic ballpoint pens. The smoke made my eyes sting, made me choke. The top copy of the betting slip was white, the carbon was pink. Dad taught me how to fill it in. He taught me what all the figures meant alongside the horses' names in the form guides. He told me what a Yankee was.

Six doubles, four trebles and an accumulator.

I don't understand.

He peeled a fresh betting slip from the Perspex dispenser on the wall and wrote on the reverse while he explained.

Four races, you pick one horse in each. A, B, C and D, right? A and B win, is a double. You got six doubles: A/B, A/C, A/D, B/C, B/D and C/D. A, B and C win, is a treble. So you got four trebles: A/B/C, A/B/D, A/C/D and B/C/D. Yeah?

What about D/A/C?

That's the same as A/C/D, innit? Dipstick.

So what's an acc . . . an accumulus?

Accumulator. All four horses win. A, B, C and D. In a Yankee, you got every combination. Six doubles, four trebles, accumulator.

I studied the jumble of letters and figures he'd scribbled on the thin pink page. One of the blokes was standing behind us, laughing. He had red stubble and his breath reeked of raw onion. He laid one hand on my shoulder and one on Dad's.

Tell you what, son, 'f you're takin' gambling lessons from your old man you might as well flush your money down the fuckin' pan and 'ave done with.

Dad was brilliant at times tables. Call one out and he would come back with the answer quicker than you could snap your fingers.

Nine eights?

Seventy-two.

Seven twelves?

Eighty-four.

If we were playing darts, he could subtract 85 from 501 in the time it took to chalk the numbers on the slate; he could tell you any "out" shot. He could study the league tables in the Sunday paper and work out Chelsea's goal average or tell you how many points they needed from their remaining games to avoid relegation. When snooker was on the telly, he'd study the screen and say: "Black with the last red leaves him needing snookers."

Mental arithmetic. With arithmetic, you can add, you can take away, you can multiply and you can divide; but there are only two types of answer: right and wrong. Arithmetic is one of the three Rs. Writing is another.

When I told Mr. Teja I didn't see the point of maths, he explained the difference between pure and applied mathematics. Pure mathematics is the abstract science of space, number and quantity, he said; a theoretical science. Applied mathematics is theory put to practical use, especially the application of general principles to solve definite problems. When I told him maths was boring, he said:

Physical exercises are boring, but we do them to keep fit. Mathematics is push-ups for the mind.

He grinned. His teeth were very white and neat and even, his moustache clipped to perfection. His thick black hair always bore the tooth furrows of the steel comb he kept in the inside pocket of his jacket and used from time to time with the absent-mindedness of habit. His English was accented, correct at all times. His skin was the colour of strong coffee.

In the back of my maths exercise book, while he was writing on the board or talking to us, I drew pictures. Cartoons. I turned geometric shapes into houses, trees, people. I made bicycles with triangular wheels, I drew children with oblong heads and round feet. I made their faces out of numbers: a zero for the head, two 3s for the ears, an upside-down 7 for the nose, lots of 1s for the hair, a sideways 8 for the eyes, a small zero for the mouth. I couldn't colour them in because there was no reason for anyone to have coloured pencils in maths. If Mr. Teja came near, I'd turn to the front of the book—naturally, no sudden or surreptitious movements—and carry on with whatever work we were supposed to be doing. After he'd walked past, boys would pinch their nostrils and make faces at each other. They would pretend to vomit or to pass out. Curry Breath.

When I told him I didn't understand maths, he said:

What is there to understand? It is only numbers, it all comes down to numbers. There is no knowledge without calculation.

Numbers, he said, are integral to our understanding of the world we inhabit. Physicists depend on numbers—mathematical formulae—for their theories about the nature of the universe, its origin, structure and time-space relationships. Those who know most about existence are not the poets or clerics or philosophers, but those who can compute. The mathematicians. He grinned again:

Numbers are creation, Gregory. Zero plus zero equals one.

I offered Mr. Teja a definition:

A statistician is someone who has his head in the oven and his arse in the fridge and insists that, on average, he is the perfect temperature.

He didn't laugh, didn't even smile. He said I'd used a bad word, that I was being irreverent. I overheard him in the corridor later that day, repeating the joke to another teacher.

What odds on me being able to trace Mr. Teja? How do you calculate such odds? What law applies: the law of probability? The law of chance? Dad said betting odds weren't fixed merely according to the probability of a horse winning, but *the extent to which the gamblers backed it.* A question of supply and demand, profit margins. The accountancy of the turf.

Betting isn't gambling, Greg, it's an investment. Spec-u-lay-shun. Ask someone with stocks and shares if they're a gambler and see what they say.

Mum said Dad was talking out of his backside.

I got it into my head that if enough people placed bets on a horse (a dog, a football team, or whatever) it was bound to win. Even if only one person backed it—as long as the stake was high enough. The sole purpose of the race itself was to confirm or refute a gambler's expectations.

I was certain I'd find Mr. Teja because the only thing I had to invest in tracking him down was time, and I had unlimited quantities of that. I had more time than you could count. As it turned out, I traced him within ten minutes of commencing my research. I checked in the local directory under Teja, S. There were three. I rang each of them in turn. On the second call, a woman answered; when I asked her if a Mr. Teja—a maths teacher—lived there, there was a long pause, then the stuttery stammerings of a reply from which these words emerged:

I am *Mrs.* Teja. His wife. His w—

I replaced the receiver. I noted down the address listed in the phone book, copied it onto the wall chart and inserted a pin in the appropriate place on the map of Greater London. The pin was black, the line connecting it to his name on the chart was also black.

Two weeks had passed since my abortive journey to Aberdeen. I was ready to resume. I didn't eat or sleep; through the night, I worked with my notepad and pencils. There would be no hesitancy this time, no misgivings, no reprieve; Mr. Teja was—to borrow the terminology of war—a legitimate target. I made measurements on the map, I calculated that he lived one and seven-eighths of a mile away from our house. My house.

Primary school reports:

> *Jul 1967 (Form 1a)*
> *Arithmetic: Gregory will only be able to make quick and accurate calculations by obeying rules which must be learnt.*
> *Dec 1968 (Form 3a)*
> *Arithmetic: Greater thought and care essential. Needs to pay attention.*
> *Dec 1969 (Form 4a)*
> *Arithmetic: Gregory seems uncertain about basic methods.*
> *Jul 1970 (Form 4a)*
> *Arithmetic: He must learn the basic principles.*

Rules, methods, principles. Accuracy. Obedience.

In infants and juniors, maths was arithmetic. The teacher was the same one who taught us English and history and geography and science and art. We would be told to take out our arithmetic books, and the teacher would write sums on the blackboard for us to copy down. Ten out of ten, you got a gold star alongside your name on a chart on the wall; nine, you got a silver star. My name came between Lineker, P., and Mitchell, J. I didn't have any stars. Our arithmetic books were smaller than the exercise books for the other subjects, a different shape, tall and narrow; the cover was shiny red. Thinner pages, without margins. I liked the smell of the paper, I liked to touch it. I liked the way the pages looked before all the numbers and lines and crossings out and the red crosses, the red ticks, the marks. Before they got spoiled.

What I hated was fractions. Long division. I hated getting a cross for the right answer because the way you'd worked it out was wrong, or because you'd done it in your head instead of writing out the whole sum. I hated the singsong voices of forty-two children chanting times tables in unison.

112

. . . nine nines are eighty-one, ten nines are nine-tee . . .

If a question said 9×9, I'd work it out: 10 times 9 is 90, minus 9 is 81. But that was wrong. You weren't supposed to do it like that. You were supposed to *know* your times tables by heart, the answer had to be automatic. You weren't supposed to think about it.

Mum used to cut Dad's hair. She used to cut mine and Janice's. When it was my turn, she'd drape an old nylon bed sheet round my shoulders, like a poncho, and tuck it tightly into the neck of my shirt. She wet my hair with a comb, then cut it with her best scissors. I had to be very still and not giggle or fuss. I sat on a stool, facing the kitchen table. I wasn't to get down until she'd swept up, or I'd tread hairs everywhere. Her fingers were cool and smooth. Dry. They fluttered at my neck like butterflies.

After Dad died, I didn't let Mum cut my hair anymore. I made her take me to the barber's. Or I cut it myself, in front of the bathroom mirror. I used scissors and a special comb with a sharp blade between the teeth. The clumps of black hair blocked up the plug-hole in the washbasin. Or I let it grow long, to my shoulders, and the form teacher would send me home with a note reminding Mum that the school insisted its boys' hair should be no longer than collar length. The first time I wore a ponytail, I was sent to the headmaster. He said I looked like a girl. He said I was a big girl's blouse. A Jessie. I was fourteen. I told him Mum's new bloke liked to hold onto the ponytail while he fucked me up the arse.

Full inquiry. Antisocial Services, police, the lot. All bollocks, of course, all *a figment of my imagination*. When I went back to school I was allowed to wear my hair long, but I had to see the educational psychologist once a week. Michael stopped coming to the house. Michael was Mum's bloke. Mike. He was an under-manager at Supashop, where she worked. He moved to a branch in another part of London after the business about the fucking, and when Mum tried to ring him he wouldn't talk to her. I heard her crying into the mouthpiece. One morning, when I'd gone down for breakfast instead of having her bring it to my room, she sat across the table from me and said:

Gregory, it's two and a half years since your father died.

So what?

So I have to make a new life for myself. We both do.

Who, you and Mike?

Me and *you*. I don't think you're being very fair.

You want to fuck men, that's fine with me.

Gregory. Greg.

I went on eating my breakfast. When she reached out and tried to touch me I jerked my head away. I stared at the blurb on the back of the cereal packet until Mum stopped watching me.

There were other blokes after that, I know; but she never fetched them home. Then she stopped going out, except for work or shopping or to visit the women whose hair she cut. She'd come home reeking of groceries or perm solution or cigarettes, her face pale and baggy-eyed. Grey shadows fading into the powdery blush of her cheeks. She got thin, scrawny. She was always tired. Some evenings, she'd fall asleep in front of the telly. A magazine, open on her lap, would slide slowly to the floor and she'd wake with a jerk and blink across the room at me as though she didn't know who I was.

I found that nylon sheet—the poncho—among the box of old bedding in the attic the week after the burning. If you looked closely you could see bits of black hair stuck to the bright orange fabric. Fragments. It was impossible to tell if they were mine or Dad's or Janice's.

I walked to the Teja house. It took thirty-three minutes and eighteen seconds. May, a Saturday morning; the sky was grey and heavy with the threat of rain. I had a notebook, a pencil and a camera. I hoped to take a photograph of Mr. Teja for my wall chart. A mug shot. The camera had a zoom lens, I'd bought it the previous day. It was important to find a discreet position from which to observe the house so that, if he came out, I could get the picture without him knowing it had been taken.

To reach Mr. Teja's house I walked up the hill for more than a mile to the small shopping parade of Asian grocers, halal butchers, fabric stores and tandoori restaurants. The street was busy. On the pavement ahead of me, a child had picked a gnarled piece of gingerroot from a display stand and was about to put it into his mouth. His mother, a slender woman in a pink and gold sari, slapped his hand away. She scolded him in words which were foreign to me, but whose tone and meaning were unmistakable. When she saw me watching, the woman smiled fleetingly and tugged a loose fold of the sari more firmly about her head. The boy had started to cry. This time his mother spoke to him in English.

Bad child. Stop it this minute, you hear.

I walked past them, taking the turn which made a right angle at the T-junction, and followed the arc of the road as the shops gave way to a tight curve of houses with brightly coloured front doors. I consulted the section of map I had photocopied from the street directory, checking the name of the road leading to the side street where the Tejas lived. A small square was marked—green on the original map—denoting a park, which was actually a dusty patch of earth enclosed by iron railings. A group of Asian kids was playing cricket with an old bat and a tennis ball, plastic no-parking cones for wickets. A bench in the park would have been the perfect place from which to observe No. 3, the Tejas' address, but I had already attracted the attention of the children and decided to move out of their sight.

Two lines of row houses face-to-face across a double-parked street. I walked to one end and back again, keeping to the even-numbered side, searching for an inconspicuous vantage point. One house had been boarded up, the grey-white brickwork above the upper windows blackened by scorch marks. A partially burnt mattress lay slumped over a clutter of charred furniture and rubbish in the small scrap of front garden. The house was directly opposite No. 9, offering an angled view of the Teja household a few doors along. I sat down on the doorstep, partially concealed by a shallow wall which ran up either side of the steps from the street to the open porch. Two youths, whom I'd seen repairing a car at the roadside, were now obscured from view, though I could hear their tinkerings, their voices, the tinny burble of their radio. I leaned back against the rectangle of chipboard that had been nailed over the front door of the empty property. Removing the notepad and pencil from my day-pack, I made a rough sketch of No. 3. I took photographs, zooming in for detailed shots. The house was constructed of the same grey-white brick as all the neighbouring buildings, black slate roof and black guttering which looked in need of repair. Two storeys and a basement, with its own front door and separate doorbell. A small arched window under the eaves suggested an attic bedroom. The rest of the windows had been fitted with double-glazing, and were made opaque by dense mesh curtains. There was a garden, of sorts, a small area of crazy-paving bordered by flower beds. Through the frosted-glass panel of the front door, I could make out a blur of red and grey patterned wallpaper. I tried to visualise the interior. I pictured Mr. and Mrs. Teja eating lunch together, reading, watching TV. Were they Hindus or Muslims? Or Sikhs? Would their walls, their mantelpiece, be decorated with religious iconography? Did they have a place in their home dedicated to worship, maybe a small shrine decked out with fresh flowers? Would the house be aromatic with incense and cooking spices? I had no idea. Nor could I be sure they lived alone, although, by my estimation, they must have been in their midsixties and any children would be grown up. I wondered whether No. 3 had a rear access: a passage parallel to the street, perhaps, with a gate into the back garden. Before returning home that day, I would check. I'd reconnoitre. Draw more sketches, take more photographs.

· · ·

Geometry: a branch of mathematics dealing with the measurement, properties, and relationship of points, lines, angles, surfaces and solids. The word is derived from the Greek *geometria*, meaning "to measure the earth." Geometric progression is a sequence in which the ratio of any term to its predecessor is constant.

I think: What the fuck kind of progress is that?

Trigonometry is to do with triangles. Trigonometric function is a function (specifically the sine, cosine, tangent, cotangent, secant, or cosecant) of an arc or angle most simply expressed in terms of the ratios of pairs of sides of a right-angled triangle.

I think: What?

According to Pythagoras, the square of the length of the hypotenuse of a right-angled triangle equals the sum of the squares of the lengths of the other two sides. (The hypotenuse is the longest side.) Pythagoras (d. 500 B.C., approx.), Greek philosopher and mathematician. Pythagorean (adjective): of or associated with the philosophy of Pythagoras and his followers, asserting the mystical significance of numbers and the transmigration of souls.

We had to draw them in our geometry books, they had to be perfect. They had to be labelled clearly and correctly. Circles, squares, triangles (right-angled, equilateral, isosceles), rectangles, trapeziums, rhombuses, polygons (regular, irregular), polyhedrons. When you draw a circle, you can see the circumference and the centre, the pinprick made by the point of the compasses. Invisible, but which can be measured (and therefore exist), are the radius, the diameter. We drew parallel lines, we drew a diagonal line bisecting them so that we could measure the interior and exterior angles with protractors made of transparent plastic. We built cones from lumps of modelling clay, we sliced them into cross sections. The conic sections are: ellipse, circle, parabola, hyperbola.

Mr. Teja dictated the following definitions:

1. An acute angle is one that measures less than 90 degrees.
2. An oblique angle is one that measures more than 90 degrees.
3. An ellipse is a closed plane curve generated by a point moving in such a way that the sum of its distances from two fixed points is a constant.

These were the definitions he did not dictate:

1. Acute means sharp, intense, sudden or urgent. Pointed.
2. Oblique means inclined, indirect, nonexplicit. Neither perpendicular nor parallel.
3. Ellipsis is when something is missing, omitted. It is incompleteness.

I sat for three hours. When it rained I was sheltered by the porch of the burnt-out house. People passed by in cars, on foot and on cycles; front doors opened and closed as people came and went. Some of them noticed me, some didn't. An old woman at No. 11 spied on me for a while through a gap in the curtains. I stared at her until she retreated from view. Nobody entered or left No. 3; I saw no movement at the windows, heard no sounds from within. Once or twice there was the muffled ringing of a phone, but I couldn't tell if it was coming from the Tejas' or a neighbouring house.

I was putting the finishing touches to another sketch when I heard a voice, someone addressing me. I looked up. One of the youths I'd observed earlier, repairing a car, stood at the foot of the steps. His blue overalls were oil-smeared and he was wiping his hands on a rag. He gestured at the empty house.

You squatting?

I shook my head.

You an artist, then, or summink? Painter.

I became conscious of the notepad resting on my lap, the pencil in my hand. Architect, I said. I'm an architecture student. (I made up the name of a college.) We have to do a project on urban design. You know, a thesis.

My mate said you was from the Social Services—snooper, like—but I said you was too scruffy. (He smiled.) All due respect, an' that.

I smiled back, without comment.

Said to him, social don't wear ponytails.

He asked if I was local. I told him where I lived—not the estate, just the area. Did I drink in such and such a pub? I said I didn't. He talked a little about cars, about engine parts. Then he went away. The two youths were still working when I left. They broke off to watch me go. The white one, the one who'd spoken to me, looked out from under the raised bonnet of the car and nodded. His mate, the Asian, just watched.

Lynn, Gregory
Form 4-3
Mathematics
Gregory has difficulty adjusting to the GCE syllabus. He has only moderate ability and is losing interest and concentration. His recent "mock" O-level result was poor (32%) and his homework is infrequent.
S. Teja

The barrister interrupts my observations on the decision to relegate me to the CSE group in mathematics at the end of the fourth year. As usual, he is uninterested, he is not concentrating on what I am saying but on what he would like me to say. He is having difficulty adjusting to my syllabus.

The Asian youth—you were unaware at the time that he was Mr. Teja's grandson?

Yes.

When did you become aware of this, ah, family connection?

On my third visit.

What happened? There was some form of confrontation, one assumes.

On my third visit?

Yes.

What about the second visit, we haven't discussed that yet?

If it was substantially similar to the first, I really don't see . . .

Depends how you quantify "substantial," and what you mean . . .

Gregory.

. . . by "similar."

(He refers to a sheaf of papers fanned out on the desk between us.) The prosecution alleges criminal damage, threatening behaviour, assault causing actual bodily harm. All arising out of your third visit to the Tejas.

The third visit arose from the second, the second from the first. The pictures . . .

Look, the court won't give a tuppenny damn about your photographs and sketches. Or your O levels for that matter.

Among the items confiscated from my bedroom after my arrest was a colour photograph of Mrs. Teja taken with a zoom lens as she put four empty milk bottles on her front step; and another, slightly out of focus, of the Asian youth—her grandson—emerging from the door of No. 3. These and other pictures were taken during my second visit to the street. A Sunday, eight days after my initial visit. I sat at my observation post for seven hours and ten minutes waiting for a sighting of Mr. S. Teja, maths teacher. He did not come out of the house, nor did he appear even momentarily at one of the windows. However, I put the time spent monitoring the Tejas' home to good use, gathering intelligence on its occupants. I was able to ascertain that the basement flat was occupied by an old Asian woman whom I presumed to be Mr. Teja's mother. Living with Mr. and Mrs. Teja in the main part of the house were their grandson and his wife and baby. Visitors to

No. 3 on that day included a middle-aged man—the youth's father, the Tejas' son?—and his family (four children, the oldest of whom appeared to be aged about seventeen). Another visitor was the white youth, the car mechanic. He called for the Tejas' grandson in the early afternoon and the pair of them were away from the house for two and a half hours. They were carrying snooker cues, inside leather cases. Neither of them saw me. I could hear them speaking, but they were too distant for me to make out what they were saying.

During this second visit, I left the steps of the burnt-out house on four occasions: once to buy food and drink from a grocery store in a neighbouring street; twice to use the public conveniences on the main road; and once to take the rolled-up piece of paper which Mrs. Teja had inserted in the neck of one of the empty milk bottles. This document was among those discovered in my files by the police, and which is now in the possession of the prosecution. My barrister has a copy. It bears a handwritten note, in block capitals, which reads: THREE PINTS SEMIS-KIMMED, PLEASE.

Three pints are three-eighths of a gallon. They are one and a half quarts.

$1^{1}/_{2} - {}^{3}/_{8} = 1^{1}/_{8}$

But: $1^{1}/_{2}$ quarts minus ${}^{3}/_{8}$ of a gallon equals 0.

Janice played a skipping game with her friends. Two of them held the ends of the long rope while the others skipped, three or four at a time. When a girl stepped out from one end of the line, another joined in at the other. They chanted in time with the rhythm of the rope, voices fractured and breathless with skipping:

> *Not last night but the night before,*
> *Twenty-four robbers came knocking on my door.*

121

As I stepped out to let them in,
This is what the first one said to me . . .

Or they simply called out numbers, counting each skip. Hop, jump, hop, jump, twist. The rope made a slapping sound against the ground; the faster it moved the more blurred it became, as though there wasn't one rope but several. If the girl who was skipping trod on the rope or it snagged on her feet, the others would giggle; her turn would be over. When Janice skipped by herself, she could switch the handles of the rope from hand to hand in midskip without tripping or having to slow down. She could skip backwards. She could skip and run at the same time. I wanted her to teach me, but she said skipping was for girls.

Daddy says boxers play skipping.

Daddy says, Daddy says.

When we played It, we all stood in a circle and held out our fists. Janice would bang her fist against ours to choose which one of us was It.

One potato, two potato, three potato, four;
Five potato, six potato, seven potato, more . . .

If it was you, you had to shut your eyes and count to 20 before chasing the others. If you caught them and touched them, they were It too. When she did potatoes, Janice had to bend down to reach my fists. She said I held my hands wrong, with the thumbs inside my fingers. She showed me how to do it properly. Her hands were bony and hard like a boy's, except when I cried or fell over and she'd wipe my cheeks or rub the place where I'd hurt myself; or when I was in bed and she stroked my hair night-night.

Auntie was dusting. I'd told her not to, but she did it anyway. Now I was working, I was too busy to keep the place spick-and-span, she said. The house lacked a woman's touch. While she was doing the downstairs, I went up to lock my bedroom door. I flushed the toilet so she would think I'd been upstairs for a pee. When she'd finished dusting, we had tea together in the lounge. Her gaze alighted, briefly, on my bare feet, the rolled-up trouser cuffs. She said I was looking very well. She mentioned the old photographs in Mum's bedroom and said it was funny to think of me in my school uniform. And Janice, with her skinny legs and one sock round her ankle. Bless her.

You were very alike, you know, you and Janice. I'd forgotten.

I stared into my cup.

Same hair, eyes. You both had your father's nose.

The tea was hot, oversweetened. It released a thin stream of vapour which flickered in the draught from an open window.

You wouldn't remember her all that much, you'd only have been . . .

Four and a half.

Yes.

I was four and a half.

Auntie helped herself to a biscuit, a digestive. Bits of it stuck to her lips. She sipped her tea and the crumbs disappeared. She asked how the job was going and I said very well, thank you. She said Uncle had seen me the other day while he was driving the bus. Sunday. I was coming out of a public convenience; Uncle had beeped his horn but I hadn't noticed him. She said the name of the road.

I was running an errand.

You'd hardly credit it nowadays, but that used to be quite a genteel neighbourhood. Before the coloureds moved in.

On her way out, Auntie pressed her lips against the side of my face. She told me to put some socks and slippers on before I caught my death. She said God was watching over me and that Janice and Mum and Dad were with Him now, and that they Dwelt in Bliss.

• • •

Mr. Teja cleaned the blackboard. He wrote "No. in class" at the top.

Anyone?

Scrape of chairs, twisting of heads, as we counted, jabbing the air with our index fingers. All except me. I faced the front, watching. A boy raised his hand.

Stephen?

Thirty-four, sir.

Thirty-five—you haven't included yourself. (Laughter.) Mr. Teja wrote "35" on the board. Shall I tell you a quick way to count a group of people? You add up all the arms and legs and divide by 4. (Groans.)

He asked those with black hair to raise their hands.

Gregory Lynn.

I raised mine as well.

He wrote the number on the board. He asked those with brown hair to raise their hands, then those with ginger hair, and those with fair hair.

Black: 8
Brown: 13
Ginger: 4
Fair: 10

Right, if I pick one pupil at random, what is the probability that he or she will have fair hair? Go on, get cracking!

Silence while the class scribbled in their exercise books. A girl put her hand up, gave the answer. Mr. Teja wrote the calculation on the board.

$$\frac{\text{No. with fair hair}}{\text{total in class}} = \frac{10}{35} = \frac{1}{3.5} = 1 \text{ in } 3\frac{1}{2}, \text{ or } 3\frac{1}{2} \text{ to } 1$$

In other words, for every pupil who has fair hair there are three and a half pupils who do not. Gregory Lynn!

A piece of chalk hit me on the head and cracked against the window, where I had been watching two raindrops trickling down the pane—wondering which would be first to reach the bottom; tracing their patterns among the droplets they absorbed in leaving their thin slug trails on the glass.

You must be the nearest thing to half a pupil. (Laughter.)

I looked up. Seven to two, I said.

What?

Three and a half to one is seven to two.

Yes, well, we are not in a betting office now. (More laughter.) Here, bring my chalk.

I picked up the broken pieces from under the table behind me and went to the front of the classroom. I offered them to Mr. Teja, but he refused to accept them. He gestured at the blackboard.

Mr. Lynn will now perform the same calculation for the other categories of hair colour. The rest of you can work out the odds on him getting any of them right.

I stood in front of the board, facing him. His eyes were dark brown, so dark that it was difficult to distinguish the pupils from the irises. I knew that one of my eyes was green, the other brown. I wrote nothing, said nothing. Eventually, Mr. Teja took the chalk from me and told me to return to my seat.

I was put on detention. I spent the entire hour drawing a sequence of cartoons in which the class watched while I forced Mr. Teja to swallow a stick of white chalk. The chalk expanded in his stomach, like a growth, and spread slowly throughout his body. Finally, it invaded the skin, diluting the pigmentation. He became lighter and lighter, he became white. In the final frame, his whiteness could not be distinguished against the white of the paper. Mr. Teja had disappeared. One minus one equals zero.

Drawings are a different reality, they are not subject to the law of probability. By drawing things, sometimes you make them happen.

The third visit, a Tuesday. I monitored the house from 8 A.M. The first person to leave, just after 8:15, was the grandson. He drove off in the car he and his friend had been repairing during my earlier visit. Mrs. Teja left at 9:42, returning forty-five minutes later with two heavy shopping bags. At 10:59 the grandson's wife went out, pushing their baby along the pavement in a collapsible buggy. The sole visitor to No. 3 that morning—at 11:02 —was me, Gregory Lynn.

I rang the doorbell. A woman's outline, distorted by the frosted-glass panel, loomed in the hall; and I knew she'd be scrutinising my tall, bulky silhouette for clues to my identity. The door opened. Mrs. Teja, dressed as usual in Western clothes— beige slacks, crimson blouse, a black choker, and sandals—held the door ajar, the expression on her upturned face one of puzzlement mingled with curiosity. A thin smile. Standing so close, I realised how short she was—barely five feet tall.

Is Mr. Teja in?

Mr. Teja? You mean my grandson, Shiraz? He has gone to work.

No, Mr. Teja. Your husband.

She studied my face. My husband is . . . no longer alive. He died.

A motorbike roared along the street, tyres screeching; we turned to watch it go. When the bike had disappeared from view I continued to stare after it, at the thick haze of exhaust fumes as they dispersed, blending into the metallic grey of the road, the parked cars, the houses, the sky.

Still half turned away from her, I said: I've been trying to find him.

He died more than a year ago.

I was in his class at ———.

Mrs. Teja nodded.

I wanted to talk to him. There was something we needed to discuss.

I am sorry.

(Facing her.) We're publishing a magazine to mark the school's twenty-fifth anniversary. I was hoping Mr. Teja would write an article for us.

(Smile.) He would have liked that. My husband had very fond memories of ————. Some of his old pupils came to the funeral, you know.

I was there from 1970 to '75. I was in Mr. Teja's maths class.

He was very popular with the children.

I smiled at her. She held the door open more widely now, her face had relaxed, though the daylight emphasised the creases etched around her eyes, her mouth. Her hair, fastened back with an arrangement of plastic slides and grips, was more grey than black.

I wonder, d'you have a photograph we could use?

Of my husband?

A lot of people would remember him.

Really, I don't know. The pictures I have of him are all in frames. They are quite old now.

Of course, I'd take care of the picture and make sure it was returned to you quite safely.

A magazine, you say?

Twenty-five years. There's a reunion later in the year. Dinner-dance, speeches, that sort of thing. Everyone will get a copy of the magazine.

The breeze got up, sending empty wrappers scuffing along the pavement and rippling the thin material of Mrs. Teja's blouse, bringing out goose bumps on her bare forearms. Spots of rain made blotches in the fine dust on the doorstep. She let go of the door.

Look, why don't you come inside a moment?

I sat on a wooden chair in the kitchen, listening to the hiss of an electric kettle while Mrs. Teja searched upstairs for a suitable picture of her late husband. She returned with a small colour snap, evidently cut from a strip of four photo-booth pictures.

I found this. It was taken when he had to get his passport

127

renewed. It must be five years old, you know. No, six—we went to Kenya that summer.

I took the photograph from her. He was wearing a check sports jacket with a white shirt and plain blue tie. The poor quality of the picture gave his neatly groomed hair and moustache a purple tint. A serious expression, no trace of a smile. He looked much older than when I was his pupil, though I recognised his face immediately. His perfect white teeth. I put the photograph in my jacket pocket.

This will do nicely. Thank you.

Mrs. Teja made tea. She placed the cup on the pine table in front of me and told me to help myself from the small milk jug and cut-glass sugar bowl which she stood on a cork place mat.

Or there's lemon if you'd rather.

Milk's fine.

She got a packet of biscuits from one of the cupboards and arranged half a dozen on a plate. I complimented her on her home. I asked how long she'd lived there and she said nearly thirty years. She talked about her children, her grandchildren, her mother-in-law; how difficult life had been for them when they came to this country.

My husband worked very hard, you know.

The kitchen smelled of spices and lemon-scented washing-up liquid and of the damp tea towels which had been draped over a radiator. It smelled of baking, of warmth. A covered saucepan simmered over a low heat, emitting an unfamiliar aroma. Mrs. Teja followed the direction of my gaze.

Channa dhal, she said. Chickpea and lentil. We have it with parathas and a little yoghurt.

Through the window, which looked out over the garden, I could see that it was raining heavily now. I finished my drink and Mrs. Teja refilled it from the pot.

I was in the O-level group and he made me drop down to CSE. He said I wasn't good enough.

(Smile.) Oh dear.

He said it was better to go for a grade I CSE than fail the O level.

These grades, you know, I never really understood them.

I said I didn't care about passing exams, I just wanted to know what mathematics *meant*. I wanted him to teach me that.

He loved mathematics, my husband. All he ever wanted to do was . . .

D'you see what I mean?

(Pause.) Of course it's all GCSEs these days. Continuous assessment.

I ate another biscuit. Did he die at school?

I'm sorry?

Mr. Teja, did he actually die while he was teaching?

His widow placed her cup back in its saucer with a slow, deliberate movement, carefully shifting the teaspoon to one side as though it was of absolute importance that the cup should not rattle or rest at an awkward angle. Her eyes still focused on the half-empty cup, she spoke so softly I had to pay close attention to hear her.

He took early retirement because of ill health. Cancer, you know. He was at home for two years.

My mother died of cancer. Four months, three weeks and four days ago. There are healthy cells and diseased cells and the diseased ones keep on multiplying until their number is so great that you die.

Mrs. Teja looked at me across the table.

Lynn, Gregory
Form 3-3
Mathematics
I am disappointed with Gregory's progress. His work suggests he has not yet fully grasped certain basic principles.
S. Teja

Mr. Teja did not discover the cartoon, he saw only that I had failed to complete the exercises during my period of detention. He spoke to me about mathematics, his sadness that I could not appreciate the beauty of numbers.

You think maths is too rational, don't you? Too logical. Well, let me tell you, it isn't.

He listed the different types of number and told me to note them down in my exercise book—prime, rational, irrational, transcendental, complex. Briefly, I became interested. Then he defined these terms, explained them; the irrational became rational, transcendental ceased to transcend; complex became simple. I switched off. Seeing that he had lost me again, Mr. Teja tried a different tack. Had I heard of the Fibonacci sequence?

No, sir.

Write these numbers down: zero, one, one, two, three, five, eight. Now tell me the next number in the sequence.

I stared at the numbers. I don't know.

Thirteen. Look, zero plus one equals one, one plus one equals two, one plus two equals three . . . You see?

I nodded. I said: So what?

It's not just an intellectual game, you know. Take a look at a plant, at the leaves growing in a spiral up the stem—nearly always, the number of leaves between two places where a leaf lies exactly above another is a Fibonacci number. (Big smile.) Numbers and nature, they are indivisible!

What I wanted to confront Mr. Teja with, all those years later —what I couldn't confront him with because he was dead—was the beauty, not of numbers, but of numerical ellipsis. I wanted to tell him, for example, that a reduction from 80 to 40 is a reduction of 50 percent, whereas an increase from 40 to 80 is an increase of 100 percent. I wanted to know why it was necessary for me to understand the mathematical processes which made this so; rather than simply relish the (seeming) anomaly created by a reversal of perspective. Why I couldn't look at a plant without having to count the fucking leaves.

The sound of a key being inserted in the front door brought relief to the awkwardness of our conversation. Mrs. Teja, seemingly glad of having something to distract her, stood up and went over to the oven, opening it to release an aroma of hot bread.

My grandson, he comes home for his lunch.

I heard his footsteps in the hallway, a coat being shaken and hung up, the click as the kitchen door opened. His greeting was curtailed when he saw that she had a guest. He was smarter than when I'd seen him working on the car; dressed in a suit this time. Shiny shoes, speckled with raindrops. We nodded and said hello, then Mrs. Teja performed the formal introductions—realising with embarrassment that she didn't know my name. I said it was Gregory. She explained the purpose of my visit, smiling animatedly all the while. The young man listened, rinsing his hands at the sink, while his grandmother busied herself with the food. She removed the parathas from the oven and laid them on a plate, which she covered with a large white napkin. Lifting the lid from the saucepan, she stirred the contents briskly with a wooden spoon. She talked as she worked, telling him about the school magazine, and the photograph of Mr. Teja which was to be published; but I could see the young man was more interested in me than in what his grandmother was saying. Taking a small towel from a hook above the sink, he dried his hands; each finger in turn, then between the fingers, then the palms, the backs of his hands, the wrists. I was reminded of the methodical thoroughness with which Mr. Teja wiped chalk dust from his hands with a damp cloth at the end of each lesson. There was little physical similarity between the young man and his grandfather, but they shared a likeness of movement.

I asked him what he did for a living. He seemed reluctant to answer at first, replacing the hand towel on its hook with excessive care before informing me that he was an accountant.

Like his father, said Mrs. Teja. And his uncle. (She laughed.)

You know, I've spent my whole life surrounded by men whose first language is numbers.

He sat where his grandmother had been sitting, watching me, while she began to lay the table. She smiled at me.

There's enough for three, if you would like to stay and eat with us.

He won't be staying for lunch, Mamima.

Mrs. Teja hesitated, then gave a nervous laugh. You hear, he calls me his mother's sister—says I am too young to be a grandmother. But I tell him it has nothing to do with age, it is a fact of life.

My auntie has been born again, I said. She says we must be ready for the Day of Reckoning, when all our sins are added up and will weigh against us.

Mrs. Teja stood beside the table, three plates in her hands. She was no longer laughing. She was watching her grandson, who was looking directly at me. When he spoke, his thin lips appeared not to move.

What the fuck are you doing here?

Shiraz!

Quiet, Mamima.

I smiled. I said: Mr. Teja.

My grandfather is dead.

I shrugged.

Why were you watching us that time? Hey?

Shiraz, what are you . . . ?

He interrupted her. He told her that he and his friend had seen me the other Saturday, sitting across the street for hours, taking photographs and drawing pictures. Like a spy, he said. He asked again what I was up to. I told him I was revising, I was doing my maths revision.

You're a fucking nutcase, that's what you are.

He struck me quickly and cleanly in the side of the face. I saw his arm move and, immediately, felt the jolt of his fist. The chair tipped back abruptly and, as I fell, my knees collided with the underside of the table, scattering various items of kitchen-ware. My head hit the floor. I saw him stand and move towards me, but I managed to deflect the second blow by rolling swiftly to one side. He must've lost his balance, or tripped over the legs of the upturned chair; in any event, he was down too. I was the faster to rise, grasping him by the tie with one hand so that I might keep his head still enough to be sure of connecting with each punch. It was at this point that the plates smashed, Mrs. Teja dropping them as I wrestled her grandson around the kitchen. It wasn't clear whether it was one of my arms or his that caught her, but the plates fell and broke into many pieces on the tiles. The young man was shouting at his Mamima to call the police. To hurry for fuck's sake. She was in another room, making that call, when I left the house. I heard her, crying, speaking rapidly and incoherently into the telephone. I drew all this later, frame by frame. I had to imagine the final scene where she ran back to the kitchen to find her grandson slumped semiconscious and bloody among the geometric shards of dinner plate.

Souvenirs from this act of revision were the mug shot of Mr. Teja, which I affixed to the wall chart; a fragment of crockery; and a calculator, which had fallen from the pocket of the grand-son's suit jacket during the fight. The calculator was one whose digits can be made to appear in the quartz display panel when exposed to light, but which are otherwise invisible.

5

physical   **1a.** having material existence; perceptible, esp through the senses, and subject to the laws of nature   **1b.** of material things   **2a.** of the body   **2b.** concerned or preoccupied with the body and its needs, as opposed to spiritual matters

education   **1.** provision/receipt of: **i.)** schooling   **ii.)** mental or moral development, esp by instruction   **iii.)** training or improvement (of faculties, judgement, skills, etc.)   **2.** field of study that deals with methods of teaching and learning

Mr. Hutchinson was a footballer. He'd been on Chelsea's books as a junior but hadn't made the grade. During his years as a teacher at ———, he played for a number of semiprofessional clubs in South London and the southern Home Counties. Midfielder, ball-winner rather than play-maker. His heroes were Tommy Smith, Peter Storey, Billy Bremner. His first name was Chris but we had to call him gaffer or boss or Mr. H. He said Chelsea were a bunch of pansies, except Ron "Chopper" Harris and David Webb. Mr. H. had hairy arms. When he took us for football, what he hated more than anything was if you pulled out of a tackle. The only bad tackle was the tackle you didn't make.

Put a foot in. Win that ball, win it! Make it yours.

To be a great goal-scorer you had to be selfish, you had to be arrogant and aggressive and single-minded. You had to be greedy. You had to want to score and to keep on scoring. When you played up front, all that mattered was the ball and the goal. You had to shoot, shoot, shoot.

You never win a raffle if you don't buy a ticket.

Mr. Hutchinson said that—in football, as in life—there was no such thing as luck. You made your own luck.

The first time he saw me, I was aged eleven and three quarters. He was picking sides: Shirts vs. Skins. Early September, we were on the main field and the grass was dry, the ground hard and cracked. He wore a plain white T-shirt and black tracksuit bottoms, he wore a stopwatch on a loop of cord round his neck. We were the same height. As we lined up, he asked my name and told me to play centre-forward because every team needs a big bugger up front. Before the kickoff, he took me to one side and said I was to make myself available, lead the line, get a head on everything—corners, free kicks, crosses; I was to put myself about.

First challenge, let the centre-half know you're there, he said. He gets a whack, next time he won't be so keen.

I played for Skins. I didn't score, I didn't give the centre half a whack. The first header, I kept my eyes shut and the ball hit me on the bridge of the nose. Mr. Hutchinson blew his whistle. He said I was a donkey. He made me run round the perimeter of the field for the rest of the match. Laps, he called it. Anyone who misbehaved or did something wrong had to do laps. My feet jarred on the hard ground, I was sweating; my eyes stung with salt. My nose dripped blood and mucus, watery pink. Whenever I slowed down, Mr. H. shouted at me to go faster; whenever the ball went out of play, I had to run and fetch it so that the other boys could carry on with their game.

Afterwards, in the changing rooms, a boy chanted: EE-YORE! EE-YORE! He was naked. I held him under the shower and turned the water temperature to maximum until he screamed for mc to stop.

I inquire if my barrister is a footballing man. He smiles, he informs me that they played rugby at his school. *Rugger.*

Well I never.

I know that he was unimpressed by the account of my nose-bleed, but the flicker of interest was unmistakable when I described the incident in the showers. Similarly, in the earlier part of this session—when we *tied up the loose ends* of my final visit to the Teja household—most of our time was taken up with my "assault" on the grandson, and in establishing how he sustained the concussion (mild) with which he was hospitalised (overnight, for observation). I understand the prosecution will make great play of the fact that, several months later, he still suffers the occasional headache. My fractured cheekbone—the result of a "legitimate act of self-defence" by the young man whose family home I'd entered under false pretences—was not a topic for discussion. Nor was my barrister concerned that, even now—on cold, damp days—one side of my face becomes quite numb. A dismissive sigh, a hand raised to still my objection.

I do not dispute that you were injured, Gregory, but I might remind you that—in the eyes of the law—you are not the injured party.

In my room—my cell—I have time to draw and to write and to think. I reflect on the latest session with my lawyers, I anticipate the next one. I appraise the tactics and strategies employed by both sides during these meetings. I take each encounter as it comes. Counsel persists in inviting me to change my plea on those charges to which I will plead not guilty. I persist in declining his invitation. I ask if he can arrange for Mr. Andrews to visit me, but he insists there can be no such access to prosecution

136

witnesses. Thus we have equalised our refusal to comply with one another's wishes. Lately, I have tried to incorporate Mr. Andrews into my cartoons. But I can't picture him, portray him, accurately. I have only a vague image of him in my head. Words, gestures, facial expressions. Trying to visualise him, what I see is not the man but the portrait I painted and which, as far as I know, still hangs on his office wall at the community arts centre. Unsigned. When I try to recall his voice, what I hear is not the words he spoke to me during my penultimate act of revision, but his testimony—his evidence to the court—which I rehearse in my imagination. Trying to picture his smile, I see only a frown.

When they burned her, I did not attend because I was too young. I was not forbidden to attend, I didn't even know there was to be a burning. It was years before I learned that a burning had taken place and I'd not been in attendance. It must have occurred on one of the days Auntie came to baby-sit, though I was no longer a baby—I was four and a half years old.

Passing, Auntie called it; if it was necessary to refer to it at all Janice's Passing. Auntie gave Mum and Dad a small lemon-coloured card, in a frame. The frame stood on the mantelpiece for years; I found it in a box in the cupboard under the stairs when I conducted the inventory of the house. The card was inscribed with words, in neat calligraphy, which said:

> Though we be denied their physical presence,
> yet shall they live within us.

The box contained a second framed card, inscribed with other words:

> Fleetingly known, yet ever remembered.
> These are our children now and always.

Those whom we see not we will forget not,
morning and evening all of our days.

This, also a gift from Auntie, was in response to the second Passing; when Janice's physical presence returned—fleetingly—to us, to be denied us again. On this occasion, I now know, the burning would have been of a different nature. No service from which I might be excluded; and, in the circumstances, the correct terminology is not cremation but incineration, i.e., burning. Different ways of saying the same thing.

> *Lynn, Gregory*
> *Form 1-3*
> *P.E.*
> *A more mature approach is needed if he is to overcome his aversion to this subject.*
> *Chris Hutchinson*

The black-and-white photographs of Mr. Hutchinson which adorned the wall chart were from the cuttings library of the local paper, also my source of information on Mrs. Davies-White. The first, a head-and-shoulders (1973—long hair, sideburns). The second, an action shot from a match in 1980 (the ball was airborne, though it was unclear whether he was on the point of kicking it or had already done so). He was wearing a plain shirt (green? red?) and white shorts. Both were photocopies of original prints from a packet of pictures and cuttings filed under "Hutchinson, C." The articles traced his career—as player, then coach—up to the late eighties, when, aged forty-four, he'd left London to manage a non-League club in Oxfordshire. The move coincided with a new teaching job in Oxford after nearly eighteen years as a P.E. teacher at —— school, the report said.

I added the new information, an orange line connecting Mr. Hutchinson to the matching coloured pin next to Oxford on the map. Directory inquiries gave me a number for the *Oxford Times;* I named a newspaper in South London, I was its football reporter researching a piece for a "Where Are They Now?" slot. The man on the sports desk was helpful. He gave details of the two clubs "Hutch" had been with in the five years since his move, and their playing records under his management. There had been rumours of a part-time coaching job with Oxford United's youth team next season. But that was now in doubt because he'd damaged his knee in a charity cricket match and would be laid up for the rest of the school holidays after a cartilage operation. He said Hutch was always good for a quote and did I have his number? No. I heard a drawer opening, the rustle of pages, lips sucking on a cigarette, then the journalist's voice again as he read out the digits.

Mum was brushing Janice's hair. Short, brisk strokes; the brush kept catching on tangles, tugging her head sideways. Janice was crying, but it wasn't the crying she made when Mum was hurting her hair. I was crying too. I was sitting at the breakfast table, not eating. The cornflakes had turned to orange mush.

You've set him off now.

Janice didn't say anything. She tried to pull away, but Mum held her by the arm and went on brushing. Janice looked pretty. She was wearing her new grey skirt, a white blouse and a blazer with a badge on it. The blazer was new too. Her white socks came up to her knees, except one of them had fallen round her ankle. Her knees were scabby. When Mum had finished doing her hair she brushed down the shoulders and lapels of the blazer, picking off one or two strands which had stuck to the coarse blue cloth. She had a cigarette in her mouth and the smoke was making her squint.

There.

Janice sniffed. She'd stopped crying, and so had I. Mum told me to eat my breakfast or we'd be late. I was looking at Janice, at the way her hair shone; at her cheeks where the tears had dried.

Mum came over to the table, filled my spoon with cereal and fed me. She fed me 'til the bowl was empty and made me finish my juice.

Fetch your satchel, Jan love.

Janice went upstairs and came back down again. The satchel was brown. It was new and shiny, it had two buckles; it had her name written inside in black ink—she'd shown me. Janice Lynn. When Mum wasn't looking, she'd got the pen and drawn a flower next to her name; the flower had a smiling face, like Little Weed in *Bill and Ben*.

We left the house, Mum was holding our hands tight and making us hurry along the street. Women said hello to her, but she didn't stop to talk. We went past the nursery and carried on to the end of the estate and under the underpass. It was dark and smelly, lots of puddles; people had written in bright colours on the walls. Janice slowed down and Mum had to tug her arm to make her keep up. She told her off. After the underpass there were more children and grown-ups and the girls were dressed just like Janice. We came to the gates. Mum bent down to straighten Janice's collar and to kiss her.

Say bye-bye to Greg.

Janice touched my forehead with her face. Her face was cool and smooth and wet where her lips were and she smelled of apricots and toothpaste. Her hair tickled. I started to cry again and Mum shook me and I cried louder.

Go on, off you go. There's a good girl.

Will you be here?

Yes, I'll watch you go in.

No, later.

This afternoon. We'll be here when you come out, me and Greg. Now you run along and be good and do what Teacher tells you.

I want a wee.

You ask Teacher and she'll take you.

When Janice walked down the steps to where the other children were and where the big lady was, I went to follow her but Mum grabbed me.

Pack it in. People will hear. They'll look at you.

She lifted me up into her arms and told me to wave bye-bye to Janice, but I couldn't see her among the other boys and girls. They were standing in two lines, each child holding the hand of the one next to them.

Wave, Greg! Wave!

I waved. I rubbed my eyes with one hand and waved with the other. I went on waving even after all the children had gone and the big lady had gone and the glass doors banged shut so you could see the reflection of the steps, and of the grown-ups. Mum and me.

Come on, or you'll make Mummy late for work.

She carried me some of the way, then made me get down and walk because I was too heavy and too old to be carried anymore. Outside the nursery, she rubbed my snotty face with a tissue and shook me and said if I didn't stop my snivelling she'd tell Daddy and Daddy would be very angry.

Dad talked about right-halves and left-halves and inside forwards, he talked about the WM formation. He talked about wingers, and leather balls that got heavier when it rained and how the ball weighed so much it hurt your foot when you kicked it and, if you headed it wrong, the laces would split your face open. He ran his thumbnail along my forehead to show where the skin would split. He said 4-3-3 and 4-4-2 was all bollocks, he said the sweeper system was bollocks. Mum said:

England didn't have wingers in 1966.

What the fuck d'you know about football?

In Dad's day, football was all about scoring more goals than the other team; nowadays the idea was to concede fewer. Mum didn't see the difference and Dad said it was the difference between winning 5–4 and winning 1–0, any fucking idiot could see that.

Ten days after the visit to Mrs. Teja, I reported to the casualty department. I told the nurse I'd sustained the injuries in a football match. Aerial challenge, there'd been a clash of heads and I'd landed awkwardly. She examined me, prodding the skin beneath my eye and down the side of my nose with a pin.

Feel anything?

Pain.

What sort of pain?

Like someone was sticking a pin in my face.

She said that was good. She asked me to rotate my eye, to look up and down, right and left. She inspected my swollen hand and made me try to move each of the fingers in turn.

When was this football match?

Yesterday.

Mr. Lynn, I've worked in E.R. for five years.

Maybe the day before, I forget.

If that black eye is less than a week old I'm a Dutchman's aunt.

I didn't answer.

Completing her examination without further comment, she made notes on a buff-coloured card and directed me along the corridor to radiography. The X rays confirmed fractures to my cheekbone and the knuckles of the middle fingers of my right hand. I was issued a prescription for painkillers and a course of antibiotics to reduce the swelling in my face and hand. The damaged fingers were strapped together and fitted with a leather sheath fastened at the wrist. I was to keep my arm in a sling for a few days and to avoid chewy food.

I lived off a diet of tinned soup, and Weetabix mashed in hot milk. I slept a lot. I didn't shave or brush my teeth, and I gave up my attempts to draw left-handed. I read, I watched TV. When handling paper—my files, a newspaper, a paperback novel—I had to refrain from indulging my habit of tearing strips from the pages and placing them in my mouth. If I forgot, the action of chewing would be an immediate and painful reminder. I'd have to remove the shred of paper, unable to form it into one of the moist pellets with which I'd taken to adorning the flat surfaces of my room. Meanwhile, I scanned the local papers for an account of the incident at the Tejas', an appeal for information, a description of a white male in his midthirties, tall, dark, well built, one brown eye and one green. Maybe a composite. There was a story, one paragraph on an inside page, which said police were investigating an assault on a nineteen-year-old man *during a tussle with an intruder.* The victim was not named, the exact circumstances were not reported, the assailant was not described. Nevertheless, I awaited the knock at the door, the uniformed officers wondering if they might ask me a few questions. But the only visitor was Auntie. When she expressed concern over my injuries, I said I'd had an accident at work. She tutted. She told me about the time Uncle hurt his back as he climbed from the cab of a bus.

I discover, from my barrister, that the police had obtained a detailed description of me from the Tejas, from whom they had also learned my first name, and that I was a former pupil of ————. The grandson's mate, whom I'd spoken to during my first visit, aided the investigation by revealing where I lived—the general area, that is. Counsel believes that, had the police followed up all this information, my arrest would have been merely a matter of time. That they chose not to pursue their inquiries, he informs me, was due to a reluctance on the part of the Tejas to press charges, were the assailant to be traced and apprehended. Only when subsequent events brought me to public attention were they persuaded to reconsider.

I ask: Why the initial reluctance?

(Barristerial smile.) Mrs. Teja.

And the grandson?

He deferred to her wishes. The matriarchal figure, you know, is really rather revered in Asian culture.

On wet days, P.E. was indoors: badminton, trampolining. Volleyball. However, if the rain was especially heavy—or the day especially cold and blustery, or Mr. Hutchinson was in a bad mood, or someone misbehaved—he'd send us on cross-country. No exemptions. If you'd forgotten your trainers, you ran in plimsolls; no plimsolls, you ran in ordinary shoes. If you had a note from your mum saying you weren't to run in the rain because you were asthmatic or had just got over a cold, Mr. H. read it aloud to the class. And made you run. If you failed to complete the course within a specified time, you did push-ups—one for every ten seconds over the limit. After each race, they lined up at the finish: the fat boys, the wheezy ones, the boys in mud-caked leather shoes; steam rising from the backs of their sodden T-shirts as they heaved themselves up and down while he stood over them, counting.

The course started with a lap of the playing field, then through the gate and along the cinder path which skirted the school's perimeter fence before rising steeply up the edge of the estate towards a wooded hill: the copse, my childhood playground, the place where I'd built my den. Here, the path petered out into one of the muddy shingle tracks that traversed the copse, bringing us onto a road looping round the other side of the school boundary, then back along the path to the playing field. Five and a half miles, six if Mr. H. made us finish with another circuit of the field. He always ran with us, making sure no one took shortcuts, chivvying the tailenders. In the woods, his voice boomed over the birdsong and rain and the gravelly pounding of boys' feet; in the streets, his words echoed dully off the concrete expanse of the flats, the houses, the fractured flagstones.

The sun was bright on the morning I revisited the cross-country route, still used, for all I knew. July, school had broken up for the summer; the playing field was deserted, the white lines of the football field had faded and become overgrown with grass, the cricket square was roped off for reseeding. The goalposts still stood but the nets had been taken down and, in the centre of one of the crossbars, a large tyre dangled from a length of rope. From behind the high fence, the padlocked gate, I looked in. By following the fence I came to a place where the local kids had breached it—a tree, a plank propped against a stout branch which overhung the line of metal posts. I remembered to bend my knees, careful not to put my damaged hand down to steady myself as I landed. The strapping had been removed and I'd long since discarded the sling, but my fingers still hurt sometimes. Now it was my cheek which twinged as my feet jarred on the hard ground beyond the fence. I stood, brushed myself down. I breathed in the scent of pollen and grass, then exhaled, erasing summer with the sensations of past winters there: the rain, the cold, the mud, the damp shirt clinging to my skin, my matted hair, steamy rasps of breath, coffee-coloured water squelching through the lace holes of my training shoes. Running, running, running. I walked the perimeter of the field, exiting via the gate, which from the inside—it was possible to scale by using its thick metal hinges as footholds. Lowering myself the other side, I followed the rise of the cinder path to the end of the estate and into the copse. Hard, after so many years, to recall exactly our route through the woods. But I'd returned there often enough since the burning of my mother to know which tracks led to the point where we rejoined the road. In the copse—where the sun was unable to penetrate the canopy of trees, and where it was cooler, damper, and the pebbles crunched underfoot in a moist bed of earth—it was easier to imagine the rain, to imagine running. To recall slipping on a wet tree root, sprawling headlong into the mulch of muddy leaves and twigs and old tree bark. I stood at the edge of the track where I'd fallen that time. I remembered lying there, winded; my mouth, gritty and dribbling

145

spittle and dirt. Mr. Hutchinson's voice, his hand tugging the collar of my T-shirt.

C'mon, Lynn. Up.

It wasn't until I stood and tried to put weight on my left foot that I realised I'd sprained my ankle. My knee buckled and I would've sunk to the ground again but for Mr. H.'s firm grip beneath my armpits.

My ankle . . .

Walk on it.

He supported me for the first few steps back onto the shingle track, one foot twisted at a grotesque angle so that the uninjured one bore most of the impact. He told me to jog, but I could only hobble. Whenever my left foot touched the ground I'd reach for his arm as he walked beside me.

I can't, sir.

It's only a sprain. Two minutes, you'll run it off.

He walked with me the rest of the way, through the copse and along the long loop of road behind the school, back to the playing field, the one last lap. The rest of the runners were huddled at the finish line, watching in silence as I completed the final circuit; slowly, the toes of my injured foot skimming the ground as I hopped lopsidedly alongside the teacher. He clicked the stopwatch.

Lynn, push-ups. The rest of you, back to the changing rooms.

Back at the gate, I stared across the playing field—dry now, grass gleaming in the sunlight—and recalled that other time in the rain, when I was thirteen years old; Mr. Hutchinson's voice, counting.

. . . thirty-eight, thirty-nine, forty . . .

Lynn, Gregory
Form 3-3
P.E.
Gregory has not shown sufficient enthusiasm. Repeated absence

*has made it harder for him to improve his general level of fitness
and his performances in the various activities. He must always
make sure he brings the appropriate clothes.*
Chris Hutchinson

Mum was fifty-six when they removed part of her lung. She'd
complained to the G.P. about a persistent cough; he'd examined
her, given her a prescription for a bottle of linctus and told her to
cut down on her smoking. When she went back a couple of
months later, still coughing, he made an appointment for her at
the hospital. They carried out tests, took X rays. On returning
for the results, she was ushered into a consulting room and informed that she had a growth, that the growth was malignant;
that it was operable. A date was arranged for the operation. She
rang her clients to cancel their hairdressing appointments and told
her boss at Supashop, who said there'd be a job for her when she
felt ready to return. Waiting for the taxi to take her to hospital,
Mum told me that—apart from "babies and whatnot"—it would
be the first time she'd been hospitalised since she was concussed
during a school netball match when she was fifteen. She had the
operation, she came home, she underwent a period of chemotherapy which made her puke and caused her hair to fall out.
When she was better she went back to work part-time at the
shop; and from home, styling women's hair. It was eighteen
months before she began to feel ill again. This time the cough
was worse, she lost weight, and rarely lasted a day without vomiting. Despite Auntie's pleading, Mum refused to see the doctor
or return to the hospital for further tests. I overheard them arguing.

You can't just give up.
I'm riddled with it.
You don't know that. Not for sure.
I know my own body.
Marion, please.
No!

For Gregory's sake, then.

Gregory's thirty-four, for crying out loud!

She stayed at home with me, she went on smoking; she continued working until she became too sick to leave the house. In the final weeks she was confined to her room for much of the time—I could hear her coughing in there at all hours, retching into the plastic washing-up bowl I knew she kept by the side of the bed. Auntie came every day to shop, to cook, to clean. She'd sit at Mum's bedside and, if Mum was up to it, they'd talk. I heard them, the murmur of their voices through the wall that separated our rooms. It was Auntie, finally, who called the G.P.; and Mum was readmitted. They discharged her on Christmas Eve with a supply of drugs for the pain.

In my bedroom, I drew cartoon strips. I drew Mum, I drew a tangle of black squiggles to represent the cancer. Frame by frame, I erased it.

Pinned to a noticeboard in the sports hall at ———— was a poster showing the fielding positions in cricket: a bright green oval dotted with little white matchstick men. The name of each position was printed beneath the appropriate figure: mid-off, mid-on, extra cover, deep fine leg, point, silly point . . . thirty-one, including the bowler, although the fielding side is only permitted to have eleven players on the field. The umpires were represented by crosses, one behind the stumps at the bowler's end of the wicket, the other in line with the batting-crease at square leg. An imaginary vertical line down the centre of a cricket field divides it into the "off side" and the "on side." The on side is also known as the leg side. A note, in small type at the foot of the poster, said: "Standard fielding positions for a right-handed batsman. The positions are reversed, as in a mirror image, for a left-handed batsman."

A cricket wicket has three stumps: off, middle and leg. The leg stump can become the off stump—and vice versa—depending whether the batsman is right- or left-handed. The middle stump is always the middle stump.

The first time I went in to bat during P.E., I took a left-handed stance at the crease. As the batsman I'd replaced had been right-handed, there was a delay while the fielders and the square-leg umpire swapped sides of the field to take up their positions. After one ball, I switched to a right-handed stance. There was a moment's confusion while the fielders and umpire returned to their previous positions. As he jogged past me, Mr. Hutchinson —umpiring at square leg—asked what the hell I was playing at. I told him I was ambidextrous.

ambidextrous *(adj)* **1.** able to use either hand with equal ease **2.** unusually skilful; versatile **3.** characterised by deceitfulness and double-dealing

My hand no longer caused discomfort when I used a can opener, when I drew pictures, when I tied my shoelaces, when I turned a door handle. Rest and the programme of exercises recommended by the hospital's physiotherapist had effected an improvement in dexterity. I was able to make a fist. My cheek, too, was better. My face had resumed its familiar shape, although a close inspection in the mirror revealed a slight depression along the line of the fracture; there would be occasional numbness, or a twinge if I yawned too widely.

Even so, I waited. I allowed time for the mental healing to take place—the confidence not to flinch from certain tasks, not to be protective—a psychological acceptance that physical recuperation is complete. I unlearnt the fear of hurting myself. Once, when Dad took me to watch Chelsea, I saw a player break his leg. They carried him off on a stretcher, legs strapped together; his elbows made twin peaks as he pressed both hands to his face. The paper said he'd be out for months. Dad reckoned he'd never be the same player again. He tapped his temple:

Every time he goes for the ball, he'll remember the tackle that bust his leg.

I embarked on a training regime, more demanding than for any previous act of revision. I became fitter, stronger. I ran the school cross-country course so many times I could have done it with my eyes closed, I did push-ups and sit-ups every morning, I swam each afternoon at the local baths, I lifted weights at the sports centre. I ate properly, I had regular sleep. Auntie said I was looking well, better than for a long time. And all the while I used my cartoons, my files, my wall chart, my memories of ———, as a focus for the mental preparations. Every day, for an hour at a time, I'd sit and stare at the photos of Mr. Hutchinson until, even with my eyes shut, I could picture every detail. I reproduced the action shot, in cartoon form, of him about to kick the ball, or having already kicked it; I drew me tackling him. I was kitted out in blue, Chelsea colours.

A little over two months after the Teja episode, I set off one morning by bus and train into London. I bought two wholemeal rolls and a carton of milk from a sandwich bar outside Victoria. I ate lunch, watched by an audience of pigeons, on a bench in a small park in Grosvenor Gardens. A woman was asleep in the shade of a horse chestnut, a filthy brown blanket over the hump of her body; two police constables—one male, one female—were trying to wake her. People glanced in her direction, then returned to their newspapers, their books, their magazines, their conversations, their sandwiches. A blond teenager closed his eyes and tilted his face sunwards, lips formed into a smile. I observed the hordes as they hurried along the pavements, lining up at bus stops, waiting for lights to halt the traffic so they might cross; I listened to the roar of engines, the hiss of air brakes, the beeping horns; the voices; each sound magnified, reverberating off the surrounding buildings in raucous mimicry of itself. I saw speech bubbles ballooning from hundreds of mouths, floating upwards until they popped and the words spilled and were dispersed in the haze of fumes, dissolving into nothing. This was outside, and I was in it, part of it; it wasn't a blankness, a white void—it was filled with colours, shapes and sounds, and I knew that my colour, my shape, my sound, were integral to it.

When I'd finished eating, I shook the crumbs from the paper bag and picked my way through the feeding birds towards the coach stop. A single-decker—red and grey, with "Oxford Tube" painted on the side—had rolled forward from the waiting bay, its door open and the side panels raised for passengers to stow their luggage. I bought a day-return and sat near the front, in the no-smoking section. I put my bag and jacket on the aisle seat; then, as the coach began to fill up, I moved them onto the overhead shelf so that those people still searching for somewhere to sit would know that the place next to me was available.

At Butlins, Bognor Regis, we played cricket on a wide stretch of grass between two rows of wooden chalets; Mum, Dad, Janice and me, Auntie and Uncle, Dad's workmate Denis and his wife and their two boys, both older than me and Janice. Three stumps stuck in the ground, an old tennis raquet for a bat, a tennis ball worn bald with years of use. Dad paced out the square and made a line in the earth with his heel to mark the bowling-crease. Janice batted first, then the two boys. If the ball came near me I had to run and pick it up and throw it to Uncle, who was wicket-keeper; except I couldn't throw very far and someone else always ended up having to fetch it. When Denis's older boy was batting, he hit the ball in the air and Dad caught it and threw it high and caught it again.

Owzat!

Then Mum said it was my turn to bat. Janice had to help me hold the raquet. She stood behind me and held my hands. Her palms were warm, and green with grass stains. Her hair hung damply against the side of my face and smelled of chlorine from when we'd been playing in the pool. Dad lobbed the ball to me, underarm, and we swung at it, Janice's hands moving mine. The ball struck the wooden part of the raquet and bounced towards Auntie. She bent down, but she was slow and it slipped through her fingers. Janice was screaming.

Run! Run!

I dropped the raquet and ran as fast as I could towards Dad. Everyone was cheering and laughing and shouting and clapping. The next time Dad bowled, we missed the ball and Uncle caught it and threw it back for Dad to bowl again. We missed, the ball clunked against the wicket.

Owzat!

Dad raised his index finger. I was out, it was Mum's turn to bat. She took the raquet from me and I followed Janice and stood next to her, ready to fetch the ball when Mum hit it. One of the boys told me to move somewhere else, pointing to the place where I'd been standing before.

You're at midwicket, Greg. Remember?

He's all right, Janice said.

You can't have two fielders at square leg.

I started to cry. Janice held my hand.

He's helping me catch.

Mum was out straightaway; then Dad batted and Denis bowled, overarm, his bare belly wobbling as he took a run-up. Dad hit the ball so hard it went over the roofs of the chalets and there was a race to see who'd be first to get it. I tripped and Janice stopped to pull me up. One of Denis's boys had the ball and was holding out of reach while his brother tried to grab it. My knee bled where I'd grazed it on a stone. Janice spat into the palm of her hand and rubbed the mud and grass away from the cut. It stung.

Here.

She gave me the stone, it was pink and white and brown and very shiny. Smooth and rounded on one side, with a rough edge where a piece had broken off. I held the stone while she wiped my knee again and made the trickle of blood go away.

After cricket, we sat on plastic chairs on the café terrace and ate ice creams. The reflection of the sun on the white tables made me squint. Denis lent me his sunglasses and everyone laughed because they were too big and kept sliding off my nose. The boys wanted to play crazy golf, but Janice complained of a headache. Dad said:

Sunstroke. Court-martial offence in the army. Self-inflicted wound.

He started telling Denis and Uncle about National Service in

Egypt, after the war. Egg-wiped, he called it. He had a blob of ice cream on his chin, he reeked of vinegar—which he rubbed on his shoulders and neck to prevent sunburn. Janice sat on Mum's lap, in the shade of one of the big table umbrellas, and went to sleep. When we left the terrace, the others went off to play golf; Mum and Auntie took the two of us to the chalet. Mum gave Janice an aspirin dissolved in a beaker of orange juice and put her to bed, with a cold flannel for her forehead. She slept all evening and all night. The next morning, when she woke up, there was a damp patch on the pillow where the flannel had fallen off.

My barrister, changing the subject, asks whether my conduct in the *Mr. Hutchinson affair* was entirely "sporting." He wiggles the index finger of each hand to signify quotation marks. I tell him a joke:

Moses, Jesus and God are playing a round of golf. On the first tee, Moses hits his drive two hundred yards down the middle of the fairway. Jesus' tee shot is shorter and lands in the rough. God tees up and slices wildly towards the out-of-bounds markers, as the ball sails over a tree it is halted in midair by a sudden gust of wind; a bird takes off from a branch, catches the ball in its beak and flies over the fairway; the bird drops the ball and, as it lands, a rabbit appears from a burrow and carries it in its mouth all the way to the green; the rabbit lets the ball go and an earthquake causes the ground to tremble, making the ball roll right into the hole.

Jesus turns to God and says: For fuck's sake, Dad, it's only a game!

Sport is about power—psychological, physical; it is about perfecting the balance of skill and strategy, strength and determi-

153

nation. It is about concentrated effort. It is survival of the fittest, the best. It is about winning. To win, it's necessary to understand your opponent, to nullify his strengths and exploit his weaknesses. Beyond that, it isn't necessary to give a fuck about him, nor the effect of defeat upon him. Handshakes, the mutual expressions of good luck beforehand, commiserations/congratulations afterwards, grace in defeat and magnanimity in victory . . . these things are bollocks. Fair play is bollocks. You play by the rules, but the first rule—the only rule—is: you win, he loses. The successful sportsman is the one who has the power to control the outcome of events. Who wins. Who wins. Who wins.

These things I learnt from Mr. Hutchinson. These things I taught him.

Gloucester Green is not in Gloucester, it is in Oxford. It is where buses and coaches arrive and depart. It is where I disembarked, early one weekday afternoon last August. I went into a newsagent's and asked the man behind the till if I might borrow his phone directory. He obliged. I looked up the address I required, noted it down and thanked him. He sold me a map of the city. The rear door of the newsagent's opened onto a broad red-brick plaza bordered by boutiques, café-bars and upmarket gift shops. Sitting on a bench in the sunshine, I unfolded the map and ran down the index of street names. According to the map, Mr. Hutchinson's home lay two miles to the north of the city centre. I walked, glad of the exercise after an hour and a half on the coach. Cars, buses and cycles blared along the main road, flanked by language schools, old people's homes, a hotel, a conservatory-style restaurant, four-storey Victorian houses with stained-glass windows and gravel drives, a long parade of shops. My shirt was clammy. Taking off my jacket, I rolled it up and stashed it in my bag. I bought a small bottle of mineral water and drained it in two draughts. Beyond the shops, where a row of narrow cottages gave way to larger, leafier homes, I turned into a quiet side street lined with trees.

The house was easy to find—a large whitewashed two-family, its number spelled out in iron scrollwork on the wall. A rose trellis framed the front door, though most of its peach-coloured blooms had shrivelled, strewing the flagstone path with their faded papery petals. No car on the drive, but a small downstairs window was propped open and one of the upper windows was ajar, a curtain being sucked gently in and out of the opening as though propelled by an invisible pair of lungs. Two-thirty. Someone was home, but I didn't know if it was Mr. Hutchinson; or, if it was him, whether he was alone. I retraced my steps to a telephone booth on the main road. The first call, to the City Council's electoral registration department, established that two names were listed for the address I gave: Christopher and Ellen Hutchinson. Secondly, I rang the Hutchinsons' number. I asked for Ellen. A voice, male, said she was at work and offered to take a message. I hung up.

The door-knocker was brass, a fox's head hinged at the jaw. I made the fox open and close its mouth three times, each metallic clunk producing an echo beyond the closed door. I waited. After a lengthy delay, there was a noise, then a voice.

Hang on!

The door swung open abruptly and a short, balding man stood before me, holding the door with one hand and supporting himself on a wooden walking stick with the other. He was wearing a short-sleeved check shirt and cotton shorts, his right knee heavily bandaged. The clumps of hair on his big toes protruded through the straps of his sandals. Although it had been eighteen years since we'd last met, I recognised him from the more recent of the two photographs which adorned my bedroom wall.

Sorry 'bout that. He gestured at his leg, smiling. I can walk okay, it's getting in and out of the chair that's a bugger.

I gave him the same story I'd told the journalist at the *Oxford Times*, that I was a sports reporter doing a piece for a newspaper in South London. He was surprised I'd driven all the way to Oxford to see him. I explained that I was covering Palace's match at Birmingham City that evening and had decided on impulse to make a detour off the M40. I apologised, I should've phoned ahead. No problem, he said, beckoning me inside. I followed him into a tiled hallway. He walked with a shuffle, leaning heavily on the stick.

I had a trial at Crystal Palace, when I was a kid.

I thought you were on Chelsea's books.

This was after. He opened a door and led me into an open-plan living room. Nineteen-sixty, it must've been. I was sixteen. Palace, Fulham, Charlton, Brentford, Millwall . . . I've had more trials than a bank robber. What'd you say your name was?

Gregory. Gregory Lindsay.

Sit down, Greg.

I sat where he'd indicated, my back to the big bay window, and watched Mr. Hutchinson lower himself with difficulty into the other armchair. He raised his injured leg onto a footstool, adjusting a cushion beneath his heel, and propped the stick against a side table. On the table, there was a newspaper, an empty mug and the remote-control gadget for the television. The TV was on, a golfer in a peaked cap was lining up a long putt.

Sky. I got the dish a couple of weeks ago. He watched the golfer miss the putt, then clicked off the picture. He patted his bandaged knee. Telly's a godsend when you're laid up.

You live on your own?

No, my wife works. Another teacher. The girls are at university.

They home for the holidays?

He shook his head. One's on a kibbutz, the other's Inter-Railing round Europe with her feller. Wife didn't want them to go, but what can you do?

He offered tea or cold beer. I declined, switching the conversation to the supposed subject of our interview. I withdrew a ring-bound notebook and pen from my bag, pretending to take notes. What I was doing was making a sketch. Using pen instead of pencil made the portrait clumsier and more defined than I'd intended, especially in rendering the play of sunlight streaming through the window behind me and casting a silvery-yellow sheen around him. The drawing was almost done when we exhausted the topic of football, so I prompted with questions about teaching. He mentioned his years at ———, and the job as deputy head of P.E. at an independent school for boys which had brought him to Oxford.

Good standards here. Good facilities, not like in London. And the boys are keen. He watched me scribbling. Maybe you'd better not put that in, eh?

Of course. I made crossing-out motions with the pen. What about cross-country running?

Cross-country?

D'you still send them out in the pouring rain?

He hesitated, then laughed. That happen at your school too?

I smiled. The sun was directly in his eyes now and he asked me to pull the curtain across. I didn't move. Completing the sketch, I studied the result for a moment and closed the notebook.

He pointed at the curtain, one hand raised to shield his eyes. D'you mind, Greg, I can't see a bloody thing.

What about laps? D'you still make boys do laps?

Laps?

And push-ups. Do you make them do push-ups in the rain?

Listen, I don't know . . .

He was still well built; good physique, muscular limbs. Broad chest and shoulders. The hairs which poked out from the neck of his shirt and which matted his forearms were slightly grizzled, and his belly bore signs of a paunch, although that may have been the way he was sitting. His hair was thinning and there was slackness in the skin around his neck, his jaw, the hint of a double chin. But he was no product of a lifetime of sedentary office work. No couch potato. This was a sportsman, fitter looking than a man of forty-nine going on fifty might expect to be. Even so, when I kicked the stool from under his leg, when I shoved his chair back so that it toppled, when I grabbed his walking stick and cracked it across his damaged knee . . . when I did these things, he struggled on the floor like a geriatric. He had tried to rise from his chair as I'd crossed the room, but I was quick, and he'd been hampered by his injury and by the dazzle of the sun. Now he was moaning. Holding his knee, the fingers of his other hand clawing at the carpet as though the most important thing in the world was for him to dig a hole and disappear into it. I whacked his leg again with the stick.

Jesus fucking Christ!

Give him a whack early on, next time he won't be so keen. Isn't that right, Mr. H.? Gaffer.

I stood over him. He lay curled up on the floor, making himself small, making himself into a foetus. Sweat pearled his forehead, and his eyes were tightly shut like a child pretending to be asleep or about to make a wish. His mouth was open, he was breathing in irregular gulps. I left him while I checked every window and door in the house to ensure they were locked shut. I looked at my watch, allowing myself an hour before Mrs. Hutchinson would be home. When I returned to the living room, Mr. H. had crawled over to the far corner and was trying to remove the phone from on top of the sideboard. So far he'd succeeded only in overturning a vase of marigolds, soaking his shirt and dandruffing his hair and shoulders with orange petals. I crossed the room, disconnecting the phone at the socket.

This is my fucking house!

It's nice, sir. Big. You know, comfy.

Who *are* you? He was slumped by the sideboard, looking up at me. Should I know you?

Nicely done out. I gestured at the beige suite and matching curtains, the glass-fronted sideboard, the alcoves filled with pine shelving, the Cotswold stone fireplace, the polished table and chairs at the end where a dining room would have been before the dividing wall was knocked through. I indicated one of the shelves. Your football medals, Mr. H.?

I asked you a question, Lindsay.

You didn't put your hand up. *Sir.*

I went over to the alcove and examined the display—medals mounted in velvet-lined boxes, miniature trophies on wooden plinths, shiny statuettes of footballers, a ball stuck to one instep; each engraved with the date and occasion, the names of the teams. I turned, holding up one of the medals.

F. A. Vase Final. Didn't know you'd played at Wembley.

I don't know what you want, but . . .

The hallowed turf. Those famous twin towers, eh? Up those steps to the Royal Box. I studied the inscription more closely. Ah, *loser's* medal.

He was using the sideboard to raise himself, careful to avoid putting weight on his leg. The knee appeared more swollen than before, the bandages tighter against the skin. When he was almost upright, I hit his knee again with the walking stick. He gave a sharp cry, crumpling forwards and losing his balance. The merest shove sent him sprawling.

You cunt! You fucking little *cunt!*

Lap of honour, gaffer. Even the losers do a lap of honour at Wembley. I pressed one of the miniature cups into his hand. Once round the room, eh?

There was a damp patch on the carpet, where saliva had dribbled from his mouth to form a small puddle. The side of his face was connected to the floor by a silvery strand of spittle. He called me a bastard, ejecting the word in a hoarse whisper between grunts of breath.

C'mon. Hands and knees will do.

Fuck off.

With a little encouragement—verbal and physical—he began to drag himself slowly around the room, using both elbows and his good leg to inch his body forwards. Every few feet he would pause to recover his breath or to raise the trophy in a white-knuckle salute to the fans whom I invited him to imagine were massed in the stands. By the time he'd completed the circuit, negotiating a route among the items of furniture, the trophy had become detached from its base and his elbows were reddened and moist where the skin had been rubbed raw against the carpet. He lay facedown, panting.

Nineteen minutes and two seconds, gaffer. That's fifty push-ups.

Fuck you.

I leaned over him, my face a few inches from his twisted profile. Make it a hundred, I said.

As Mr. Hutchinson looked directly into my eyes—one brown, one green—his expression changed. He lifted his head slightly, his eyes widening. *I know you.* I know you! Your name's not Lindsay, it's Lynn. Gregory Lynn!

I stepped back.

You were at ———, weren't you? The headcase who got expelled.

I left because . . .

Jesus, how many years ago was that?

You . . .

It is you, Lynn, isn't it?

I hit him so hard the black rubber tip flew off the end of the walking stick and struck the wall, the blow to his face leaving a livid welt above the left eye. I'm in fucking charge here, not you! *Me!* I'm in control! You . . . you just shut the fuck up and do what I say. The second blow brought a cherry-red bubble of blood from the bridge of his nose.

All right, all right! Jesus!

I breathed in deeply, held my breath, breathed out. I inhaled again. The words came out calmer, quieter. I can fucking erase you, sir.

He did the push-ups, blood dripping from his face. If he stopped or failed to complete one, I gave him a whack. Once, when he made a grab for the stick, I had to stamp repeatedly on the back of his injured leg until he let go. The push-ups were slower after that, more erratic. While he heaved himself up and

160

down, I read aloud from the newspaper clippings I'd brought with me—faded reports of football matches played two decades ago:

> . . . McAllister was taken off with suspected concussion in the 33rd minute after a hefty challenge by Hutchinson . . .
> . . . Chris Hutchinson received his third booking in as many weeks for a late tackle on Gerry Davies . . .
> . . . Hutchinson—in only his first game back from suspension—was in the thick of a fracas . . .
> . . . Barnes could be out for six months after breaking his leg. The incident resulted in the sending-off of Chris Hutchinson . . .

The bandages were soiled now, a deep red stain the size and shape of a thumbprint had seeped through the layers of gauze. A bloodshot eye peering out of pure white face. The knee itself had ballooned, distending the hairy skin above and below the strapping, stretching the bandages to accommodate its grossness. Mr. Hutchinson was moaning persistently, a low guttural sound that became a high-pitched whimper with each blow of the walking stick. He had reached a count of 80 when there was the sound of a key being inserted in the front door, of the door jarring against the chain.

Would you have, ah, killed him, d'you think, if Mrs. Hutchinson hadn't come home when she did?
Am I charged with contemplated murder?
I'm only . . .
Interrupted homicide, is that a criminal offence?
(A barristerial shrug.) Gregory, we . . . that is, I'm merely

161

trying to establish your state of mind during this incident. Your motivation.

I smiled. We're having enough difficulty agreeing on what *did* happen, never mind what *might've* happened.

You of all people, I would've imagined, ought to appreciate the "what if?" line of inquiry.

I turned to the solicitor, who glanced up from her notepad. Put a tick next to that. Put v.g.

As I made my way through the living room to the kitchen, I heard her voice: puzzlement giving way to irritation, and then to alarm. I heard her calling his name, his muffled cry in response; the front door jarring once more against the chain. Metal versus wood. I unlocked the back door and ran into the garden, along a path which divided an expanse of lawn, and across a raised flower bed. At the foot of the garden, in an area of nettles and unkempt grass, stood a chest-high wooden fence. Beyond it lay the long rear garden of the house backing onto the Hutchinsons'. A grey-haired man was mowing the lawn, his back towards me. Glancing over my shoulder, I saw Mrs. Hutchinson coming round the side of the house and making for the back door. She didn't see me. I gripped the top of the fence and lifted myself up and over, crossing the next garden in a crouching run, never taking my eyes off the back of the old man as he steered the mower. A trickle of piss escaped into my pants. As he stooped to unclip the grass-box, I slipped by and was halfway across a patio at the rear of the house when I heard his shout.

Hey!

I kept going. I didn't turn round or show any sign of registering that I'd been seen.

Hey, you there!

I went through a wrought-iron gate and along a path which led to the front of the house. Another shout, the slap of footsteps

162

behind me. Inside the house, a dog was barking. I crossed the front garden, hurdling a low wall. No people, only lines of parked cars shimmering in the sunshine. I turned right, sprinting now. A backward glance to see that the man stood at the foot of his driveway, still holding the grass-box. He gave a cry which I couldn't make out, dropped the box with a metallic thud, and hurried indoors. At the end of the street I headed left, then right at the next turning, almost stumbling over a loose paving slab. I slowed down to a jog, a brisk walk. My breathing eased and I mopped my forehead with the cuff of my shirt, leaving a dark stain on the light blue material. It was then I realised I'd left my bag behind, as well as my jacket, my notebook and the map of Oxford. The Hutchinsons had them now. Soon, they'd hand the items over to the police, along with my description. My name.

I kept walking, slower now; a man out for a stroll. The schoolchildren I passed paid me little attention as I improvised a zigzag route through the side streets; each step, each twist and turn, taking me further from Mr. Hutchinson. His wife would be with him, kneeling beside him on the soiled floor of their living room, tending his injuries while they waited for the ambulance, the police. She'd be comforting him. At a busy road, I crossed to the opposite pavement and followed it for a short way, in what I took to be the direction of the city centre. Then, hearing sirens somewhere in the distance, I veered off again into a quieter neighbourhood where the larger houses gave way to a network of narrow red-brick houses dotted with pubs and corner groceries. I became lost among them. I became a missing person.

6

art **1.** skill acquired by experience, study or observation **2.** humanities as contrasted with science **3.** conscious use of skill and creative imagination, esp in the production of aesthetic objects **4.** (adj) composed, designed or created with conscious artistry

Mr. Andrews told us to help ourselves to art paper from the supply cabinet. When we were back at our desks and had quietened down again, he told us to close our eyes and visualise where we lived; our homes. As soon as we were ready, we were to open our eyes and draw what we'd pictured in our minds.

Ink, charcoal, paint . . . use whatever you like.

No other instructions. We worked for forty-five minutes, then he came round and collected the pictures. He pinned them to the corkboard which filled most of one wall of the classroom. Flats and houses in red, brown, grey, white; some pictures were unfinished, some showed people standing outside in gardens, on doorsteps—family groups, posing in front of their homes as if for a photograph. Mine was the darkest. Mine was the only one drawn from the inside looking out: a sepia room illuminated by a single shaft of white light from a window through which only vague shapes could be distinguished beyond the dense curtains. Inside, the furniture was large—out of proportion to the dimensions of the room—and the walls, floor and ceiling met at odd angles, as though the house was constructed of some flimsy material which had been tilted out of alignment. Small pale faces, featureless, peered from behind chairs or from shadowy corners where brown cross-hatching deepened to black. The only vivid colour was the scarlet shirt of a figure at the window, looking out; his elongated shadow cast diagonally across the dull yellow floor of the interior.

Mr. Andrews didn't say anything, didn't ask us any questions; he just stood with his arms folded and looked at the pictures. And because he was looking at them, we looked at them. At the end of the lesson, once we'd rinsed the brushes and water jars and put the HB pencils and sticks of chalk and charcoal back in their boxes, he let us go.

Thanks for coming.

He always said that, as if we were doing him a favour by being there. As if we had a choice. As we filed out of the room, he said my name. He asked if I'd stay behind for a moment. I was already halfway through the door and got jostled as I turned back against the tide of pupils. A heavy bag banged against my knee. Someone said my nickname: Odd Eyes; another voice whispered "weirdo." I pushed past, into the room. After the last pupil had left, Mr. Andrews told me to shut the door. He said please. He walked over to the arrangement of pictures and I followed.

Yours?

I nodded.

Unsigned.

Yes.

(Smiling.) But unmistakably yours.

I shrugged.

He turned away from the wall and sat on one of the desks, pulling a chair out from underneath and resting his feet on it. He wasn't wearing shoes. He never wore shoes, except in the corridors or the dining hall or on the bicycle he rode to and from school. In class he went barefoot, the legs of his jeans rolled midway up his shins. In class he wore T-shirts in spring and summer

165

and long-sleeved sweatshirts during the autumn and winter months. That morning he was wearing a black T-shirt with the slogan "Art Is a Tart." He hadn't shaved for several days.

Why so sombre?

(I looked at the picture.) It's the way I see it. The house.

Not the picture, *you.*

Me?

If I'd done a picture that good I'd be walking round with a grin this wide. He stretched his arms out as far as they'd go. He smiled, the delta of creases at the corners of his eyes deepening. The eyes were grey and always looked straight at yours whenever he spoke to you. Mr. Andrews seemed permanently to be on the point of winking.

You ever use oils, Greg? Acrylics?

No.

(He sniffed, tapping his nose.) Don't, they fuck up your sinuses.

I looked away, trying not to laugh.

Mr. Andrews pulled something from the back pocket of his jeans and put it in his mouth. It was a small strip of paper. He was always chewing paper in class, removing the soggy wads from between his teeth every now and then and pressing them against the wooden surround of the blackboard, where they'd dry and harden. The wood was peppered with little grey-white lumps, like blobs of dried putty stuck to a window frame. Sometimes he'd arrange them into shapes: a circle, a star, a diamond. Spit Sculpture, he called it. The papers were Rizlas, for rolling cigarettes; only he'd quit smoking and taken up chewing instead.

My lungs are okay now, but my shit comes out A4.

He told that to the class once and everyone laughed because he'd said "shit." One of the boys told his dad and his dad wrote to the head and Mr. Andrews got a verbal warning.

You paint at home, Greg?

Drawings, that's all.

What sort of drawings?

Just drawings. You know, cartoons and stuff.

D'you have somewhere you can work? Privately, I mean.

My bedroom.

What about your mum?

She's not allowed.

Mr. Andrews nodded. Anytime you want to come in and use the materials here—paper, paints, brushes and that—just tell me. Evenings, I mean. Weekends. There's a drawer where you can lock your work away after.

She's not allowed.

He nodded again, his eyes on mine. Anyway, the offer's there.

I looked at the floor, at the space between us. I thought he was going to let me go but he indicated the desk opposite and asked me to sit down.

I hesitated. I've got double science.

Mr. Boyle?

Yes.

He was chewing, I could hear the kissing sounds of paper between his teeth as his lips opened slightly and closed, opened and closed. I watched him pick the white pulp from his mouth and press it onto the underside of the desk. He spread his hands, palms outwards, the thick blunt fingers splayed. The yellowy-brown discolouration of the index and middle fingers of his right hand testified to his former habit. My hands, he used to say, are not those of an artist but of an artisan.

Okay, Greg.

I moved slowly towards the door. Mr. Andrews didn't call me back, didn't say it wouldn't hurt to be late for double science. He just said:

I'll see you . . . when is it, Thursday?

Friday.

Friday. You sure? Okay, Friday. Mind how you go.

I let myself out and walked along the corridor and down the stairs. I collected the books from my locker, put them in my day-pack and looped the pack over one shoulder so that it banged against my hip as I made my way to the science department. Class would've started. Mr. Boyle would not allow my late arrival to pass without comment, some snide remark. I pictured him: straight pale brown hair swept across his baldness, glasses, a line of pens in the breast pocket of his jacket, metal tie clip. Mr. Boyle never went barefoot in class, nor neglected to shave. He never made Spit Sculpture. Opening the door to his classroom, I noticed that my fingers were tacky with paint, leaving a bright red stain on the handle.

Colour

1. Primary colours:
   RED
   BLUE
   YELLOW
2. Secondary colours:
   VIOLET (Red & Blue)
   GREEN (Blue & Yellow)
   ORANGE (Yellow & Red)
3. Complementary colours:
   RED/GREEN
   BLUE/ORANGE
   YELLOW/VIOLET

GREY results from the mixing of BLACK and WHITE. GREY also results from the mixing of any two complementary colours.

If grey is a mixture of black and white, then greyness is not vague or indistinct; it doesn't blur the two extremes but *embodies* them, makes them whole. And if grey is a mixture of two complementary colours—say, yellow and violet—it is no longer a "dull" colour, it is no longer a dreary or depressing colour once you discover that grey is actually a combination of brightnesses.

168

. . .

There are grey areas in the account of my escape from Oxford following the visit to Mr. Hutchinson, the return to London; my subsequent time as a fugitive. Counsel wants these events clarified, distilled into black and white. He wants facts. How, exactly, did I get from Oxford to the M40? In what type of vehicle did I hitch a ride to London? (A yellow one, I inform him.) Did I return home? If so, how did I evade capture? If not, where did I live? When I tire of being helpful, my barrister cites the necessity of establishing my state of mind in the period prior to the final incident. For the purpose, as ever, of mitigation. My responses dissatisfy him, but this is not something about which I give a fuck. In his preoccupation with the ultimate act, typically, he neglects the *penultimate* one. No crime here. Nothing of concern for the court. What he fails to appreciate—and about which I refrain from enlightening him—is that the penultimate episode was characterised by as many shades of grey as any other, for all their vividness, their semblance of blackness and whiteness.

In my cartoon, the barrister is in one frame and I am in the adjacent one. The thin black line between the frames bulges in the shape of his hands and feet as he attempts to break through. But it does not admit him.

Horses grazed on the meadow, and cattle; Canada geese squabbled at the river's edge some distance away. A thin column of smoke rose above the cut, where houseboats and green and red canalboats were moored alongside short wooden jetties. From the humpbacked bridge, I followed a muddy track across the pasture to the moorings. A man, chopping firewood, glanced up but didn't speak. I crossed a bridge over the cut to the river, turning along the towpath and across another bridge to the opposite bank where a small boatyard was set back in a gravelled clearing overhung by trees.

In the chandlery window, among displays of coiled rope and cans of engine oil and navigation charts, hung a framed watercolour depicting the meadow—lime green beneath a sweep of pale blue sky whitened by clouds. The painting represented a view looking northwest from the boatyard, away from the city skyline of honey-coloured spires and towers and green domes. I paused to examine the picture, turning now and then to compare it to the scene it portrayed. There were discrepancies—telegraph wires, a missing chimney stack, trees where there should have been rooftops. The colour was unnatural, anaemic with age and exposure to sunlight, exaggerating the flat featurelessness of the landscape. And the angle was wrong, the point of view; the artist must have set up his easel nearby but not at the *exact spot* where I was standing. It occurred to me to enter the shop, remove the picture and take it with me so that I might identify the place on the riverbank where it'd been painted; so that I might share the artist's perspective. But I was tired and hungry and my hand hurt from the beating I'd given Mr. Hutchinson. Sunshine had given way to cloud, it began to rain. I moved away from the chandlery window and continued along the towpath.

By the time I reached a road, my hair and clothes were damp and the day's light was leaking from the sky. The road twisted through a cluster of houses, rising to join a highway choked with traffic. I bought peanuts and chocolate and a can of drink from a petrol station and walked to a lay-by. I ate and drank and raised my thumb at the stream of vehicles; counting them. Dad taught me Traffic Cricket—a car is one run, a van is four, buses and lorries are six each, and a motorbike is a wicket. In the rain at the roadside, I played cricket while I waited for a lift to London.

Lynn, Gregory
Form 3-3
Art

Greg's work is impressive and original—he shows a natural flair for the subject, combining enthusiasm and application with a high degree of artistic skill and boldness of approach.
Andy Andrews

Sooner or later, the police would be at the house. Unable to obtain an answer, they would force the door and conduct a thorough search of all the rooms, my bedroom. They'd find the wall chart, the files, the photographs, the cartoons. My fingerprints, everywhere. What they would not find would be me, Gregory Lynn; orphan, bachelor, only child from the age of four and a half. Missing person.

When I was picked up at last by a man in a yellow van, I divulged nothing by which I might be identified (I told him my name was Andrew); nor did I disclose my precise destination, other than to say I was bound for London. Coming in on one of the western approaches, the driver asked where I wanted letting out and I said any tube station would do. It was dark, still raining. I had enough cash for the tube and bus fares across the river, to within walking distance of the place where, even at that hour, I hoped the object of my penultimate act of revision would be working. Where once, some years previously, I'd been apprentice to an artist.

Janice taught me how to make pictures by painting a funny shape on one half of a sheet of paper and then, while the paint was still wet, folding the paper over and pressing down hard so that when you opened it out again the shape would be there twice. Each shape was identical but together they made a completely different shape, symmetrical—like two wings. Butterfly Painting, she called it. Mum let us put the pictures up in our bedroom or on the wall in the kitchen, or Sellotape them to the fridge door. If we wanted to paint we had to go out in the yard, so it didn't matter if we made a mess. On rainy days we went to our room and Mum spread newspaper and an old bed sheet on the carpet, stood the water jar and paints on a metal tray.

One summer, the year Janice went away, Mum bought us a face-painting kit. We took turns to paint each other, using the thin, tickly brushes that came with the kit or dipping our finger-tips in the paint and daubing one another's skin with greens and blues and reds. Sometimes we'd do our own faces, only it was hard using a mirror because your hand became awkward and moved in the opposite direction to the way you'd intended, as though it wasn't your hand at all. I liked it when we painted each other, when we used fingers. Janice used her middle finger for my cheeks, chin, forehead and nose, and her index finger or little finger for the places around my eyes and mouth, my ears, or if she wanted to make a special pattern. The tips of her fingers were hard and soft all at once, they tickled and made me laugh and she'd tell me to keep still or I'd spoil it. I liked to paint her face too. I liked the smoothness of her skin. I liked the tiny hairs on her upper lip and the way she'd make herself go cross-eyed to put me off. Sometimes she'd close her eyes—not tightly, but like she was asleep—and sit perfectly still, her lips curled in a slight smile, until I'd finished. Then she'd hold the mirror in front of her face, tilting it at different angles. Laughing. Other times, while I was painting her, she'd shake her head or push my hand away and I knew I'd been too rough, too clumsy, too sudden. And she'd tut and roll her eyes, the way Mum did, and say: Don't be such a *boy* all the time.

Her face was painted the day the ambulance came. I'd given her cat whiskers, a pink nose, one black eye and one white. I asked if it was the paint that was making Janice's head hurt and Mum said not to be so stupid. Dad was wearing work clothes, hands grimy with paint and grease, the toe caps of his boots spattered with dry white flecks. Him and Mum went in the ambulance, Auntie stayed at home with me. She cooked fish fingers and chips and told me to eat it all up and to stop carrying on. When she took me upstairs at bedtime she told me to kneel beside the bed and say my prayers. I was to pray for Mummy and

Daddy and Janice and to ask God to bless them all, especially Janice; and to ask Him to make her well again.

We called them rulers. So did Mr. Andrews. Mr. Boyle called them *rules,* insisted we did too or he'd pretend not to know what we meant.

Use your rules to obtain a precise measurement, he would say.

(Dad told me a joke: My dick's twelve inches long, but I don't use it as a rule.)

At the beginning of one art lesson, Mr. Andrews stood at the front of the class and held up two 12-inch rulers side by side, one in each hand. He asked a boy in the front row:

Which is the longest?

Puzzlement. Nervous laughter. Then the boy replied that they were both the same length. Mr. Andrews extended his left arm fully towards the boy so that one of the rulers was close to his face, kept the other where it was.

Now which is the longest?

The boy didn't answer.

Okay, which one *looks* the longest? The biggest.

The boy touched the ruler closest to his face. Mr. Andrews withdrew it, held it alongside the other one again.

Twelve inches is twelve inches is twelve inches. Except when it isn't. Anyone know what I'm talking about?

Silence. I raised my hand.

Greg.

Perspective?

(He smiled.) Perspective. Perspective, in painting or drawing, is the art of creating reality by means of deception; the attainment of truth through falsification. (Gestured towards the supply cabinets.) Right, grab some paper and pencils—today we're going to tell lies.

> **perspective** *(n)* **1.** (the technique of accurately representing on a flat or curved surface) the visual ap-

pearance of solid objects with respect to their relative distance and position   **2a.** the aspect of an object of thought from a particular standpoint [try to get a different perspective on your problem]   **2b.** (the capacity to discern) the true relationship or relative importance of things

We've gone metric now, so it isn't inches anymore, it's centimetres. A 12-inch ruler is a 30cm ruler. It is a different way of saying the same thing.

On the pavement, in the drizzle, in the dark evening, looking through railings at the red-brick building, formerly a church. Stained glass mostly intact, and a dull stain in the shape of a cross above the iron-studded wooden doors. A rectangular sign bore the Borough Council crest beneath the words, in rainbow lettering, "The Picture Factory." Light from a first-floor window illuminated the haze of raindrops, fragments of crystal momentarily suspended between blackness above and below. I could picture the interior of the building, even after the passage of years: the nave, divided into two storeys, each partitioned into studios; the chancel, used as a screen-printing workshop and retaining the ornate altarpiece and altar with its plaster crucifix; the vestry, converted into a photo studio and darkroom; the cluttered office, where Mr. Andrews sat with his bare feet on the desk, slurping coffee from a mug the size of a child's beach bucket. Where he had his easel, his acrylics, his oils, his watercolours. Where he played Mozart tapes, full volume, on a dusty radio-cassette while he worked. Where we talked. Where, on the wall behind his chair, hung a painting—a portrait of him in gouache, his features picked out in a patchwork of odd geometric shapes that paid scant regard to proportion, to alignment. The painting was unsigned; its frame, like every surface in the room, Spit Sculptured with dried misshapen pellets of Rizla paper.

Thirteen months I worked there. Six more as a *voluntary helper,* after the cuts in the Leisure Services budget. Andy—Mr.

174

Andrews—called it a scandal, but I didn't mind the loss of earnings as long as I could go on working with him. Then Social Services intervened, said I wasn't "genuinely available for employment" because of the hours I was putting in at the arts centre. I took the painting along to the benefit office, held it up to the shatterproof glass. Canvas, 120cm by 80cm, wooden frame. The man behind the screen must've pressed a concealed button beneath the counter, because two uniformed attendants—one black, one white—appeared either side of me. One tried to relieve me of the painting as they escorted me from the building. But I resisted, I said I could manage quite well by myself.

M y hair is dark, almost black. But when shaved close to the scalp, as it is now, the whiteness of skin shows through, rendering the stubble into a charcoal grey. I share this observation with my barrister, who suggests the little time remaining in today's session could be more usefully spent in addressing the *Mr. Andrews affair*. If nothing else, I have succeeded in engaging his interest in this particular act. I scratch my head, watching the dusting of white flakes form on the table. The solicitor looks up at me over her notepad with an expression that may or may not be one of mild distaste mingled with fascination. I smile at her. I say:

Prison shampoo.

(Clearing of the barristerial throat.) Gregory, your, ah . . . encounter with Mr. Andrews . . .

I rub the palm of my hand vigorously over my scalp. Snowfall. Counsel is paid fuck-knows-how-much an hour to watch me do this.

I t didn't happen the way the cartoon said it would. In the cartoon, I hid in the shadows until Mr. Andrews left the arts centre and followed him home on foot, keeping my distance, waiting

175

until he inserted the key in his front door before saying his name aloud. He turned, puzzled at first, then smiling as he recognised me. I drew all this on a piece of cardboard—the inside of an empty cereal box I'd found in a dustbin and which was torn and stained and smelled of stale tea bags. I used the only pen I had, a ballpoint, careful not to press too hard in case the point punctured the places where the cardboard had softened with damp. I drew speech bubbles and thought bubbles, I drew Mr. Andrews clapping his hand on my shoulder, saying how good it was to see me again after all this time, holding the door ajar, inviting me in. But that's not how it happened. As I stood outside the Factory, clothes damp and clinging coldly, there were three people with him as he came out—students, I supposed, two women and a man. Talking loudly, laughing at something one of the women had said. I watched them cross the road and go into a pub. I waited, concealed in the dark mouth of a passage which ran between the arts centre and a neighbouring house. The rain had stopped, at least, but my joints ached and the backs of my eyes hurt and I couldn't stop shivering. Twice I had to move on because of people walking their dogs, taking a circuitous route back to my hiding place once the street was quiet again. I was beginning to worry that Mr. Andrews had left the pub during one of these absences when—fifty-seven minutes after he'd gone in—he emerged alone, silhouetted momentarily in the yellow glare of the doorway. A gust of jukebox music escaped with him into the silent street as the door heaved open and then closed. He passed within a few feet of my hiding place, so close I could smell beer on his breath as he exhaled grey clouds of vapour into the darkness. I watched him walk over to the railings at the front of the arts building and stoop to unchain an old black bicycle. He hooked the loop of chain over the handlebars and tugged at the bulging pockets of his denim jacket, removing two lights and clipping them in place front and back. He switched them on, spilling two dim beams onto the pavement—one white, one red. In picturing our meeting I'd forgotten the bicycle, how easy it would be for him to swing himself into the saddle and ride away —oblivious of my abandonment at the roadside. As he wheeled his bicycle to the kerb and prepared to mount, I stepped out from the shadows and uttered his name. My throat was dry, hoarse; I had to repeat the words to attract his attention.

Mr. Andrews, it's me—Greg. Mr. Andrews, I think I'm sick.

He fixed me a drink: whisky, hot water, a teaspoon of clear honey, juice from a plastic lemon. Two paracetamol. I scalded my mouth trying to swallow the tablets with one gulp. Through the closed door connecting the lounge to the kitchen, I heard muffled voices. I couldn't make out what they were saying, but they were arguing about me. Someone was banging cutlery into a drawer, slamming the drawer shut. The kitchen door opened and she came into the lounge, went over to another door and out of the room without a word or a glance in my direction. She was wearing a silk purple dressing gown over white pyjamas. Tall, slender and very black—African, not Caribbean. Constance. Mr. Andrews was standing in the doorway to the kitchen, a huge mug cupped in his hands.

D'you want any more to eat? Toast or something? Biscuits?

I pointed at the other door. I said: She doesn't like me.

He walked over to the chair nearest the window and sank heavily into the cushions. It's the situation she doesn't like, Greg. Me, actually. Not exactly flavour of the month.

His hair was as long as ever, but greying, thinner on top. He'd grown a beard. I could barely make out his features in the dimly lit room, which was illuminated only by a small lamp. The floor was bare boards, partially covered by a large patterned rug, and the plain white walls were sparsely decorated with prints and pictures, some of which were recognisably Mr. Andrews's own work. No clutter, the room was perfectly tidy. He reached into the breast pocket of his shirt and removed a pack of cigarettes, took one out and placed it between his lips. Ignited it with a disposable lighter from the same pocket.

You don't chew paper anymore.

(He laughed.) Gave it up. Doctor's orders.

His face was partially obscured by a thick veil of smoke. The smoke dispersed, drifting upwards to form a grey haze suspended above his head like a halo. He stared at me across the room. I blew on the hot drink and sipped slowly, inhaling its bittersweet tang, savouring the whisky-burn at the back of my throat, spreading into my chest. In another part of the flat, a toilet flushed, doors opened and closed. Beyond the wall, I heard the creak of bedsprings. Mr. Andrews cleared his throat.

Constance . . .

The sentence petered out, terminated by a wave of the hand, another suck at the cigarette. He asked again if I was hungry and I thanked him, said I wasn't. I was warm and sleepy, I was wearing a navy-blue bathrobe he'd lent me; in the kitchen, the washing machine—loaded with my filthy clothes—whirred into spin cycle.

The way you wolfed those chips down was like you hadn't eaten for, I don't know, a week or something.

I smiled. I sneezed twice in rapid succession, felt my eyes water. Mr. Andrews fetched a box of tissues and placed it on the coffee table.

He'd bought two bags of chips on the way home, balancing his in the basket of his bike as he'd wheeled it along the pavement, catching the cuff of his trousers on the pedal every now and then, or knocking into me with the handlebars. Between mouthfuls of food, we'd talked: about ————, about the time I'd worked at the Factory, about what I'd been up to since then. I told him about Mum, how she'd died of cancer; how they'd burned her. I told him I was *between jobs* at the moment, and the bastard Council had evicted me and I didn't have anywhere to stay. And I was sick. He listened, nodding now and again; nothing was said by either of us about my sleeping at his place—I simply fell in step alongside him as he wheeled his bike home. It took twenty minutes to reach his flat, the top floor of a three-storey house in a broad, shabby street lined with parked cars. The street's nameplate was spray-painted with luminous silver swirls of graffiti so that the name was obscured, illegible. He bumped his bike up the uneven concrete steps to the front door and into the hallway, leaning it there unchained. The hall smelled of damp and dog hairs. Relieving me of my chip wrapper, he deposited it with his in the bicycle's wire basket and nodded at me to follow him upstairs. It was only at the door to the upper flat that he'd explained about Constance—his *partner,* he'd called her—and would I mind waiting while he went inside and spoke to her? He'd exhaled in my face and asked if he smelled of beer.

Lynn, Gregory
Form 4-3
Art
Greg has produced some fine pieces again this year and has applied himself keenly. He doesn't always stick rigidly to the set assignments, but the quality and originality of his work consistently impress.
Andy Andrews

Art outings weren't like geography field trips or history tours; or visits to a science museum, when Mr. Boyle would give us long questionnaires to fill in as we went round and then check each answer to make sure we hadn't skipped any of the exhibits. On art trips, Mr. Andrews would say:

If you get bored, go to the cafeteria and have a Coke.

Or he'd send you into the gallery with instructions to choose just one painting—one you hated—and stand in front of it for as long as it took to write down a list of all the things you didn't like about it. And the thing was, when you did that, you found you didn't hate the picture as much as you thought; sometimes you even ended up quite liking it.

After an outing, he'd hand out photocopied sheets filled with notes or quotations connected to the exhibition we'd just visited. He'd say:

Read these, think about them, discuss them; and, next time you paint a picture, dismiss them totally from your mind.

Notes on the Association of Mood/ Emotion with Colour

> The French Impressionists . . . broke away from the traditional technique of painting clearly defined objects in continuous brushstrokes. They discovered that if we look at nature in the open, objects do not have their own individual colour. Instead, they are made up of a medley of tints which blend in our eye. The Impressionists used small touches of pure colour to capture an immediate visual impression of what they saw. Result: LIGHT and ATMOSPHERE.
>
> When you go out to paint, try to forget what object you have before you, a tree, a house, a field . . . merely think "here is a little square of blue, here is an oblong of pink, here is a streak of yellow." [Claude Monet]

When I imagine Janice, I blot out the frightened white face, the crimson blanket the ambulanceman wrapped round her as he helped Dad take her away; nor do I see her tiny baby body, slimy pink and blood-red against creamy sheets and the flesh of Mum's bare legs, Dad's hands lifting her, enclosing her in white. What I see is honey and apricot, the blush of rose petals, tree-bark brown; I see gold and copper, and burnished bronze; I smell the colours of her hair and her skin: warm, woody scents of autumn.

Mum didn't die of cancer. She had cancer when she died, but it didn't kill her. Not directly. When I told Miss McMahon and

Mr. Andrews that Mum died of cancer, I was lying. I was also telling the truth, because if she hadn't had cancer she wouldn't have died the way she did. Probably. I've tried to represent this concurrence of truth and falsehood by drawing different endings to the cartoon strip of her death. In one version, I divided the final frame—diagonally, top right to bottom left—and drew two endings, side by side. But this was unsatisfactory, and it took a long time to understand why. The "why" is this: there can't be two or more endings to one event, but there can be one ending (the actual one) with multiple interpretations. One ending, different conclusions; or no conclusion at all. Problem being, how to render this with any certainty that someone studying the sequence of drawings will reach the same conclusion as the artist? I discussed this with Mr. Andrews while I was in residence at his flat. He said once your picture is hanging on the wall it no longer belongs to you, it belongs to the person looking at it.

I found her. Me, Gregory Lynn. I went to her room one morning to wake her, to tell her that Auntie had phoned to say she'd be popping round later and did Marion want anything from the shops? It was early in the new year, the Christmas decorations were still up and the mantelpiece and window ledges were dotted with greeting cards. Outside, the temperature had dropped and the sky was bleak with the threat of snow. The wind had got up, beyond the door to Mum's bedroom I could hear the arm of an open window rattling against the catch. Otherwise the room was perfectly quiet, not even the rasps of her breathing or the racking coughs which punctuated most of her waking hours and recurred intermittently during the night. I knocked twice, no answer. I turned the handle and went inside. The room was gloomy, curtains drawn closed and flapping madly in the breeze. Beneath the yellow counterpane, made grey in the half-light, the humped outline of Mum's body resembled a range of snow-blanketed hills. I switched on the light. She lay half on her side, turned away from me, dark hair untidy, and one bare arm hanging stiffly over the side of the bed. When I spoke, she didn't respond.

When I shook her, she didn't stir. When I held her shoulder and eased her fully onto her back, vomit glugged from her half-open mouth and seeped down the side of her face and neck. There was more vomit on the pillow, its stench permeating the room despite the gusts of fresh air from the window.

Mum?

Her eyes were wide open, pointing in my direction. But they were not looking at me, or at anything at all. I didn't detect the bottle and glass, both empty, on the bedside table. The doctor noticed those. Paracetamol, he said. Several tablets were identifiable in the puddle of vomit, and later the pathologist found others, partially digested, in her stomach. Enough to constitute a potentially lethal overdose, he informed the inquest, had she not become sick and aspirated the vomit, thereby suffering acute heart rhythm disturbance. (I've looked all this up, and what it means is: Mum's heart stopped because she choked on her own puke.) With the medical cause of death established, it remained for the coroner to determine whether the overdose had been deliberate or inadvertent. Witnesses—me, the doctor, Auntie—testified that she had left no note and, in the days preceding her death, had said nothing to suggest she might've been contemplating suicide. Confirming that Mrs. Lynn had been terminally ill with cancer at the time of death, the G.P. said she had displayed symptoms of clinical depression. It may also have been possible, he agreed when prompted by the coroner, that the morphine she'd been prescribed for pain relief during the latter stages of her illness had made her confused. Confused to the point where she might have swallowed a handful of paracetamol without really knowing what she was doing. The coroner, in his summing up, said the available evidence was inconclusive. In the circumstances, he could not be satisfied beyond all reasonable doubt that the deceased, Mrs. Marion Lynn—albeit in a state of depression—had intended to take her own life. He therefore recorded an open verdict. So Mum *caused her own death* (swallowing the pills that made her choke), but she didn't *take her own life*. And, anyway, she was already dying. Of cancer, which wasn't the cause of death at all. So I lied.

I was ill for three days. Mr. Andrews—Andy—made me drinks, soup, toast; he fetched pills, mugs of hot lemon and whisky, a supply of tissues as well as books and magazines. He placed a transistor radio within reach beside the bed, and a thick A4 pad and pencils. I didn't request these, he just brought them one morning with the breakfast tray. He invariably paused for a chat, trivial stuff—the weather, gossip from the arts centre—or to ask how I was feeling. If I was up to it, he'd stay for a longer talk. Once, he pressed his hand to my forehead, said I was running a temperature. His palm was rough, like Dad's, dry and with knobs of hardened skin at the base of each finger joint. I told him Dad had been a painter too—car bonnets, wings, door panels—and he laughed. But we didn't talk much—I was sick, tired; most of the time I slept or dozed, or listened to the radio with the volume turned low, or read, unable to concentrate for more than a few pages. I didn't do any drawings. I left my room only to use the bathroom, or—if I was sure nobody else was home—to make myself a drink. Mostly, though, I stayed in bed, huddled beneath the heavy duvet, wearing borrowed pyjamas a couple of sizes too small for me and a pair of thick woollen walking socks. The spare bedroom was small and partially decorated—one wall papered, the others bare plaster. There was a narrow single bed, and a radiator that required regular bleeding but which, when working properly, issued a soporific heat. A solitary sash window, too stiff to open, overlooked an overgrown back garden cluttered with abandoned tools and lengths of wood and a rusted bicycle wheel. The first morning, when I drew the curtains, I saw Constance pegging out washing on a plastic line. Some of the clothes were mine. She was singing the whole time, I could see her lips move, but she didn't once look up at the window.

Being in Andy's flat reminded me of living at home in the years before Mum's burning: occasional sounds—footsteps, a cough, a tap being turned on, a door closing, a voice talking into a telephone—made me conscious of sharing a residence; but, enclosed in my room, it was as if my entire world existed within the confines of four walls. Each external event reduced to a sound equivalent to the burble of a distant radio, everything observed through a window was as two-dimensional as images on a television screen.

The morning of the third day, Andy came in as usual with breakfast. I sat up, shoving one of the pillows behind my back, took the tray from him and set it on my lap. He went over to the window and opened the curtains.

Looking better.

I'm feeling better.

Not you, the weather. *You* look like shit.

Thanks.

Don't mention it.

He had his back to the window now, the narrow window ledge taking most of his weight as he settled himself, one foot braced against the end of the bed. He was barefoot, the legs of his jeans rolled halfway up his shins; his sweatshirt had a large underarm hole where the seam had come apart. I picked up a slice of slightly burnt toast.

D'you think I need a haircut? Constance says I need a haircut.

Don't know.

She says now I'm going thin on top I should wear my hair shorter.

I ate. Andy became preoccupied with his fingernails, picking at each cuticle in turn before using his teeth to pare away the excess skin. He didn't look up when I spoke.

She wants me to leave, doesn't she?

Constance?

Yeah.

He took so long to answer I wondered if he was going to respond at all. Finally, he said: Greg, if you're in some kind of trouble.

There were two paracetamol in a twist of foil on the breakfast tray. I held them up. I said: Mum swallowed a whole bottle. (Smile.) Must've been some fucking headache, eh?

Mr. Andrews—Andy—was staring at the foil. You ever paint a portrait of her?

I shook my head.

What was she like? Dark, like you?

Floating. She floated. She had long hair.

That one you did of me is still hanging on the wall in my office, you know. Students are always commenting on it, how good it is. How it captures my "fragmented personality." They read too much art crit, if you ask me.

When they burned her I wanted to keep the ashes and paste them into my scrapbook.

(He smiled.) Collage. *Mother and Coffin,* ash on paper. Unsigned, of course.

(Tea, too strong. I made a slurping noise and my breath was hot when I exhaled.) If she hadn't died I wouldn't have found the reports.

He asked what reports, and I told him about the box in the attic. I told him what the other teachers had written about me, and what he'd written. Verbatim. I asked if what he'd said about me failing to adhere to set assignments had been intended as a criticism. He said no, not in his terms. I said I thought teachers were cunts.

Me included?

No.

Well, if *you* can pick and choose who the cunts are, then so can everyone else. And that means we're all potential cunts.

I was expelled.

The momentary anger in his voice dissipated; the words became slower, quieter, more measured. I know, I was there when your case was discussed. (His fingers made quote marks in the air around the word case.) All your subject teachers were. Miss what's-her-name, the English teacher?

McMahon.

Her and Mr. Teja were the only ones who argued in favour of letting you stay on.

Mr. *Teja?*

Maths. He said you were the only pupil who ever *discussed* mathematics with him. Said you had, what was the phrase he used? . . . an "organised mind."

(Pause.) What about you?

I said my piece. But, I mean, the head had said right at the outset that any assault on a member of staff was a matter for automatic expulsion. So the rest of the meeting was a sham. Christ, Greg, even the educational psychologist wanted you out.

I put the unopened paracetamol down and lowered the tray to the floor, sliding my legs out from under the duvet and sitting on the edge of the bed. Silence. I kicked the tray so hard it cartwheeled against the wall with a loud crash, knocking over the empty mug and tipping the plate upside down, scattering toast crumbs on the carpet. Andy stared at the mess. When he spoke, his voice was gentle.

You know all this.

Not all of it. Not the bit about Mr. Teja.

He's dead now. I heard he died.

I nodded.

Andy eased down from his makeshift seat, went to the radiator and pressed the flat of his palm against it. He got the small brass Allen key from the window ledge and inserted it into the valve, turning it to release the air, then shutting it off as soon as a thin jet of water spurted out.

Fucking thing.

He had cancer as well, his wife said. His widow.

You met her. Mrs. Teja?

Her plates got smashed.

I picked up the breakfast things, conscious of him watching me. There was a mark on the wall where the corner of the tray had chipped the plaster. Andy took the tray from me and left the room, returning with a dustpan and brush. He swept up the toast crumbs. I was sitting on the bed. Without looking up, he said:

Look, Greg, we're going away tomorrow. For the weekend.

You and Constance.

Yes. For a couple of days. It's something we arranged weeks ago.

So I have to leave?

I mean, d'you have somewhere to stay?

I like it here.

Your aunt and uncle or somewhere?

If you just told her . . .

It's not Constance. Mr. Andrews stood up, still holding the dustpan and brush. It's not just Constance. We talked about it this morning and we both agreed . . .

Yeah, sure.

. . . that now you're a bit better . . .

Yeah.

(His eyes, on mine.) Greg, what I'm saying is, if you're in trouble of some sort. If you need help.

Where are my clothes?

He put down the pan and brush, reached into his back pocket. He took a cigarette from the pack and lit up, expelling smoke towards the ceiling.

Just get my fucking clothes. *Sir.*

I can't give you any work, you know. Or money. Is that what all this is about?

All what?

How can I help if you won't say what's wrong? You hardly talk at all, or if you do you just go on and on about school like it was last week or something. And, Christ, the Picture Factory was how many years ago?

All what?

He went over to the window, sucking on the cigarette. Constance has never even met you before. I tell her about you—

187

about ————, and when you worked with me—and, to her, it's just . . . something that happened. In the past. You know?

All *what?*

(Gesture of the hand, encompassing the room, the chipped plaster, the faulty radiator, the smoke haze; me, Gregory Lynn, sitting on the narrow bed.) All *this,* Greg.

I have access to a dictionary here, and to other reference books. I look up "collage." One definition is: "an assembly of diverse fragments."

>   **Art Deco:** decorative style . . . distinguished by bold colours, ornateness, geometrical lines and lack of symmetry
>
>   **Art Nouveau:** decorative style freely ornamented with . . . organic or natural forms; characterized by the use of curves and the absence of geometrical lines
>
>   **Art trouvé:** found art. Not the direct creation of the artist but adapted from "found" or natural objects which have been primarily shaped by circumstances, nature and the elements

. . . *lack of symmetry . . . use of curves . . . absence of geometrical lines . . . shaped by circumstances . . .*

You returned home?

I nodded.

Three days after he . . . that is, after you began residing with him and his, ah . . . partner?

Yes.

He knew the police were looking for you?

I told him.

But you didn't tell him why.

Yes, I told him why. Some of it.

Did it not concern you that by returning home you might, as it were, expose yourself to the risk of being apprehended?

I shrugged. I wanted him to see.

See what, exactly?

Just to see.

When my case comes before the court, the barrister will *represent* me. It interests me, representation. This acting on behalf of, this standing in for, this conveying of an impression, this symbolism, this depiction. The barristerial art is a representational one in the sense, also, that its primary concern is attention to detail, to accuracy, to realism. To facts. Andy is averse to realism. Real in relation to what? he always asks. He is averse, too, to the notion that the role of art (and, therefore, the duty of the artist) is to represent; that a picture ought, necessarily, to be *of* something or *about* something.

Andrewsian aphorism: My sole duty as an artist is to fill the canvas with whatever I please, or leave it blank if I choose.

This was daubed on a banner above the fireplace in his office at the Picture Factory; may still be for all I know. Alongside it hung a notice, in stark red letters: NO SMOKING. Mr. Andrews referred to these signs as the "guiding principles" of his life. If he broke the second more frequently than the first, he said, it was merely because it took less time to smoke a cigarette than to paint a picture.

My barrister, when pressed, defines *his* duty as one of seeking to obtain justice for his client. In the case of the Crown against me, Gregory Lynn, "justice" is taken to mean a sentence which reflects the extent of my diminished responsibility. To that end, he says, he will represent me. His difficulty is that I am unwilling and, in any case, entirely unable to furnish him with coherent data which might assist the court. I am, it seems, as elusive in custody as when I was at large. Despite his attempts to blame *me* for this, counsel's dilemma is, of course, of his own making. He is the type who, when confronted with an abstract painting, asks: What does it *mean?* This obsession with facts, the gathering of incontrovertible information. When I was received into custody, I had my photograph taken—showing my face from different angles. If I were to escape, to go on the run, these images would be published in the newspapers and displayed on television. Fair enough. Identity, where it is a question of mere physical resemblance, is inevitably reduced to the superficial. Unfortunately for him, this is the sort of profile my barrister seeks to elicit from our conversations. His intention being that the *workings of my mind*— like the photographic records—can be indexed, date-stamped, filed away. A series of mental snapshots; a psychological waxwork bust moulded from a cast of my brain; a sketch of my personality which an observer might compare with the subject and exclaim: "My word, what a truly remarkable likeness!"

Bollocks, is what I say.

I entered from the rear, via the alley which ran along the ends of the gardens. The wooden gate was bolted, as usual, but easily scaled; and I had a key for the back door. It was a cloudy night. The house was silent, no lights at the windows. No sign of disturbance. I opened the door and went inside, quietly, as though I was an intruder. The kitchen was cold and musty, with a distinct aroma of mouldy food. I switched on the light. The room appeared no different to the way I'd left it—pans and plates stacked in the draining rack, an unpaid phone bill on the table where it had been on the morning of my departure for Oxford. The other downstairs rooms bore more obvious signs of disturbance— drawers and cupboards not properly closed, furniture out of position. The rooms were dusty, unaired. Post was strewn on the front doormat, junk mail, pizza home-delivery leaflets and free newspapers; notes—recognisably from Auntie—which I left unopened. I went upstairs. The door to my room was closed but unlocked, the handle was loose and I saw that the wooden door frame was dented and splintered at the point where the lock would have engaged.

They'd taken everything: the wall above the desk was stripped bare, lumps of Blu-Tac the only evidence that the wall chart and maps had ever been there; the desk drawers had been emptied and left open, one of them pulled out so far it had become detached from its runners and fallen to the floor; the boxes of files were missing; the folders and loose papers I'd left stacked on top of the desk had gone. They'd even taken my pens and pencils, the ruler, the tub of glue I used to paste the photographs to the chart. I stared at the wall, the desk, the square dust marks on the carpet where the boxes had stood, as if the missing items might reappear at any moment. All that came to my notice, however—and these visible only on a closer inspection—were the scores of grey-white lumps which peppered the surface of the desk, the drawers, the underside of the chair—tiny pellets of paper, chewed to a pulp, pressed against the smooth wood in various patterns—or randomly, patternless—and left to harden.

Notes on Representation

Some ancient alphabets were developed from stylised pictures of the objects to be represented. For example, around 1500 B.C. the Semitic character for the word "ox" was ⩖ based on a simplified drawing of the head of an ox. This written symbol, in turn, was represented by a spoken sound—a glottal stop—which meant "ox" to anyone familiar with the language. What must be borne in mind, however, is that the picture is not the ox and the word is not the picture and the sound is not the word. Many so-called primitive tribes—the Yukaghir of Siberia, for instance—have evolved subtle systems for transmitting often quite complex messages graphically (i.e., in pictures), without reference to spoken words—that is to say: thoughts, images and ideas for which no word or series of words exist in their language. In Chinese the same written character (or morpheme) can be pronounced quite differently by two people from different regions of the country, *to the extent that one will not understand the other at all.*

The police, in ransacking my room, neglected to confiscate the dozens of exercise books filled with cartoons depicting scenes from my life; from that first one, of Dad's death, to the one of Mum floating, adrift because I was unable, with my coloured pencils, to represent heaven. To the police, these drawings must have been irrelevant, the incoherent scrawl of a child. Counsel for the Crown has copies now, however; now that my barrister has been persuaded to use them in mitigation on my behalf.

The exercise books had been stacked neatly on sheets of newspaper in the bottom of the wardrobe. Now they were dumped in a corner, along with my clothes and shoes and the dishevelled bedding the police had stripped, no doubt in their haste to search under the mattress (my cum hanky was missing too). I arranged the books on the bare bed—making a multicoloured patchwork of cardboard covers—sorting them into chronological order, then reading them in sequence. Every page of every book. Each cartoon telling its story and all the cartoons, in combination, telling *their* story; the stories were the same: this happened, then that happened. Different ways of saying the same thing. And when I shuffled the books, reading the cartoons out of sequence—at random—the events occurred in a different order, but the story was unchanged: this happened, then that happened.

By the time I'd finished reading, it was 3 A.M. I'd dozed off sitting upright, my back against the headboard, only jerking awake when one of the books slipped from my lap to the floor. I gathered them all up and, using a pair of Mum's hairdressing scissors, cut out those pages depicting scenes at school and those depicting scenes at home. I separated them into two stacks— school and home—rereading each series of pictures in turn. And again the stories were different yet the same: this happened, then that happened. When I tried to reassemble them in the correct order, however, I found that I couldn't. Too confused, too tired; the cartoons' details became indistinguishable from one another until the only characters I was able to identify with certainty were me and Janice. Even then I couldn't differentiate between the twelve-year-old me and the twenty-year-old me and the thirty-four-year-old me; nor between the first Janice and the second one. As for the teachers, Auntie, Mum and Dad, they blurred into one composite figure. It was only by referring to the numbers written at the foot of each page—rather than to the drawings themselves—that I eventually restored the exercise books to their previous state. Except that the individual folios were loose now, unbound, and might easily slip out from between the covers.

Dawn. I switched off the bedroom light and went downstairs. A thorough search of the kitchen cupboards produced an empty box, and items with which to fill it: tins of food, biscuits, cheese crackers, jars of peanut butter and jam, a tin opener, cutlery. I filled saucepans and empty milk bottles with tap water. These were the most awkward to carry into the loft without mishap. Once the provisions were safely installed, I collected the duvet and pillow from my room, as well as my winter jacket—the one with the hood—and the blank pad and pencils I'd fetched with me from Mr. Andrews's flat. After replacing the lightbulb in the loft with one I'd taken from the bedside lamp in my room, I flicked the switch. It worked. I paid a final visit to the bathroom —from now on, piss and shit would be ejected into a flip-top bin partially filled with water and floor-cleaning fluid. When I was satisfied that all the preparations were complete, I climbed into the loft for the last time, nearly losing my balance as I knelt at the open hatch to haul up the retractable ladder. I lowered the flap. It closed with a dull wooden click, shutting out all natural light.

> **cunt**   *(n)* **1.** the female genitals, the pudenda   **2.** an unpleasant person (use vulg.)

Mr. Andrews—Andy—proscribed my use of this word in the context of a general or selective term of abuse for members of the teaching progression. That is to say, *profession*.

The cunts, all the fucking cunts with their chalk and their textbooks and their do this/do that, don't do this/don't do that, their this-is-the-way-things-are. With their *teaching* and their *learning*, their assignments and assessments, their marks, their fucking do-as-you're-told. Their rules. Their role as rulers.

I have looked up pudenda; it derives from the Latin *pudere*—to be ashamed. If I am not to use the word cunt (in its anatomical or vulgar meaning) to describe teachers, then I claim etymological authority to refer to them as pudendal (adj).

I know what Mr. Andrews would say in response to this (I know, because I've drawn him saying it):

We are all potential cunts, we are all potentially pudendal.

I have touched Janice's pudenda (while she was pissing), I've seen Mum's—the second time Janice went away. I called Mum a cunt once, just to see the expression on her face.

I lied when I said Mr. Andrews has seen the cartoons, the books full of drawings depicting scenes from my life. "Mr. Andrews" has seen them, but Mr. Andrews hasn't. "Mr. Andrews"— "Andy"—was with me in the loft during the ten days of my solitary retreat. He was with me, as Mr. Mistry Man was present when me and Janice retreated there; by drawing things (by imagining things to be true), sometimes they happen. Because truth is to be found in your imaginings. I represented Mr. Andrews, I represented him. In some of the pictures I made him the way he was when I was a pupil at ———— (same appearance—no beard, no cigarette—same attitude); and in others I made him the way he was when I stayed at his flat. We talked, in speech balloons that filled most of each frame of each cartoon. And there were hundreds of cartoons. In every cartoon, I was trying to make him see. I was trying to make him see the story—the stories—of the twenty-three years of drawings that lay loose and unbound between soft cardboard covers. We talked, as we'd talked on that last morning, the day I retrieved my clothes and left, so that he—Mr. Andrews, minus quotation marks—and Constance could be unencumbered of the presence of myself. Which as any decent Miss McMahon knows is incorrect English. That morning, I revealed to him the (f)acts of revision (more or less)—those completed and those still outstanding: his own, Mr. Boyle's. I admitted my fugitiveness. My fugitivity. I put him in the picture.

(In the loft, we talked, me and "Mr. Andrews.")

Sometimes I draw things and they happen, or they unhappen.

What about Janice? Your mum, your dad . . . do they still happen? Do they become alive again, Jeggy?

Don't call me that.

Do they?

(Pointing at the neat piles of exercise books.) They're there! They're there! I draw them!

So what are you in control of? The page, the pencil? Your ideas, if you're lucky.

You said . . .

What, Jeggy?

Nn.

What?

The things you *said*. The way you *were*.

I didn't say . . . I didn't say *this*. If you thought I said this, you . . .

195

What you said belongs to me now. I heard it, it's mine. It belongs to me, not you!

You can't . . .

I can. (Turning to face him.) I can do what the fuck I like.

I never taught you to hurt people.

(In the loft we shared strips of paper, me and "Andy," chewing them into moist pellets and Spit Sculpturing every flat surface: walls, floor beams, rafters, empty food containers, the covers of the exercise books. Sometimes he'd spoil it by lighting a cigarette. This was easily remedied—in one frame he'd be holding the cigarette, in the next he would extinguish it and resume chewing paper. Slowly, frame by frame, the smoke would disperse. In the loft, I chewed paper and defecated daily in the flip-top bin. My shit came out A4.)

I heard noises downstairs. Voices. It would've been day five or six, I think. I can't remember. There wasn't much food left, so it could've been later—day eight. I stayed still and quiet while they moved around in the rooms below, listening to them talking in their men's voices but unable to make out what was being said. I shut my eyes tight, the way Janice taught me, and made my brain shallow, silent.

The monsters will go away, Jeggy. The dinosaur, the sabre-toothed tiger, the mammoth. They won't even know we're here.

I kept still until the voices and the noises ceased.

Mr. Andrews is about 5'10", 5'11". Shorter than me, except when I was sitting or lying down and he was standing over me. When he was across the other side of the room or in the garden and I stood at the window, looking down, he was much shorter. In my drawings "Mr. Andrews" is smaller still, sometimes only a few centimetres high. But the portrait which dominates his office wall at the Picture Factory shows him to be huge. When he sits at the desk, with the picture behind and above him, he is dwarfed by himself.

(In the loft, we discuss matters which are either related or unrelated to the above, depending on your point of view. "Mr. Andrews" expresses the opinion that my sense of perspective has become distorted. I have things *out of proportion.)*

I say: Never confuse proportion with quantity, nor perspective with relativity. You taught me that, *sir.*

Remember the trick with the rules, Jeggy? Twelve inches is twelve inches, whichever way you look at it. It's only your *perception . . .*

Rules: you sound like Mr. Boyle.

Mr. Andrews taught me the art of meaning. He taught me that art is not an exact science. You can't give marks for painting. There was no revision necessary for art exams, he said, because art exams test your talent rather than your ability to remember. Presupposing, of course, that talent is measurable. Revision was required for other subjects—history, for example, geography, English lit, maths, science. Mr. Boyle believed in thorough revision. He said it was essential, for prospective examination candidates and scientists alike.

Boylean aphorism: If we are not conversant with what has been learned before, how can we begin to understand what is known now or to become known in the future?

Hear! Hear! is what I say. Here, here.

"Andy's" last words to me, in the loft, were:

For God's sake, Jeggy, Mr. Boyle isn't to blame.

With eraser and pencil, I inserted "fuck's" in place of "God's"; I rubbed out the word "Jeggy"; I erased "n't" from "isn't" to leave "is."

I'd intended to designate Mr. Andrews as yellow, had my chart not been torn down. Yellow pin, yellow line connecting map to biographical details, the photograph which I would've obtained. Not yellow for a specific reason, although colours—traditionally —do have symbolic associations. We learnt this in art. Another handout to be read, considered, then disregarded. In blazonry, yellow signifies faith, constancy and wisdom; but in modern art, it signifies jealousy and inconstancy. The French daubed yellow on the doors of traitors, while the Nazis made Jews wear yellow Stars of David. In Christian art, St. Peter is arrayed in golden yellow; so is Judas. So much contradiction, so many different representations. In Mr. Andrews's case, however, I'd used up all but two of the colours on the other teachers and simply chose yellow at random from the remaining felt-tips—he could just as easily have been brown. So, no symbolic significance at all.

7

science   1a. department of systematized knowledge
1b. something that may be learned systematically
1c. the natural sciences (e.g. physics, biology, chemistry)   **2a.** coordinated knowledge of the operation
of general laws, esp as obtained and tested through
scientific method   **2b.** such knowledge of the physical world and its phenomena   **3.** system or method
based on scientific principles

Janice ate a worm. Muddy and wet and pinky brown; she bit it in
two, swallowed one half and held the other between her middle
finger and thumb.

Look, Jeggy! Look, he's still alive.

When I was born she couldn't say Gregory, it came out as
Jeggy. She went on calling me that even when she was old
enough to pronounce my name properly. Mum used to tell her
off for *talking like an imbecile*. No one else called me Jeggy. As the
piece of worm writhed in her fingers I grabbed it and tried to
put it in my mouth. She stopped me, threw the worm away.

If we eat both bits he won't be alive anymore, she said.

Janice found me another worm to play with, a whole one, as
long as I promised not to eat it. It was wriggly cold on my
fingers, but it wasn't slimy like a snail or a slug. I stopped crying.
One time we found two worms tangled, like strips of red liquo-

rice, gooey and gunged up so it was hard to tell them apart. Janice said they were making a baby. Whenever we had tinned spaghetti for tea, Janice called it worms-on-toast and Mum didn't know how many times she had to tell her not to say that in front of Greg.

He's fussy enough with his food as it is.

Mum gave Dad worms-on-toast and he pushed the plate away so hard it knocked over the ketchup bottle. *Fucking kids' food*.

Dad liked to catch daddy longlegs and pull their legs off one by one.

There: daddy no-legs!

His party piece, he called it. And Mum would call him Patrick instead of Pat. Made her ill, she said. When Janice said she'd eaten a worm, Mum scrubbed her mouth out with a washcloth and made her drink two glasses of juice. Janice's top lip turned orange, like she had a moustache.

But it was still *alive,* the bit I didn't eat!

Dad said if you chop a chicken's head off she doesn't die right away, she carries on running around and laying eggs—but the eggs won't hatch because the hen can't see where they are to sit on them.

We did worms and chickens in biology. There were free-range chickens in the caretaker's garden, and a clear-sided incubator in the science lab so we could watch the chicks hatch. There were locusts in a glass tank, and another with goldfish, and gerbils in a cage. At juniors we had terrapins. A terrapin is like a tiny tortoise. We were gathered around the tank when the boy next to me jogged the table and a slab of rockery fell onto one of the terrapins and killed it. The boy said I'd pushed him. In juniors, we wore short trousers and if you did something naughty you got slapped on the bare backs of your legs. Teacher slapped me. She said I'd caused the death of an innocent creature and she hoped I was proud of myself.

• • •

On the tenth day—when the provisions had run out and the stench from the makeshift toilet had become intolerable, and once I was satisfied that my preparations (artistic, psychological and tactical) were complete—I emerged from retreat. Stiff-legged, eyes adjusting to the daylight which poured through the landing window as I climbed down the retractable ladder. I left the house by the back gate, pausing to untie the plastic clothes-line and stow it in my duffel bag along with the kitchen knife, pad and pencils, and the thermos flask of strong black coffee. I followed the alley along the rear of the houses and, keeping to the quieter streets, took a circuitous route via a small grocer's on the far side of the estate, where no one would know me. It felt good to be walking, to be inhaling fresh air. I bought crisps, cans of Fanta, three packs of ready-made sandwiches and several choc-olate bars. The bag was heavy now, I slung it over one shoulder so that it banged against my hip with each step. Approaching the school from the copse, I descended the slope between the perim-eter fence and the playing field to the point where the path was hidden from the main building by a landscaped grass mound. The mound was known as the Shag Heap, because it was where kids went to shag; and to smoke or do drugs or to fight, or just to be out of sight of the teachers. I never went there when I was a pupil. Miss McMahon said I didn't require solitude to be alone because I carried my personal supply of privacy around wherever I went—a snail with a shell into which it could retreat at will. *Underdeveloped social skills,* the educational psychologist called it. The shrink. I was *socially dysfunctional.*

Quarter to ten. Assembly would have finished, the first classes of the morning would be under way. The sky was hazy, the sun pale and indistinct behind a bleary sheen, yet bright enough to make me squint so that one eye—the green one—was almost shut. I was too warm in my winter jacket, even with the hood lowered and the zip unfastened. Taking the length of clothesline from the duffel bag, I closed the bag and lobbed it over the fence.

201

I made a secure loop of the line, hooked one end over a metal fence post and used the other as a stirrup. Once I'd scaled the fence and lowered myself onto the worn turf the other side, I reached up to retrieve the clothesline. The mound—not a natural remnant of the hilly common which predated the school, but a perfectly sculpted hummock of recycled soil—afforded me cover as far as the Sports Hall. From here it was necessary to hurry along a cinder path which separated the hall from the expanse of empty playground before disappearing behind the Science and Technical Studies Block. Here, I paused to regain my breath, to compose myself before ascending the short flight of steps to the rear entrance. For the first time in eighteen years, six months, two days, twenty-three hours and ten minutes—since the morning my suspended status was formally *upgraded* into one of expulsion—I entered the school building. Unaccompanied by my mum, on this occasion; uninvited, unobserved. The stairwell smelled of floor polish, the creamy light dimming to grey as I let the door click shut behind me. Children were drilling, hammering, sawing—sounds dulled by thick cinder-block walls dividing the workshops and classrooms. Metalwork. Woodwork. Technical drawing. Compulsory (for boys) up to third year, then an exam option for those who didn't want to do French or English lit or music. I learnt these facts: concealed lines and angles are represented by dotted lines; certain metals (e.g., tin) cannot be soldered because they melt on contact with the soldering iron; never plane against the grain. These are technical truths. They are technicalities.

Technical studies was on levels G and 1, as it had been during my days at ———, with the science labs on levels 2 and 3. I went up two flights of stairs, through a set of swing-doors, along a corridor and through another set of doors that shrieked as they swung shut. More doors, another flight of stairs. Then three classrooms on either side of an empty corridor, all closed. Each door bore a metal plate, next to the handle, inscribed with numbers—S3:06, S3:05, S3:04 . . . ; like the other doors I'd passed, each had a panel of glass at head height through which it was possible to peer into the room, unobserved if you stood far enough back. Two of the labs were unoccupied. In another, a female teacher was drawing plant sections on a blackboard. I crossed the corridor and made my way along the other side. Room S3:01. First I saw the pupils—second-years, by the look of them—in neat rows, facing the front, bent over their exercise books. A slightly nasal male voice, accentless and muffled by the closed door, was dictating:

. . . are similar in principle to [conventional?] stations in that water is heated into steam to drive turbines [. . .] produce electricity.

A pause, presumably to allow the pupils—all writing furiously —to catch up, then the dictation resumed. I moved, bringing the speaker into view through the glass panel with its crisscross of embedded wire mesh.

However, the heating process, instead of burning [oil?] or gas, is the fission of uranium 235 nuclei in a central core—known as the reactor . . .

The teacher was standing at the front of the room; neatly parted hair, a line of pens clipped in the breast pocket of his jacket. Spectacles, the lenses catching light from the windows. I raised my hood, rummaged in the duffel bag, then hooked it securely onto my back. As the teacher turned—still speaking—to indicate a diagram on the board, I twisted the handle, opened the door and went in. My hand was moist, cool. I had an urge to piss, to shit, as I strode between the desks and the blurred rows of faces. The sound of the door opening, and of my brisk movement towards him, caused the teacher to break off in mid-sentence, to look round. Bespectacled eyes found mine, his expression one of irritated distraction, of perplexity. But any words of interrogation he may have been about to assemble were mislaid as his attention shifted from my face to my hand. To the knife. To the knife in my hand. Mr. Boyle became utterly fascinated by the sight of the knife in my hand.

I draw my barrister's attention to the fact that the word "nuclear" is an anagram of "unclear." I laugh.

Unclear Family. *Unclear* Power. *Unclear* War.

He changes the subject. You were confident that the, ah, object of your ultimate act of revision would be there. At the school, I mean.

Mr. Boyle was head of science.

You knew this?

Mr. Andrews let it slip, during one of our bedside chats.

Mr. Andrews, of course, couldn't have suspected your intention.

Of course.

So your assertion . . . I have it here, somewhere . . . in a statement to the police, that he—that's to say Mr. Andrews—was an, um, *accessory* (counsel looks up from the document) . . . it doesn't really wash, does it?

I smile.

P hysics deals with matter and energy; also with the physical properties and phenomena of systems, whatever the fuck that means. It is about properties and interactions.

Physics asks questions: Why is iron magnetic, copper not? What happens when solids melt? Why do some liquids flow more easily than others? Why do some things conduct electricity well, others badly, some not at all? How long is a piece of string? (Metaphysics.)

Before such questions can be answered, other questions must first be raised and solved. In particular: (i) of what nature are the invisible particles of which matter is composed? and (ii) how are those particles arranged?

It is in the field of particles, and the forces that particles exert on one another, that physics represents science at its most fundamental; breaking matter down into its minutest components so that its basic workings might be understood, described, predicted.

Physics is about physicality. It is about the quest for knowledge. It is about mind over matter.

Boylean aphorism: It is not in man's nature to live in a world which he does not seek to explain and over which he does not seek to exert control.

Physics, the Lynn conundrum: When you travel on a bus or a train it is apparent—by the jolting of the vehicle or by looking out the window at the passing scenery—that you are moving. Yet "you" are not moving, as such; you are *being moved*. You sit quite still, reading, daydreaming, at rest, maybe even asleep—motionless at 60 mph. And the people seated all around you are motionless too. However, to the bystander in the street or on the railway embankment, watching your bus or train go by, you are a blur of motion. Streaks of colour, of clothes and flesh and glass and metal. Perspective. And we haven't even begun to consider the invisible force of gravity which keeps the bus, the train, the bystander, the passengers you—from floating weightlessly, helplessly, away from the surface of a planet which is itself rotating on its axis at 1,041 mph yet appears not to be moving at all.

How long is that piece of string, Mr. Boyle? How many exclamation marks are there in a bottle of ink?

Mr. Boyle shaved so scrupulously that the lower half of his face seemed to be sculpted from wax, buffed and polished; smoothly, consistently and permanently stripped of whiskers. It was as though the very hair follicles had been sealed to ensure stubblelessness. His jaw, his cheeks, his chin, *gleamed*. Similarly fastidious attention to the minutiae of neatness was required of us in our work. Notebook inspections were regular and rigorous. Homework was frequently rejected because of "unsatisfactory presentation," irrespective of whether the answers, the calculations, were correct.

Untidy notes smack of untidy method.

I have seen facsimiles of Einstein's notes—they're a fucking mess. It took teams of mathematicians and physicists years to make sense of them. I mentioned this, in passing, to Mr. Boyle during a third-form physics class and he observed that if I considered my work to be comparable to that of Mr. Einstein, perhaps I could enlighten everyone with my theory of relativity.

My auntie is my mum's sister—they are relatives. Sir.

He waited for the general laughter to abate. Ah yes, *humour,* Lynn. The first refuge of the nincompoop.

Einstein wasn't a nincompoop, he was a genius. In 1939 Einstein wrote to President Roosevelt on behalf of a group of eminent scientists to warn of the danger of uranium research in Nazi Germany. He stressed the urgency of the need for the U.S. to investigate the use of atomic energy in bombs.

We did bombs in physics. Or, rather, we did falling objects. Mr. Boyle divided us into teams and nominated one pupil from each team to stand on a table. He handed that person a small metal contraption about the size and shape of a retractable tape measure. From the mouth of each device emerged the tip of a strip of ticker tape, to which various objects were fastened—a coin, an apple, a magnet, a box of matches, a wooden rule(r).

Raise them above your head and, when I give the signal, let them drop.

As the objects plummeted to the classroom floor, each trailed a length of tape punched with dots made by the device. Each team's task was to weigh its object, to time its descent, to measure the distance from hand to floor so that the rate of descent might be calculated, and then to examine the series of dots on the tape to assess whether or not the rate of descent was constant. When we'd finished, the teams presented their findings to Mr. Boyle and he drew comparisons for us.

So what can we observe about the apple, say, in relation to the coin?

A girl raised her hand: The apple falls faster.

And?

She was flummoxed. Another pupil said: The apple falls faster than the coin but they both . . . speed up in the same, I mean, they speed up the same.

(Mr. Boyle, nodding.) They have the *same rate of acceleration*— all the objects, irrespective of weight or *velocity* of descent, accelerate as they fall—and the rate at which they accelerate is *identical*.

He permitted himself a smirk of self-satisfaction, like a conjuror who has just astounded his audience. So I acquired this fact, this demonstrable scientific truth, from Mr. Boyle—he taught me it, this knowledge; he must have done so because it is still with me. Remembered. But what I don't recall, what I haven't learnt, is: why do we need to know that all falling objects accelerate at the same rate? I must've said this aloud, at the time. There was a minor adjustment of his spectacles so that he might peer over them at me, a long sigh of exasperation, a singsong of imitation in his voice:

"Why do we need to know that?"—the Familiar Refrain of Gregory Lynn. (Pause.) If you would be so kind as to allow me to continue . . .

It may be that he did go on to explain the usefulness of this fact—its application—and I simply couldn't grasp it, or grasped it but haven't been able to retain it. All I remember is ticker tape and coins and rates of acceleration, pupils standing on tables and the *clunkclunkclunk* of objects hitting the classroom floor.

Among my cartoons from that period is one of Mr. Boyle, plummeting, his head an apple bursting on impact. Pips and skin and pulp.

Lynn, Gregory
Form 3-3

Science
Gregory has shown very little effort and has wasted much of the time. He doesn't find it easy to concentrate for any length of time without distractions and, as a result, has achieved little progress.
Mr. D. Boyle

M̲y barrister, untypically, requests that I proceed more slowly. Not in deference to the note-taking solicitor, but because we are encroaching upon what he describes as the "confusion of events" which have given rise to the most serious charges. Any prospect of counsel being a potential convert to the Unclear Age is undermined, however, by his qualifying statement:

We must establish the events—that is, the sequence of events and their precise nature—in order that any confusion and, ah, discrepancy can be cleared up at this stage.

It is my assumption that the heavy emphasis on the last three words is intended to imply that there must be no confusion or discrepancy at the next stage—in court, where trial succeeds trial and error as the process by which "the truth" is educed. When I refrain from responding, my legal representative adds:

We don't want any, what shall we say . . . *nasty surprises* being sprung on us during cross-examination, do we?

(I smile.) Us? You and me?

If there is any unravelling to be done, it's better that we do so now. I have to know everything, every detail of what occurred that day, to the best of your recollection, and . . .

The best of my recollection.

(He glances up from his interlocked hands, which he has been studying throughout our conversation.) . . . Yes. And then, perhaps, we can clarify the question of, ah, state of mind. Motive, if you like.

You may care to send out for fresh supplies of pink ribbon.

He smiles, he actually smiles. Fingering the neat bow binding one of the sheafs of documents on the table, he turns to the solicitor and (still smiling) says: I'd describe it as more cerise than pink, wouldn't you?

A brief silence, an exchange of glances and then, momentarily, we are united in laughter—the three of us—laughing into the parcel of air that separates us and from which we extract breath.

Mr. Boyle was unsmiling, laughterless, that morning, as I presented the blade of the knife close enough to the fleshy part of his throat that any abrupt movement on his part or mine would have resulted in a puncturing of tissue, the release of fluids. Movement for him, in any case, would have been problematic in his situation, pinned against the blackboard, my free hand gripping his jaw so that his head was tilted back at an unnatural angle. He started to speak but I squeezed, and his lips pursed into a tight little "O" of shrivelled pink as though his mouth had mutated into an anus. The diagram of a nuclear power station had been partially erased by the action of his head against the board and I saw that one or two wayward strands of brilliantined hair were peppered with chalk dust.

Out, all of you.

I'd considered allowing the pupils to remain, but decided against it. Too much potential distraction, too great a risk of interference. I was aware that by ordering them out I'd be freeing them to raise the alarm, but the school authorities would have been alerted one way or another and, once they were, one hostage would be as valuable as thirty in maintaining a position of standoff. Planning, precision, methodical attention to detail.

Go on, out!

A cacophony of scraping chairs, the rustling of bags being hurriedly gathered, feet scuffing the floor, a jumble of pushing and shoving. No one said a word. I heard the door bang against an obstruction, then bang again before shutting with a thud that reverberated off the classroom walls. I propelled Mr. Boyle over to the door and made him lock it with a key he'd denied possessing, then produced, with persuasion, from his jacket pocket. Door locked, lights on; a *flick-flick-flick* of neon strips. Taking the key, I pocketed it and conducted him to the windows along the side of the room which overlooked the playground three floors and some thirty feet below. As instructed, he lowered each blind in turn. I released him, backed away. He massaged his throat, the lower half of his face, gingerly dabbing at the skin along the jawline where the red imprints of my fingertips would develop into a string of purple bruises. He let his hand drop.

You can't do this, you know. You absolutely can't do this.

Any physicality, and I will deploy this knife. That is an irrefutable fact.

I swung the duffel bag from my shoulders and placed it on the nearest desk, loosened the drawstring and removed the contents, laying them side by side. I began to unravel the length of clothesline.

You must give me back the key, he said.

Here. (I handed him the notepad and pencils.) Anything to say, draw it. Or shut the fuck up.

This is . . .

Draw. It.

He threw the pad and pencils down and walked over to the desk at the front of the classroom, his desk. He sat in the chair, larger than all the others and made of upholstered wood rather than a scoop of orange plastic screwed to legs of metal tubing. Patted his dishevelled hair into place. Sitting there, gazing into space as though he was waiting for his pupils to arrive for their lesson, the index finger of his right hand stroking his naked upper lip. The classroom was like any other, distinguishable as a science lab only by the wall posters—a pH chart, an anatomical diagram of a man and a woman, a list of abbreviations for chemical symbols—and the line of sinks, the Bunsen burners. I dragged three desks over to the door and stacked them against it, tearing a page from the notepad and taping it over the glass panel.

I don't know wh—

I gestured towards the pad.

. . . who you are or what . . .

I'd made a choke collar at one end of the clothesline. I looped it over Mr. Boyle's head in one swift movement, pulled it taut, yanked him from the chair and onto the floor. One tug brought him to a kneeling position, two more caused him to crawl to where the pad and pencils lay.

His first drawing was of a stick man labelled "Derek Boyle" beside another, unnamed stick man. He drew a question mark beneath the second character.

My name is Gregory Lynn, I said. Orphan, bachelor, only child from the age of four and a half. I have one brown eye and one green. Tell me, sir, is there a scientific explanation for that? To do with pigmentation, is it? Something genetic?

Lynn. His voice was made hoarse by the constriction of the plastic line. I made him write my name alongside the anonymous stick man.

Two n's. L-Y-double N.

A banging on the door, the handle being turned, turned, to no effect. A loud voice.

Security, open up!

I fastened Mr. Boyle's leash to a table leg and went over to the door. I told the voice I was equipped with the means and the will to terminate Mr. Boyle's existence and would do so unhesitatingly should any attempt be made to gain forcible entry to the classroom. I may have used fewer words—fewer syllables—to express this. The voice, angry and insistent at first, became less so. It said it understood and that, whatever I did, I should not do anything rash. I assured the voice that none of my actions would be ill considered. Shortly, another voice: introducing itself as the head teacher; a more gentle voice, coaxing, solicitous, the voice of an adult addressing a small child. I told it to fuck off.

The last night, when her head hurt most, Janice woke up crying and Mum fetched her a glass of aspirin dissolved in water and sat on the bed with her, stroking her forehead with a damp wash-cloth and whispering her to shush because Daddy had to be up early for work. Janice said everything looked funny, fuzzy; she felt hot. If she wasn't any better in the morning, Mum said she'd phone the doctor—get some proper medicine. When Mum had gone, I sneaked out of my bed and into Janice's. She smelled of flannel and warm sheets and her hair was tickly on my face. She told me my feet were cold, said I had knobbly knees and pointy elbows *like a skelington,* and I wasn't to tickle her or make her laugh because it hurt her brain.

In the morning, Janice said she was feeling better; well enough to play face-painting. That was the day I gave her a cat's face.

Boylean fact: Chemical compounds vary not only in the number of elements combined but also in their proportions. For example: carbon *di*oxide contains twice as much oxygen per carbon as carbon *mono*xide. *Di,* two; *mono,* one. However, the relative amount of each is characteristic and definite—what we call the law of constant composition.

We noted this in our exercise books, alongside diagrams depicting the composition of various common chemical compounds. From this, I formulated my theory of the fatality of disproportion, by which usually harmless or even life-sustaining chemical elements can become life-threatening. Oxygen is good for us, we inhale it, blood carries it from our lungs to our brain, we live; oxygen—when combined with carbon in the appropriate proportion—forms carbon monoxide, which is bad for us, we inhale it, blood carries it from our lungs to our brain, we die.

Water, we drink it; we may also drown in it. I was thirteen years old. I raised my hand, awaited Mr. Boyle's permission to speak, then summarised this theory aloud. When I'd finished, he peered at me over his spectacles.

Your point, please?

Your law of, what was it?

Constant composition.

It isn't constant. Is it, sir?

(A smile.) H_2O is H_2O—I assure you, Gregory—whether one is drinking it or drowning in it.

(General laughter.)

No, you don't understand . . .

Forgive me, a mere humble teacher, but I do my best to keep up.

It's not the actual composition I mean, it's the way . . .

No, please—go on

It's the way things—a thing, I mean—can be the same and different.

That smile again, an adjustment of the centimetre of crisp white cuff protruding from each sleeve of his jacket. With the middle knuckle of the index finger of his right hand, he nudged the spectacles back into place on the bridge of his nose. I see, the same and different. (A pause, to allow the chorus of sniggers to subside.) And this, er, coincidental sameness and difference has a chemical manifestation, does it? According to your theory.

I didn't answer.

Or perhaps the chemical compound of the water itself remains constant, the difference being that in the case of—say—drinking, the water is on the inside of one; whereas in the case of drowning, one is on the inside of the water? Eh?

(Eyes lowered, mumbling.) Yes, sir.

Well, Gregory, as soon as the examining board offers an O level in the science of the incredibly obvious, I shall put your name down.

. . .

A chemist is a scientist, expert in the structure and behaviour of organic and inorganic compounds, an inventor of synthetic substances, a replicator of natural substances; an alchemist, one who transforms something common into something precious.

A chemist is a pharmacist, an apothecary; one who prepares and dispenses medication on receipt of a G.P.'s prescription. The senior member of staff in a shop which sells toothpaste and sanitary towels and toilet tissue.

They were out there, beyond that locked and barricaded door: the head teacher, school security staff, the police (armed, presumably), paramedics. Adults. People of importance, of social standing; out there because of me. I could even hear voices, footsteps, hurried movements, beyond the cloaked windows—noises echoing off the hard Tarmac of the playground three floors below us. I imagined the school had been evacuated, classes halted, pupils sent home—or at least shepherded beyond a makeshift cordon of blue-and-white-striped tape. The press would've been alerted by now, newspaper and radio, television; cameras zooming in from various vantage points. After an hour of fruitless attempts to engage me in conversation, the policewoman who spoke through the classroom door yielded to another, older-sounding officer. Male. More polite, more sympathetic, more genial; a kindly, soothing voice like a car being driven slowly over damp gravel. I ignored him totally.

Mr. Boyle, gagged with his own tie, was learning to behave himself. His hair—what there was of it—suited him shorter, though the vegetable knife hadn't been the ideal implement. However, the worst of the abrasions were more the consequence of his own struggles than any inadequacy as a barber on my part. Regrettably, his spectacles became dislodged and broke underfoot (his, not mine) during the procedure.

My mum was a hairdresser, I said. Hair*stylist*.

Mr. Boyle, sitting trussed to a chair, breathed heavily in and out of his nose. Barefoot, trousers rolled halfway up his shins. His eyes were on mine, never left me wherever I went in the room even if he had to twist his head—the upper half of his body—to follow my movements.

I'd given up on making him communicate by drawing pictures. Boring. He couldn't draw, anyway. Fucking stick men. Christ. At one o'clock precisely—lunch break—I unwrapped one of the packs of sandwiches (ham and tomato) and opened a can of Fanta.

You know (belch) . . . 'scuse me. You know anything about meningitis, sir?

He raised his eyebrows.

Meningitis. (I tapped my head.)

The slightest of nods.

D'you want to tell me about it? If I undo the tie.

Another nod.

No shouting to them (a jerk of the thumb in the direction of the door), or all ungagging privileges are withdrawn with immediate effect. Hn?

He nodded again.

I loosened the tie, easing it free from his mouth. The tie was sodden with saliva. I went to the row of books propped between two bookends on the teacher's desk. The bookends were polished wooden busts of Einstein and Newton. Selecting a large medical dictionary, I flipped through the pages.

Go on, then.

Why are you doing this?

"Meningitis is an inflammation of the meninges . . ." Have I pronounced that correctly? *Men-in-ges*. A hard *g*, or soft—like a *j*? What are the meninges, Mr. Boyle?

Look . . .

Mr. Boyle?

(An exhalation, a rolling back of the head.) The . . . the meninges are the covering . . .

"Membrane," it says here.

Yes, the membrane covering the brain.

And?

What? Oh, the brain and the spinal cord.

Tick v.g., Mr. Boyle. And what, would you say, causes this inflammation of the membrane covering the brain and the spinal cord?

Oh I don't know . . . an infection of some sort.

Mmm. "Blood-borne infection," yes. "It is commonest in the years from infancy to the early twenties," apparently. Symptoms, sir?

Severe headache, I suppose. And, er . . . I don't know, nausea . . .

"Headache, vomiting and fever" . . . blah, blah, blah . . . "the headache can be *so severe as to cause the patient to scream with pain."* Fatal?

Yes, sometimes.

"Not *usually* fatal," it says, ". . . with early diagnosis and appropriate treatment." Not usually fatal. I snapped the book shut, replaced it.

> *Lynn, Gregory*
> *Form 2-3*
> *Science*
> *Gregory will not appreciate science subjects until he learns to behave in a mature way. His attitude gives me concern for his future.*
> *D. Boyle*

After third year, I was advised to drop physics and chemistry. I had no aptitude for these subjects, Mr. Boyle said. But you had to choose at least one science option for O level, so I did biology. Plants and stuff. Enzymes, photosynthesis. Life cycles. Reproduction. *Describe the passage of a cheese sandwich through the digestive system.* Mr. Boyle pronounced it *systim.* I wanted to know what type of cheese; any tomato or cucumber to be taken into account? Or pickle? Brown bread or white, margarine or butter?

216

Clearly, I was in one of my argumentative frames of mind, he said. I might think I was being amusing or clever, but I was merely being tiresome.

Biology embraces the study of all living things, also the recognisable remains of those that are extinct. Living things include apparently simple microorganisms (viruses, bacteria) and the largest animals and plants.

I looked this up in *Pears Cyclopaedia*, 96th edition, printed and bound by Richard Clay Ltd., Bungay, Suffolk. It says every living organism has a "metabolism." Metabolism is the process of continual physical and chemical change: processing of food, production of waste materials [shit, piss, etc.] and the "intermediate stages . . . whereby energy and matter are provided for the operation, maintenance and growth of the organism." When its health or existence is threatened by alterations to its environment, an organism can adjust in reaction to the external change. Or reproduce in a modified form, the modifications being passed on from one generation to another to ensure the survival of the species, even if this results in an evolutionary change so that a new species of organism is ultimately formed.

Lynn conundrum: Does this mean the old species is (a) dead, (b) alive, (c) dead *and* alive or (d) neither dead nor alive? (Delete where appropriate.)

This is what *Pears* says under the heading "Living Processes": "The enormous variation and complexity of living processes make the task of understanding and defining life a very difficult one."

In a lesson on diet and nutrition, Mr. Boyle handed out charts from which it was possible to calculate whether your weight was appropriate for your age, sex, height, etc. I took the chart home. I asked Mum how tall she was and she said five-foot-three. I checked the chart and told her how much she should weigh. She said:

In that case I must be five-foot-five.

Mr. Boyle (speaking loudly so that he might be heard through the locked door) informed the gravelly voiced police negotiator that he was fine, he was all right, that everything was under control and he was being treated as well as could be expected in the circumstances. No, he wasn't hungry or thirsty—Mr. Lynn had very kindly supplied him with a round of sandwiches.

The statement about the provision of sustenance was a fib, a line he'd learnt by heart and repeated verbatim. Divulging my name was a blunder. Mr. Boyle realised that right away—apologised to me profusely, said it was a *slip of the tongue*. He hadn't thought . . . I gagged him, lit one of the Bunsen burners and held his hand in the flame.

According to my watch (two minutes faster than the clock on the wall) we'd been in room S3:01 for four hours and twenty-three minutes. This had been the third request by the police that my captive be allowed to speak to them, to reassure them that he was unharmed; the first such request with which I had complied. I was content for them to believe I was weakening, relinquishing control of the situation.

You know what we used to do with these? Not me, *the lads*.

Mr. Boyle raised his moist eyes. He looked puzzled, disoriented, as though I'd disturbed him from a deep sleep.

Bunsen burners, sir.

He shook his head.

The lads would take the rubber pipe off the gas tap and fix it to the water tap, use the Bunsen burner as a water pistol.

I demonstrated. Mr. Boyle flinched, covered his face with both hands, then withdrew the injured one as soon as the jet of water shattered against the scorched flesh. The shoulders and lapels of his blazer jacket darkened, patches of bare bloody scalp glistened between the spiky tufts of his hair.

Teacher's contributions, gagged or ungagged, during the discussions that had punctuated our time together, were predictable, unsatisfactory. A scientist's contributions: adherence to the facts, to what can be proven to be true; a determination to deal objectively with measurable phenomena. His phrases, echoes from my past. No flexibility, no readiness to recognise any inherent ambiguity in the "laws" of science. I told him about Mum, Dad, Janice. I asked if he recalled that time I'd shoved him aside when he'd tried to prevent me from walking out in the middle of one of his lessons—how he'd stumbled and fallen heavily against the wall; how he had reported me—for assault—succeeding in getting me expelled. *Excluded,* they call it nowadays. He said he remembered the episode only vaguely, it had been a long time ago. I told him how long, precisely.

D'you recollect what you were teaching us that day?

Oh really, I haven't the foggiest.

He had these moments of exasperation, impatience, when his voice—the expression on his face—betrayed a resentment at being held hostage, and a pedantic aversion to being told anything by anyone about any fucking thing whatsoever. There were various physical means by which I could reduce him to a more amenable disposition, but a stern glance or a word of admonition was usually (though not always) sufficient.

Infant mortality, sir. Incidence, and causes thereof:

> **control** *(vb)* **1.** to check, test or verify **2.** to exercise a restraining or directing influence over; to have power over; to rule
>
> **control** *(n)* (organism, culture, etc. used in) an experiment in which the procedure or agent under test in a parallel experiment is omitted and which is used as a standard or comparison in judging experimental effects

Sometimes, when I draw things, I make them happen. I've tested this. I've selected ten events with two possible outcomes, labelled "desirable" and "undesirable." Prior to each event, I've depicted the desirable outcome in cartoon form. Meanwhile, I've selected ten other events with desirable and undesirable possibilities, and haven't done any drawings at all. The results showed the occurrence of desirable and undesirable outcomes to be entirely random in both the main experiment and the control, but that those events which occurred as I'd drawn them *assumed a greater significance in my mind.* Conclusion: when I draw things, sometimes I make them happen.

Mr. Boyle—ungagged again—was impressed with my method, but not the conclusion. Said it was unscientific. I instructed him to turn to the pages at the back of the sketch pad, where he discovered cartoons depicting him shorn of his hair and with a blistered, livid hand; others of him saying—apparently to a door—that he was being well treated, of him being doused with water from a Bunsen burner. He studied them briefly, squinting without his spectacles, before closing the pad. The corners of his mouth were red where the gag had chafed the flesh.

You really are . . .

(I indicated the pad, which had slipped from his lap.) There's more.

I don't wish to see them.

(Pause.) Tell me, sir, do you plan your lessons?

Naturally.

And do they always turn out the way you intended?

Yes, usually.

Usually. (I permit myself a smile.) But not today.

More sandwiches, more Fanta. Chocolate. Mr. Boyle watched me eat, the meal interrupted by yet another police attempt to engage me in dialogue. I feigned affability, an openness to persuasion. When the officer desisted, I resumed my scientific negotiations with the hostage.

D'you think that's what ghosts are, sir—people who exist only in the minds of those left behind?

There are no such things as ghosts.

Christ, you don't fucking *listen.*

I wanted to inflict pain, but that would've meant gagging him again to stifle his cries and I wanted him ungagged so we could continue our lesson. I went over to the blackboard, erased the diagram of a nuclear power plant and used a stub of white chalk to sketch four portraits: Mum, Dad, Janice aged seven and Janice as a tiny baby.

My family. I stepped aside so Mr. Boyle could see the board from his position, fastened to a chair in the middle of the room. All dead. Brown Bread, as Dad would've said. And yet (I held up the chalk) here they are.

Your sisters both died?

Janice. She went away, came back, went away again.

I'm afraid I don't understand.

You have any kids, sir? Little Boyles.

Look, I really don't . . .

She had an acute inflammation of the membrane covering the brain. Not usually fatal.

(Pause) How old was she?

Seven. I was four and a half.

Mr. Boyle looked at me. He leaned his head back, his hands clasped in his lap—the unharmed one cradling the other, adjusting the piece of lint I'd found in one of the storage cupboards and permitted him to use as a dressing. He winced. We have two daughters, both grown up now.

Teachers?

His laugh was abrupt, more of a snort. He shook his head. They don't live near us anymore. We . . . my wife misses them very much.

I moved over to the windows, eased one of the blinds back slightly and peered out into the daylight. Two police cars were parked in the centre of the playground below, several figures standing beside and behind them. They were all wearing sleeveless flak jackets. One man had a pair of binoculars trained on the school building, another was aiming a rifle.

Do you miss Janice? Your sister.

I let the blind swing back against the window and stepped away. The swollen membrane—the meninges—must've been pressing against her brain. Can you imagine that, sir?

He lowered his head, said nothing.

Dusk outside. Inside, the neon lighting seemed brighter in contrast to the gloom projected onto the translucent fabric of the window blinds. The heating had gone off. I had another snack, consumed in silence—completing the meal free, for once, from the interruptions with which the police negotiator had disturbed our afternoon. Mr. Boyle remained silent, too, speaking privileges having been suspended indefinitely after the discussion about Janice. I had whiled away the time browsing in the books on Teacher's desk or making rough cartoons. Once or twice, he'd begun to doze and had had to be roused with a spurt of water from the Bunsen burner. He was fully awake now, gnawing at the one half of a cheese sandwich I'd permitted him, drinking the dregs of my coffee. I watched him eat: the regular twitch of the muscles in his jaw, the self-conscious dabbing at his lips to remove flecks of food, the rhythmic swallowing motion of his throat. He never took a sip of coffee without first blowing into the rim of the beaker, even though the drink must already have become tepid. As evening had closed in and the temperature in the classroom had continued to fall, I'd put back on the layers of clothing I'd removed during the day—the jacket, the sweatshirt. Mr. Boyle's garments, however, were folded according to instruction in a neat pile on one of the desks. Jacket, shirt, vest, trousers, underpants. As he'd removed each item and added it to the shoes and socks he'd taken off earlier, the pens in his jacket pocket had fallen to the floor. He went to pick them up but I told him to leave them, to finish folding his clothes and then to sit down again so I could refasten his bonds. He obeyed without comment, offering no resistance when I secured him to the chair with the plastic clothesline.

I drew him. Anatomical sketches. Spindly white limbs, goose-pimpled and virtually hairless, flabby breasts with a corona of frizzled hair around each salmon-pink nipple, slack belly underscored with a florid scar running diagonally from left hip to pubic fuzz. His penis was the size and colour of a cocktail sausage. I'd seen nude models at the Picture Factory. Sitters, they were known as, even when they posed standing up or lying down. Men, women; young, old; fat, thin. Bodies don't bother me. Bodies are just lumps of meat and flesh that haven't died yet. At school, in biology—in *sex education*—we never saw naked bodies, we were never shown films or photographs or illustrations of naked men and women, of people copulating. What we saw were diagrams, line drawings of dismembered genitalia.

The Penis
The Vagina

We were instructed as to the method by which penetration was effected. I learnt a new word: "engorged." *The penis becomes engorged with blood.*

My barrister is endeavouring to dissect what he labels the "enforced nudity" of Mr. Boyle.

You were, ah, seeking to humiliate him? Is that it? To degrade him.

To degrade him. Yes, I like that.

I can tell by his expression that he considers, then decides against, pursuing this line of inquiry. Instead he asks about Mr. Andrews.

Auntie had been the first. The police permitted her to speak to me for a few minutes, from the other side of the locked door.

223

She'd brought God with her. I let her say what He had to say, and what He said was that we must hate the Sin but love the Sinner. She said the Lord's will was for me to open the door. I gave her shrift of the short variety. A couple of hours later, another knock. Detective Inspector Gravel-Voice. He didn't have to tell me who the appellant was on this occasion, because I'd drawn it and knew it would be only a matter of time.

Greg, it's me . . . Andy.

I smiled.

Can you hear me?

I stood up, retrieving the knife from the desk where I'd left it among the books and cartoons. I crossed the room. This time his voice was louder, very close. I was conscious of Mr. Boyle watching me as I stood with my head inclined towards the rectangle of paper taped over the glass panel.

Talk to me, Greg. Please.

I listened, straining for the sounds of him breathing, the shuffle of his clothes; I imagined the tips of his fingers pressed against the other side of the door, his head inclined like mine. I imagined the kissing sound of his lips as he sucked on a cigarette.

I don't want to come in, I just want to talk.

Mr. Boyle is helping me with my revision. (Sounds of movement in the corridor, indistinct; footsteps, people whispering.) Tell them to fuck off!

(More whispering.) Okay. Okay, Greg.

Tell them!

I've told them. It's okay. No one's going to do anything to you.

I rested my forehead against the door, shut my eyes and took several deep inhalations. You knew I was here.

I heard on the radio. On the news.

They say my name?

No. No names. They said there was a siege . . .

Mr. Boyle is here. Derek Boyle. Mr. D. Boyle.

I know Derek Boyle.

He's head of science.

I know.

You can't speak to him.

I . . .

His speaking privileges have been withdrawn indefinitely.

(Pause.) Greg, are you okay?

He's helping me with my revision. Physics, chemistry. Biology.

That's good.

Don't fucking patronise me, Mr. Andrews.

Greg, I'm not. Look . . . listen . . .

I ceased listening. I walked over to the desk, sifted among the papers strewn across the shiny wooden surface, sorting the drawings into sequence. I looked up at Mr. Boyle, who was staring at me. I winked, keeping my voice low, and nodded in the direction of the classroom door.

This man could save your life.

He went to say something in reply but I raised a finger to my lips and he fell silent. I returned to the door, the sheaf of cartoons splayed like a hand of cards.

Mr. Andrews . . . pick a number between one and ten.

What?

A number.

Greg . . .

Come on, sir. Any number.

I don't know . . . seven. Number seven.

I removed one of the cartoons, folded it away in my pocket. I handed the remainder to Mr. Boyle and watched while he examined the variety of ways he might have died, or been spared. I winked again, tapping the pocket in which I'd concealed the other drawing. Then I informed Mr. Andrews that I was terminating all communication until morning; that any attempt to engage me in conversation—by him or the police—would have as a consequence the abrupt cessation of the life of my hostage, Mr.

Boyle: teacher, husband, father of two, head of science. Two eyes, both brown.

Notes

A miscarriage is a spontaneous abortion occurring in the first twenty-four weeks or so of pregnancy, and often within the first twelve to fourteen weeks . . . One in five pregnancies ends in miscarriage. (So they are common, but not *usual.*)

Main Causes:

> —a genetic defect in the foetus which causes the body to reject it
> —abnormalities in the uterus
> —fibroids (benign tumours) in the wall of the womb
> —a weakened or damaged placenta
> —a weak or incompetent cervix, resulting in the neck of the womb opening as the uterus becomes heavier
> —infection during pregnancy (e.g., high fever, German measles, listeriosis)

Consequence:

> —out pops baby, dead.

A miscarriage is the expulsion of a human foetus before it is viable.

> *expulsion*
> *viable*

A miscarriage is when a baby dies before it is born.
Lynn conundrum (Birth–Life–Death): If life starts with birth, can you be said to be alive before you are born? And if life

precedes death, can death occur to that which is not yet alive? When you die, is it possible to be born again?

miscarriage   (n): a failure in administration [————
of justice]
miscarry   (vb): to fail to achieve an intended purpose

I was going to have another little baby brother or sister. I knew that, I'd been told often enough. I'd been allowed to put my hand on Mummy's tummy, to rest my head against Little Bump and listen. Hadn't I? And it would be a baby, a little tiny baby; and it would be *brand-new*. I knew that, didn't I? So why did I keep asking when Janice was coming? Why did I keep asking when Janice was coming out of Mummy's tummy?

Janice is . . . she isn't here anymore. She was sick and didn't get well. She's gone away for good. Forever. We've been through all this, Greg.

I stared at her tummy.

For Christ's sake, Gregory . . . it *isn't* Janice!

Greg, your mum . . .

Oh you! Oh that's right, you tell him.

What?

You tell him. You were the one who put the stupid idea in his head in the first place.

Me?

Another little Janice to play with.

I never . . .

You did! You lying git, you did!

Dad went over to the kitchen cupboard, opened it and took a packet of cigarettes from the shelf and threw it across the room. It skidded off the table where Mum was sitting and landed on the floor.

Go on, smoke one. Smoke the whole fucking lot . . .

Patrick.

. . . if it puts a stop to these fucking tantrums.

You're enough to make anyone smoke.

Go on, then.

Mum breathed out loudly and pushed her fingers through her hair, which was thick, knotted. The clinic said smoking . . .

What is it, four months?

She looked at him. Sixteen weeks.

Feels more like four fucking years.

Eff this, eff that. Don't you know any other words?

Like one long fucking period.

Nice.

Eh, you must be the first woman in history to have PM-fucking-S while you're up the spout.

That's lovely. In front of Gregory.

Dad pointed at me. You're the one who's screwing him up, not me. You and your fucking moods. He picked up the packet of cigarettes and slammed them on the table. Go on, smoke one. Put us all out of our fucking misery.

See, you've set him off now.

Later—that night or the next one or the next week, I don't remember—I was woken by noises. Voices. Crying. I sat up in bed. I couldn't see anything and then it got less dark the longer my eyes were open, grey-black, and I could see things: shapes, shadows. I could see the curtains and the chest of drawers and some of my toys and my nursery school pictures on the walls; I could make out the oblong shapes of the pieces of paper, but not the actual pictures. I got out of bed, and it was cold. I had my jim-jams on. I could see the white door now, the black blob of the handle. I opened the door and went onto the landing. The landing light was off but Mum and Dad's door wasn't shut properly and there was yellowy light coming out and making a triangle on the landing carpet. I could hear the voices better now, loud whispers; the creak of the bed and of footsteps. Mum was crying and talking at the same time and her throat was making a sound like someone gulping a drink of water. I went up to their door. Dad was saying "All right, it's all right . . ." over and over; calling her "love" and "Marion love," he was saying "Sweet Jesus." I pushed the door and went in.

I thought it was pee. I thought I'd peed myself.

I know, I know. Here.

It's wet everywhere. The sheet. I thought . . .

It's all right.

Oh Jesus, Pat.

Here, let me.

My waters . . .

I know. Keep still.

Dad was wearing stripy pyjamas. He was bending over the bed. Mum was lying propped up on her elbows. Her nightdress was up round her tummy and her legs were open wide, knees bent. Her legs were very white. In between her legs, where the tops of her legs met, she was black and red and hairy and wet, and the wet was browny-pinky-red and it had dribbled onto her bottom and onto the sheet. There was something on the sheet, between Mum's legs. Dad's big hands were reaching for it. The something was slimy, small, as small as a pear, and pear-shaped; and its head was sticky red, it had tiny hands and feet and arms and legs which were tucked up into its body like they weren't arms and legs at all but were part of the body; and it had eyes. The eyes were shut tight. Mum was sitting up, watching Dad pick up the pear-thing. He picked it up gently with both hands and laid it on an empty pillowcase, folding the pillowcase over it so that it went away and I couldn't see it anymore. Then Mum saw me, standing in the doorway, and Dad saw Mum's eyes looking at me and he turned and saw me too. I was breathing and crying at the same time, only there weren't any tears, and when I tried to speak, nothing came out because of all the breathing. Dad came over. His hands, the insides, were red and sticky. He held me under the armpits and carried me. His fingers were hard and hurt under my arms and he carried me very fast, banging my feet against the door frame.

Back to your room, you.

I went on kicking, and swinging my arms, and my jim-jam top was rucked up round my shoulders and the bottoms were coming down. And I was grunting. My throat was going *ug-ug-ug*.

Come on!

He threw me on the bed, pulled the covers across and tucked me in tight. I started to cry properly now, arching my back and kicking at the bedclothes and screaming and rolling my head from side to side on the pillow until my face was wet with spit. Dad switched the light on. His face was yellowy white like a skeleton's. If I didn't pack it in, if I didn't stop crying and go straight back to sleep, I'd get the biggest smack of my life. I screamed for Mummy.

Mummy's sick. Her tummy's been sick.

Mum came into the room. Her nightdress was messy, her face was pale—paler than Dad's—and she was walking wobbly. There was wet running down the insides of her legs. She held the pillowcase in front of her tummy. The pillowcase was dirty with red and there was a white stringy thing hanging from it and going under her nightie.

Oh fucking hell, Marion . . .

Dad held her shoulders, steered her through the doorway. He turned out the light and shut the door. I heard the key turn in the lock. And I heard Mum's voice telling me to be good, to be a good boy for Mummy, to be ever so good, like when it's Christmas and Santa is coming and if you aren't a good boy he won't bring you any presents. Her voice got further and further away until I couldn't hear it at all.

I read aloud to Mr. Boyle from one of the books on his desk: "At sixteen weeks, the eyebrows and eyelashes will be starting to grow and the foetus will have fine downy hair." (I glanced up at him.) Janice didn't have fine downy hair, far as I remember. "The foetus will be about six inches long and weigh approximately four and three-quarter ounces . . . it will have joints in its arms and legs and will be able to suck its thumb." Did you ever suck your thumb, sir?

No. I mean, yes. I . . . I had a dummy, I think.

Me too! (Pause.) ". . . the foetus will move around a lot but the mother may not necessarily feel it at this stage." (I read to myself.) Did you know that at sixteen weeks "the sex of the foetus will be evident." (I snapped the book shut and put it down.)

The skin on Mr. Boyle's naked limbs and torso had a faint bluish tint. His scalp wounds had become scabby and encrusted with dried blood and his hand, where the lint had come away during the night, was yellow with pus. A large blister had formed over the thumb joint. His eyes were red-rimmed and moist, bloodshot, the eyelids—when they fluttered closed—were made almost translucent by the pale sheen cast over the room from the lowered blinds. Mr. Boyle was unshaven, the lower portion of his face peppered with light brown stubble that grew thickest on the upper lip and the chin.

So what d'you reckon?

He raised his head jerkily, squinting as though unable either to find my face or to focus on it. Sorry?

Genetic defect in the foetus? Abnormal uterus? *Benign* tumours? Or did she have something wrong with her placenta, d'you think? Perhaps she'd had an infection during pregnancy. Or maybe her cervix was *incompetent*. Eh?

I . . . Mr. Boyle swayed in the chair, prevented from toppling onto the floor only by the tight bindings of the plastic clothesline. He steadied himself. I've really no idea.

I walked over to one of the windows, fingered the blind away so that I could peep out. Dawn. The sun's fractured orange reflection adhered to the upper windows of the school's administration block, which formed an L-shape with our building. The police vehicles were still there, three floors below us, in the centre of the playground. Three of them now. Officers wearing flak jackets were handing a beaker back and forth. Vapour issued from the beaker, and from their mouths after they'd sipped from it. The one with the binoculars had let them dangle from the strap round his neck while he took his turn to drink. I withdrew from the window. Our supplies of food and drink were exhausted, the last of the sandwiches and coffee consumed in the early hours. By me. I turned on the tap at one of the sink units, testing the water to see if it would run warm. It didn't. I washed anyway, removing my jacket and rolling up the sleeves of the sweatshirt to sluice my face and hands. I sucked water from my cupped palms and swilled it around my mouth, gargled, and spat into the stainless-steel basin. I dried myself on coarse paper towels from a dispenser on the wall.

They told Mum the baby would've been a girl. Mum said, when she came out of hospital.

Mr. Boyle didn't respond or look up.

She referred to the baby—the foetus—as "she," but Dad called her "it." You know what he told my mum, Mr. Boyle? Mr. Boyle.

Sorry?

He told her: "You can always have another one." Except she couldn't.

I pulled the sweatshirt over my head, took off my shirt, my shoes and socks, trousers and underpants. I had Mr. Boyle's attention, gawping at me with his rheumy eyes.

She'd have been thirty now. My little sister. Janice number one would have been thirty-seven and a half.

Gregory . . .

If they'd lived.

I'm so cold and tired. I'm *tired*.

Tired of all this?

I began dressing in Mr. Boyle's clothes, which had remained in a neat pile on the desk throughout the night despite his repeated requests that he be allowed to dress, to keep warm. His shirt was cold against my skin, smelling faintly of stale perspiration and deodorant. Cotton/polyester mix (65% polyester,

35% cotton), size 15 collar. St. Michael. M&S. Too small, the material strained over my torso. Trousers, jacket. The trousers were scratchy, the jacket tight across the shoulders and short in the sleeve. I put on the socks and shoes last of all—loosening the laces to get my feet inside the shoes, and wearing them with the heel trodden down. Size 8.

I take an eleven myself, but nines are so comfortable I wear tens. My Dad, one of his *little jokes*.

Mr. Boyle didn't smile.

(I pointed to him.) What's the foot bone connected to, laddie?

I . . .

Come on, come on, we haven't got all day.

The toe bone.

Ah! Or the ankle bone, perhaps? See, it rather depends, doesn't it? On one's perspective, on one's point of view. On which way you care to look at it. Would you agree?

I found his spectacles on the floor. One of the lenses was cracked and the frame was slightly buckled, but I managed to put them on. Everything became blurred, as though I was viewing the room through a glass tank filled with water. I gathered up his pens and clipped them one by one in the breast pocket of the jacket. I severed Mr. Boyle's bonds, instructing him to stand up; to dress himself in my clothes, which were strewn about tables and backs of chairs. He stumbled nakedly from item to item, until his spindly shrunken form was covered in the garments I'd discarded.

And the jacket, sir. Nice warm jacket, that.

He put on my jacket, zipped it up. When I told him to raise the hood and to fasten the drawstring beneath his chin, he did so —his cold, clumsy fingers fretting at the ends of the toggles until he'd managed to fashion something resembling a bow. I handed him the knife, handle first. He seemed reluctant to take it, but I insisted. He held it gently, nervously, as if it were made of tissue paper or fine porcelain.

Open the blinds, will you?

Sorry?

(Pointing.) The blinds.

He had the shuffling gait of a geriatric; debilitated by the stiffness of spending a long night bound to a hard plastic chair, confused by fatigue and hunger, numbed with cold. As he began working the blinds, I sat in the chair where he'd been sitting. The blinds went up one after the other with a succession of loud swishes, bathing the classroom in daylight.

Wave to them, Mr. Boyle.

Who?

The police, down there in the playground. See them? Show them you've assumed possession of the knife. Let them see it's all over.

He turned to me, fully—so that his view of me wasn't obscured by the hood of the jacket. My jacket.

(I smiled.) It's all right. It's all right.

The teacher turned again to look out the window. I could no longer see his face, but his stance—the slight movement of his head—suggested he was searching in the sudden brightness of morning for the police officers. His body became alert, a curious noise escaped from his throat and I saw him jerkily raise his hand. It was the hand which held the knife, and he was waving it from side to side above his head in an awkward sweeping motion. The blade of the knife glinted in the sunlight. He was crying now, I could hear him. His throat was making the noise a throat makes when a person is crying. Then the window exploded.

In the cartoon (No. 7, chosen at random by Mr. Andrews), Mr. Boyle fell forwards, plunged face-first through the shattered pane and—somersaulting once—landed in a jagged heap in the playground, head bursting on impact like a piece of ripe fruit. In the cartoon, a perfect crimson circle darkened the material of the jacket over the place where his heart would be. But it didn't happen that way. It didn't happen the way any of the cartoons

234

predicted. How it happened: he staggered two steps back from the exploded window and momentarily regained his balance before slumping hard against his desk. The desk tipped, sending books and sticks of chalk over the floor; leaving him half sitting, half lying, his head and shoulders dandruffed with tiny shards of glass. How it happened: the bullet blew away the lower part of his face, transforming the teacher's throat into a paint gun that was still coating the blackboard with its fine scarlet spray when they broke down the door.

EPILOGUE

They burned him. A chilly morning, October; four months ago. It was chilly but the burning of him was not for warmth.

I didn't attend. I was otherwise detained and, in any case, uninvited. *Persona non grata.* I drew no pictures of the cremation. For all I know, Mrs. Boyle may have knelt in the gardens of remembrance and tried to consume a handful of her husband's ashes. For all I know.

I have an image of Mr. Boyle in my head: a solitary figure standing at a window, looking out, his silhouette casting an elongated diagonal shadow across the floor. He has his back to me, he is wearing a jacket with the hood raised. I have an image of a blackboard drenched in blood, four chalk characters partially erased—white lines obliterated, or overlaid with a scarlet sheen which is itself rendered burgundy by the black of the board. And the blackboard is not truly black, but a very dark green.

I inquire whether the police marksman is to be charged with murder. My barrister stares at me, doesn't respond—even when I repeat the question—but, instead, attempts to direct our discussion back to what he calls the *point of deviation*.

It's an interesting issue, though, isn't it? Who *actually* killed him.

Gregory, we've been over this ad nauseam.

But not ad infinitum.

I am to be charged, among other things, with manslaughter; while the officer who tugged the trigger is to face nothing more serious than an internal inquiry into the incident. Whether disciplinary action is likely to be taken against him remains unclear and depends, partly, on the findings of the court which is to sit in judgement on me. The degree of our respective guilt (or innocence)—his and mine—is inextricably bound together. My barrister says:

Who fired the, ah, shot doesn't come into it, strictly speaking. Not in a legal sense.

He's said this before, using these or similar words. He says I caused Mr. Boyle's death in the sense that I created the circumstances in which his death occurred. Deliberately or otherwise, that's the question. The Crown will focus on my actions—their apparently calculating nature—as a conclusive indicator of intent. Counsel for the defence will prefer to divert the court's attention to my state of mind. It all hinges on my being unhinged. As for the police marksman, he was under orders to shoot—to kill, if necessary—should the opportunity arise. And I afforded him just such an opportunity.

(I smile.) But he was under orders to shoot *me*.

A barristerial shrug.

The jury will weigh the evidence presented to it and reach its own conclusion about my intentions in that classroom—my orchestration of events—and to what extent I can be deemed legally culpable for the outcome. The upshot, as it were.

> manslaughter, the slaughter of a man
> murder, the slaughter of a man

Different ways of saying the same thing.

. . .

237

A trial date has been set. I have already made a number of appearances before the magistrates, prior to the committal proceedings. The solicitor, contrary to my express instructions, omitted to request that reporting restrictions be lifted during these preliminary hearings. So the newspapers have had to confine their reports to one or two paragraphs listing my name (Gregory Lynn), age (thirty-five), occupation (unemployed) and address; the offences with which I am charged; and other mundane procedural matters. The purpose of such restrictions is to ensure that the impartiality of any potential juror should not be prejudiced before the case comes to Crown Court. Once the trial proper is under way, the solicitor assures me, the press will *go to town*. In the meantime, she and my barrister are concluding their efforts to establish a defence of mitigation and to prepare me for the witness box. It amuses me to be unhelpful.

Science is about questions, not answers. It assumes nothing. It is a rejection of dogma. It asks "how?" and "what?" and "why?" When you begin an experiment, you don't know what will occur. This is what I have learned, not what I've been taught.

Art is about questions, not answers. It assumes nothing. It is a rejection of dogma. It asks "how?" and "what?" and "why?" When you begin a painting, you don't know what will occur. This is what I have learned, not what I've been taught.

The Lynn perspective: In conducting an experiment, you (the scientist) alter that which you seek to test or observe or measure, simply by your presence. You are a factor. You bring yourself into your work, in a mental as well as physical sense. You are no different to an artist who, in applying paint to a surface, leaves an indelible signature in each brushstroke.

These are matters I endeavoured to discuss with Mr. Boyle, that I tried to make him see during our period of enforced proximity.

I'm not against *science,* sir, just your representation of it. The black-and-white, the right-and-wrong. The triumph of facts over factors. You didn't learn us nuffink.

No satisfactory response. He said something about having to get the facts straight before you can presume to improvise.

Children (he pronounced it *childrin*) require knowledge before they can aspire to genius. My job is merely to furnish them with that knowledge.

What about *ideas?* Abstraction? Unknown quantities?

Ideas are not my sphere, I'm afraid.

This is what I'd like to discuss with Mr. Andrews, too, only we are not permitted to meet. We never developed these themes while I resided with him because I didn't really have the ideas straight in my own head then. By the time I did, it was too late— the "school siege horror" (as one newspaper described it) was under way and Mr. A. was the other side of a locked door, colluding with the police. I could write him a letter, but I wouldn't be allowed to send it. *Interfering with a prosecution witness.* Because, the thing is, if Mr. Boyle was black-and-white, Mr. Andrews— Andy—was white-and-black, and that's bollocks as well. In rejecting the "truths" of convention and conformity, he didn't embrace "absence of truth" but devised his own definition of what is true. His truth is that everything is a lie. Which isn't the same as an absence of truth. This is what I've learned.

lying
absence of truth

I don't know if this is a valid differentiation, or if it just sounds good. Wordplay. I don't know whether it's a *specious* observation. Miss McMahon taught me that word. Specious (adj). I looked it up today, as a reminder to myself—because we think we know what words mean and then we look them up and find that we are surprised.

    1. having deceptive attraction or fascination

    2. superficially sound or genuine, but fallacious

The word specious has its roots in the Latin *specere,* meaning "look" or "appearance." From this origin we also derive the words species and spy. I want to tackle Mr. Andrews on definitions. Their plurality of meaning. How one leads to another and to another. And about the responsibility of the one who is empowered to define.

McMahonism: Words are as slippery as a bar of soap in the bath.

As a remand prisoner, I'm innocent until proven guilty. Technically.

Auntie has been to see me in here, three times. She may also have been instrumental in the visit by the prison chaplain. They share a belief that the Lord is with me even if I am not with Him. I asked the chaplain:

Fuck me, what's *He* in here for?

I refrained from inflicting this quip on Auntie. There are other, more subtle ways of upsetting her. My presence, for example. Auntie brings me cake. She talks about Uncle's bad back, about the Pakis who've moved in next door, about the weather. She makes no eye contact with me whatsoever.

Auntie is Mum's sister. There is no discernible physical resemblance. When Mum used to do Auntie's hair she'd say she wished hers was as curly as Auntie's. Mum's hair was thick and straight, like mine. *Clumpy.* Janice had fine hair. It floated in the breeze when she ran or when she skipped or when she jumped from the branch of a tree. Janice cried the day she started school. They made her wear slides and grips. Mum fastened them for her each morning, or she'd sweep the hair back beneath a wide yellow band which kept Janice's fringe out of her eyes and left her ears and forehead exposed.

If you can't see or hear, how d'you expect to learn anything? Eh?

When I draw Janice, I draw her with her hair down, around her face and neck; or loose in the breeze—only you can't draw breeze, so it's the wildness of the hair which suggests an invisible force.

This morning, while the barrister is out of the room answering *a call of nature,* the solicitor asks about my family. About Janice. We talk. She tells me she has a younger brother—still at school—whom she loves very much and I tell her that must be *very nice* for her. Her voice is cool, quiet. Confiding. But for all her subtlety, this is no different to school: first the imparting of information, then the asking of questions.

Do you think things might have been different at home if Janice had lived?

At *home?* What the fuck's home got to do with anything?

Between you and your mum and dad. If Janice had lived.

Always Janice, not "your sister." The solicitor is pretending to be my friend, but her voice is rich with superiority even though she's in awe of me. She is in awe of me because I am awesome—what I've done is awesome—and I make her afraid and a little disgusted.

Would things have turned out differently? (I smile, scratch my scalp and make it snow.) Yes, Mr. Onassis wouldn't have married Mrs. Khrushchev.

A memorial service was held at the school in honour of Mr. Boyle. I read about it. I drew that service: packed assembly hall, row upon row of smartly, soberly attired people. Miss McMahon, flame-haired, in a navy cardigan and pleated tweed skirt; Mrs.

Davies-White (naked, eyes lowered). Mr. Hutchinson, on crutches; and Mr. Patrick, sitting on his hands to stop them shaking. No Mr. Teja, of course; but Mr. Andrews, in the front row, barefoot, trouser cuffs rolled up, chain-smoking; stubbing cigarettes out one after another against the underside of his plastic chair, unconsciously creating patterns with each combination of scorch marks. Pupils, past and present, in their hundreds; faces devoid of features, dressed uniformly and impeccably behaved. In my cartoon, the head teacher is at the lectern, a large speech balloon issuing from his open mouth. Mr. Boyle—Derek—was *much-loved and respected,* and will be *sorely missed by all of us who knew him.* Hundreds of thought bubbles, one for each member of the audience, so that the space above the rows of heads is entirely occupied by a montage of overlapping ovals of white. And the bubbles ought to contain an image of Mr. Boyle, the dearly departed, in whose memory this gathering is supposed to be dedicated. But they don't. Each thought bubble, without exception, is filled with me: Gregory Lynn.

My name is Gregory Lynn. I am thirty-five years old, an orphan, bachelor, only child from the age of four and a half. I have one brown eye, one green. In a few weeks' time I will plead not guilty to the catalogue of charges against me. I will be tried, and declared guilty. We shall agree to differ, the jury and I. There will be a unilateral appreciation, by me, that there isn't necessarily a clear distinction to be drawn between "guilty" and "not guilty." That they are different ways of saying the same thing. Then the judge will describe me and the nature of my offences in unflattering terms, and he will pronounce sentence. Which is pronounced *sen-tence.* Which is both a term of imprisonment and a sequence of words terminating in a full stop. The ending of his sentence will be the beginning of mine.